Jan Costin Wagner

Light in a Dark House

TRANSLATED
FROM THE GERMAN
BY

Anthea Bell

Harvill *Secker*

LONDON

Published by Harvill Secker 2013

2 4 6 8 10 9 7 5 3 1

First published with the title *Das Licht in einem dunklen Haus* in 2011
by Galiani Berlin

First published in Great Britain in 2013 by
HARVILL SECKER
Random House
20 Vauxhall Bridge Road
London SW1V 2SA

www.rbooks.co.uk

Addresses for companies within The Random House Group Limited
can be found at: www.randomhouse.co.uk/offices.htm

The Random House Group Limited Reg. No. 954009

A CIP catalogue record for this book is available from the British Library

ISBN 9781846556531

The transla...on of this work was ...ported by a ...institut

The F... ...Council... ...ion.
Our b... ...r.
FSC ...
en...

FSC responsible sources
FSC® C016897

Typeset in ITC Berkeley Oldstyle BT By Palimpsest Book Production Limited,
Falkirk, Stirlingshire

Printed and bound in Great Britain by
Clays Ltd, St Ives plc

For Venla

PROLOGUE

18 August 1985

Something's happened. I must write it down. Write it all down so that I can remember it later. Describe everything, and then there'll be a picture of it in my mind.

That's what Lauri said.

Right, then. She isn't crying. And she isn't laughing. She's just sitting there. I'm sitting on the piano stool beside her, and there's kind of a humming in my head. Like bees or flies or something. Dear diary. We're sitting side by side. At the piano.

She's looking at the keys, concentrating on them. Then she strikes a key, and it makes a clear sound. It's a hot day, we're both sweating. Her dress is still all crumpled up. Sort of creased and messy. It's the blue-and-white dress that I told Lauri about. Kind of a light summer dress, and you can see the shape of her breasts quite well underneath it, or maybe it's more like you can guess at the shape of her breasts.

The dress is all creased and rucked up; I can almost see the place where her bottom begins. The sound of the piano note is clear, a little louder than the humming, but anyway the humming isn't real, it's only inside my head.

The window's open. The wind is blowing in, but it's a warm wind. Laughter and splashing from the lake. That'll be the kids from next door.

Outside it's very hot. I sweated quite a lot when I was riding out to see her on my bike.

And then we're sitting side by side, after all that happened.

But she's trembling too. I'm sure she can't be cold, because she's sweating and kind of breathless, but she's trembling, and she strikes another note on the piano. A little higher than the first, so it's even clearer. It sounds somehow high and clear and quiet all at once.

Like a whispered scream.

AUTUMN

I

In an autumn when no rain fell, Kimmo Joentaa was living with a woman who had no name. The anticyclone keeping the weather fine had been christened Magdalena. The woman told people to call her Larissa.

She came and went. He didn't know where from or where to.

In the evening, when he came home, he would sit in the car for a while, looking for signs of her presence behind the windowpanes. Sometimes there was a light switched on that hadn't been on when he left in the morning. Sometimes it was dark.

If there was a light on, she usually wasn't there. If it was dark, she would be sitting on the sofa with her knees drawn up, and she laughed when he asked how her day had been. She laughed and laughed, until after a while Kimmo Joentaa joined in.

He'd asked her several times why she always switched on the light when she went out, and why she was sitting in the dark when he came home. She didn't reply. She just looked at him and said nothing. That was what she usually did when he asked questions. If he looked like beginning to ask them again, she would come over, put her arms round him, undress him, push him down on the sofa and move above him in a practised rhythm until he came.

Before the snow and ice melted, she'd played ice hockey on the lake with the kids. She ate huge quantities of ice cream, and liked vanilla and tundra-berry flavours best. She enjoyed action films, with shoot-outs and exploding cars. She didn't like comedies, but she laughed a lot, mostly at him. He didn't even have to say anything; often just the expression on his face, or a movement that he made, would make her laugh.

She had blonde hair, and insisted that she was 1 metre 60 tall – not 1 metre 51, as Joentaa suggested now and then, because he liked her furious look – and she was very slim, which surprised Joentaa in view of her consumption of sweet things.

Sometimes she disappeared. If he rang her mobile number, he reached the strange, anonymous voice of a recorded answer. He left messages, and sensed his words seeping away into the silence. He wrote to the email address that she had given him, and never got any answers. He sat in front of the laptop in an empty house, with his mobile in his hand, and waited.

He began switching on the light when he left in the morning, and he felt a tingling in his stomach when at last, after days or weeks, the house was dark again when he came home. Then she would be sitting on the sofa with her knees drawn up, and she would turn to look his way and say she was back.

If he asked her where she had been she said nothing.

She liked walking. At weekends they walked through the forest together for hours at a time, and she told him about films she had seen or books she was reading. She read anything and everything so long as it was a story. She liked stories that she could tell him. Her books gathered in piles in various corners of the house. He listened to her attentively, and tried to find the storyteller behind the characters who came to life on the stage of her imagination.

She worked as a prostitute, Joentaa didn't know where. He once began asking her about it, but she just gave a wry grin and said he didn't want to know. When summer began she had told him that she'd also taken a part-time job selling ice cream, and Joentaa said he was glad.

'If I fix it right I'll be able to eat all the sweet stuff I like,' she said.

He asked her to tell him her name, her real name, and she said that names didn't matter.

She cried in her sleep, and if he woke her, or asked, when she was awake again, why she'd been crying, she couldn't remember having any dreams at all.

2

In mid-September they went to a birthday party together. Nurmela, the Turku police chief, was celebrating his fiftieth birthday in the huge garden of his house, which went down to the river and had a picturesque view.

When they arrived, Nurmela's wife Katriina welcomed them. Joentaa had met her several times at Christmas parties at the police station. She was tall and slender, and always seemed to be aware of her physical presence as she moved.

The garden was already full of guests, and Joentaa made for Petri Grönholm and Paavo Sundström, who were sitting at a large table in the sun. Larissa held his hand tight as they walked, and when Joentaa cast her a brief glance she smiled at him. He felt her hand in his, and the heat of an autumn that was much too warm, and he was suddenly glad they had come to the party. He went up to the table where Sundström and Grönholm were sitting, and introduced the woman standing beside him, snuggling close to him, as Larissa.

'Hello,' said Grönholm.

'Wow,' said Sundström.

Larissa laughed. The loud, abrupt laugh that he liked, because it was genuine and for a few moments it gave him the feeling that he knew her.

Sundström stared at Larissa, until an idea seemed to bring him back to reality. 'My own worse half is around here somewhere,' he said, half-heartedly looking for her. 'Probably at the prosecco bar.'

'Sounds a good idea,' said Larissa.

'Yes . . . in a moment,' said Joentaa.

'Come on, let's get sloshed today,' said Larissa.

Sundström laughed, Grönholm laughed, Joentaa nodded, and Larissa let go of his hand and walked up the slope to the drinks table. Joentaa watched her go, and was aware that Sundström and Grönholm were doing the same.

'Good for you, Kimmo. The new woman in your life, right?' asked Sundström.

Joentaa nodded. The new woman. Or whatever.

'I'm glad,' said Grönholm. 'Really glad for you—'

'What a . . .' Sundström interrupted him.

'What a what?' asked Grönholm.

'What a cracker,' said Sundström.

'What did you say?' asked Grönholm, smiling, and he glanced rather uncertainly at Joentaa.

'I only meant . . . oh, hello, darling,' said Sundström. 'May I introduce Kimmo Joentaa, another of my unfortunate subordinates? Kimmo, Sabrina. Sabrina, Kimmo.'

'Hello,' said Joentaa.

Sabrina Sundström raised a glass of prosecco to her mouth, took a sip, lowered the glass and gave Joentaa a ready smile. Joentaa didn't know her, but he knew she must have a sense of humour. A good one. How else could she live with Paavo Sundström?

Violin music began playing in the background, and after that Police Chief Nurmela, standing on the terrace in expansive mood, spoke into a microphone, thanking them all for coming and for their generous presents, which he would unpack at the appropriate time. He just hoped there weren't too many references to pensions, retirement and the evening of his days, because this was only half-time for him, there was a lot he still planned to do. His wife Katriina was standing behind him, and when he had finished she said that the buffet would be open in a few minutes' time.

The violins struck up again. The black-clad quartet of musicians was sitting at the side of the broad terrace, three young women and one young man. Larissa came back, balancing a bottle of sparkling wine and glasses on a tray.

'Plenty for everyone,' she said.

Sundström laughed, Grönholm poured the wine, and Larissa sat down and was immediately deep in conversation with Sundström's wife. If Joentaa got the gist of the remarks that he caught from time to time correctly, they were talking about summer fashions.

Out of the corner of his eye, he saw Nurmela coming towards them with his wife. Walking with a spring in his step, wearing a beige suit with a yellow tie. There were laughing, blue Donald Ducks all over the tie. Katriina moved fluently and gracefully, easily keeping up with his staccato pace.

'Great outfit,' said Sundström, as soon as the couple were in earshot. 'The tie, I mean. And of course your wife's dress.'

'Thanks, thanks,' said Nurmela. Katriina smiled, and Joentaa got the impression that something had changed in Nurmela's face.

'Hello there, August,' said Larissa.

'Hmm?' That was Grönholm.

'Who?' said Sundström, and Grönholm's eyes wandered off, presumably in search of August.

'Oops,' said Larissa, clapping her hand to her mouth, and Joentaa sensed that, beside him, Nurmela was swaying slightly as he quickly excused himself. Katriina was staring at Larissa. 'Come along, darling, I must . . . must go and see to the guests . . .' said Nurmela. He made off in the direction of the drinks table.

They all watched him go. Katriina tore herself away and followed him.

'What was all that about?' asked Grönholm.

'Since when was Nurmela's name August?' asked Sundström.

'His first name isn't August, you know,' said Grönholm, turning to Larissa.

'My mistake,' she said, with a wide smile for Kimmo Joentaa. 'Who wants some more fizz?' She picked up the bottle and refilled their glasses. Joentaa gratefully held out his, and drained it in a single draught. He suddenly had the sure and certain feeling that he could only spend this summery autumn day appropriately in a state of mild intoxication.

'Cheers,' said Larissa, and they all clinked glasses.

'Is his name really August or not?' asked Sabrina Sundström.

'Not as far as I know,' said Grönholm.

'Nope,' said Sundström.

'Just a mistake,' said Larissa.

'Names don't matter,' said Joentaa.

He caught Larissa's eye. She was giving him a glance that he couldn't interpret. He went to find another bottle of fizz.

3

The rest of the party passed in a soft, pleasant haze, with the clink and clatter of the cutlery, with lines of guests winding their way over the freshly mown lawns, going over to the buffet on tables covered by snow-white cloths. Larissa ate with a hearty appetite. She liked the eggs on salmon and the curried herring best.

'Mm, delicious,' she said several times, laughing, and Joentaa felt an urge to put his arms round her and hug her until they were both breathless. He had emptied his glass of sparkling wine eight to twelve times – he didn't know exactly how often, because at some point he had lost count – and was vaguely aware of Sundström raising his eyebrows.

'Er, Kimmo . . . everything okay so far?' he asked.

Joentaa nodded. He felt curiously sober, apart from the soft veil of mist that had come down over his mind.

Larissa was in animated conversation with Sundström's wife, and Grönholm was leaning back, relaxed, drinking beer after beer with a glass of sparkling wine or so in between, and seemed to be listening to them. Joentaa wondered why Grönholm never brought a woman to any occasions of this kind, and whether that accounted for Grönholm's good humour and generally equable temperament, but rejected the idea, and for a while watched Nurmela talking to the guests surrounding him in the centre of the garden. Now and then he glanced at the table where Joentaa was sitting. Presumably he was trying to work out how the little blonde had found her way into his birthday party. Joentaa had a feeling that Nurmela's eyes were lingering

Then he let go of him again. Joentaa followed his eyes to the windows at the front of the house. Katriina in the middle of the room, in the light from the chandeliers. Tall and slim. A smile for every guest.

'I'm sorry if Katriina . . .' Joentaa said.

Nurmela let himself drop on to a white folding chair. Joentaa fetched another for himself. Sat down.

'I'm sorry if Katriina . . . was annoyed . . .'

'She didn't notice anything,' said Nurmela.

'She didn't?'

'No. Well, yes, but I can smooth it over,' said Nurmela.

Smooth it over, thought Joentaa. Soft, gentle rain was falling, the first in a long time. Inside the house, no one seemed to notice that their host was missing.

'I'll tell her some kind of shit,' said Nurmela.

Joentaa nodded.

'Doesn't matter,' said Nurmela.

Joentaa nodded again, and saw Larissa on the other side of the windows. Deep in animated conversation with Nurmela's wife. They were laughing together. Nurmela stared into the darkness. He had begun to stumble over his words.

'None of it matters,' he mumbled.

'No,' said Joentaa. He saw Larissa beyond the windowpane. Larissa. With Nurmela. He found it difficult to give distinct outlines to the image.

'Half-time,' said Nurmela.

'Yes,' said Joentaa.

'Time for the next half.' Obviously in an attempt to put this statement into practice, he stood up wearily and marched towards the house. 'Come on, Kimmo, let's have another drink,' he called.

Joentaa followed him.

'Are you two . . . together?' asked Nurmela as they walked on.

Larissa beyond the windows at the front of the house. Dancing to the rhythm of soundless music.

Joentaa nodded.

'Mhm. Mhm,' said Nurmela, and it struck Joentaa that maybe Larissa was about to lose one of her best clients. Although why should she? Now that everything was adequately explained.

Nurmela, Larissa.

Nurmela nodded to himself. The blue ducks laughed, a peal of laughter like Larissa's on the other side of the windows.

When Nurmela opened the door, and at last they could hear the music to which Larissa and Katriina were dancing, Joentaa thought that there were two questions he must ask him some time.

Why his house had soundproofed glazing.

And why . . . why August?

4

'Why . . . why August?' asked Sundström, either because no more risqué jokes occurred to him or because Grönholm had just gone to fetch another beer.

He leaned over to Joentaa, who was sitting at the other end of the sofa. There was a red-haired woman whom Joentaa didn't know between them, and Sundström for one seemed to take no interest in including her in the conversation. His head hovered in the air just above her lap as he made the question more specific. 'What was all that just now about this August?'

'No idea,' said Joentaa.

'Larissa's been trying to kid me that she never said anything about any August. But you heard her too, mentioning August. And she seemed to mean Nurmela.'

'No idea,' said Joentaa again.

'But . . .'

'Doesn't matter. A misunderstanding,' said Joentaa.

'All I mean is . . . well, Nurmela's first name isn't August. I haven't been able to think what it is, but certainly not . . .' murmured Sundström, removing his head from the lap of the redhead, who didn't bat an eyelash.

The music was loud and atmospheric, the basses hummed and growled, and Larissa and Katriina danced and laughed at each other, and Joentaa thought that Nurmela threw a really remarkable party. A few last guests still here. The string quartet had left long ago. Grönholm was staggering towards them in high good humour, and Nurmela was lying back in an armchair to one side of the room, smiling as if transported to a better world.

Half-time, thought Joentaa. In view of the picture before his eyes, that seemed a mild way of putting it.

Larissa. And August.

Or whatever they were called.

Then Larissa came over to him, took his arm and led him on to the dance floor in Nurmela's living room. With strength that allowed no contradiction. He wondered where on earth Nurmela got this weird music from, and Larissa was hanging around his neck, her lips to his ear. A faint suggestion of her voice, but he couldn't make out the words. Too loud, he signalled, and she smiled and dismissed it with a wave.

In the background, Sabrina Sundström was smoothing down her husband's tousled hair, and Petri Grönholm raised his beer glass to his mouth. Larissa was laughing. At him. Of course. He returned the laugh and exaggerated his ridiculous style of dancing by adding some nervous twitches. On the sofa, Grönholm laughed and egged him on. Sundström had closed his eyes, and seemed to be enjoying Sabrina's scalp massage. After that there was quieter music, piano and a vocalist. Larissa wound her arms around him and said the singer could hardly have survived that song.

'How do you mean?' asked Joentaa.

'Too sad.'

'Hmm,' said Joentaa.

She let herself drop, laughing as she dragged him down towards the floor. 'Oops,' said Joentaa, holding on to her tightly, and Petri Grönholm threw up on Nurmela's golden-brown fitted carpet.

The redhead screeched, jumped off the sofa, and landed in the arms of a drugs investigator.

'Oh dear,' said Sabrina Sundström, and Katriina walked across the room, upright and graceful, and bent over Grönholm, who was clutching a table leg and trying to get up.

'It doesn't matter,' said Katriina.

'The carpet's the same colour as the beer you brought up,' said Sundström.

'Paavo, please,' said Sabrina.

'What about it? They match,' said Sundström.

Nurmela came up and put an arm round Katriina, and together they looked down at Grönholm, who was mumbling, 'Sorry . . . didn't notice . . . didn't realise I was so . . . it was the last beer, one too many.'

Katriina began mopping up, and Nurmela took the cloth from her hand. 'Let me do that,' he said.

'Another glass of wine?' asked Sundström, as he helped Grönholm to get to his feet.

'Kimmo's fault,' said Grönholm. 'Your silly dancing finished me off.'

'Sorry,' said Joentaa, and Grönholm began giggling. Nurmela was scrubbing for all he was worth, and Katriina said, 'Not so hard, darling, or the carpet will fade.'

'What?'

'That patch of carpet. If you scrub too hard, the detergent won't come out.'

'Oh.'

'Salt,' suggested Sundström.

'For wine,' said Sabrina. 'That's for wine.'

Then they all sat round the table, and Nurmela offered a nightcap of an apricot liqueur from France.

'I don't know if that's a great idea just now,' said Katriina, but even Grönholm said, 'Sounds good, sounds good.' And there was no stopping Nurmela anyway. He brought out the bottle, and they all clinked glasses.

'Hm. Very good,' said Larissa, emptying hers at a draught, and Nurmela cleared his throat.

The redhead and the drugs investigator were first to leave. Joentaa and Sundström supported the swaying Grönholm, who kept muttering to himself, 'Oh, man . . . oh, wow, would never have thought . . . thought a thing like that . . . of all people . . .' Then he giggled again.

Nurmela and Katriina waved, the drugs investigator and the redhead waved, and then the other five were in a car driven by Sabrina Sundström. The Sundströms sat in front, with Joentaa, Larissa and Grönholm in the back.

'Where first?' asked Sabrina.

'Better take Petri home first,' said Joentaa.

'Don't bother about me . . . I . . . I can drive myself if . . . if I have to,' Petri Grönholm assured them.

It had really begun raining now.

'Here comes autumn,' said Sundström.

'It's supposed to be going to stay warm,' said Sabrina Sundström.

Grönholm thanked everyone for the nice evening and insisted on getting out of the car and going into his apartment by himself. It was in a comparatively tall building in the centre of Turku, right on the marketplace.

'See you tomorrow,' called Sundström from the passenger seat, and Petri Grönholm grunted something that Joentaa couldn't make out. Then they drove along narrower streets through the increasingly heavy rain.

'Are you sure this is right?' asked Sundström, when Joentaa asked Sabrina to turn off along the forest path.

What's for sure? thought Joentaa.

The house in the dark.

Larissa beside him.

Her hand in his.

'Well, goodnight then, you two,' said Sundström.

'Sleep well,' said Sabrina.

'And you,' said Joentaa, and he followed the woman whose name he didn't know and who was already halfway to the front door.

5

She cried in her sleep, and couldn't remember any reason when Kimmo Joentaa woke her and asked if everything was all right.

'I have to get some sleep now,' she said.

'You must have been dreaming something.'

'Kimmo, I can't remember what. Let me sleep, okay?'

'If you promise me not to cry.'

'Sometimes you really get on my nerves.'

'What's he like, then – August?'

She did not reply, but sat up a little way.

He felt a pang in his stomach, in his chest.

A burning behind his eyes.

'Kimmo, go to sleep now.'

'Sorry.'

'Just go to sleep.'

'Sorry.'

'Goodnight, Kimmo,' she said, turning over on her side.

Some time passed. A sentence formed in his mind. He weighed it up on his tongue for a while before bringing it out.

'I need something from you,' he said at last.

There was no answer, and he didn't know whether she had heard him.

'I need your name,' he said.

But perhaps his words were only sounds or colours in the dream that she was dreaming, the dream that she would have forgotten as soon as she woke up.

6

Dear diary,

That's what people say, don't they? Yes. I think so.

Write it down just as you saw it at the time. So that you can remember it. Later.

The hospital is sparsely furnished. The walls are green, white and blue. I walk through wide spaces with a sense of being alone. Glances fall on me but do not linger. They glide away again. There are medics wearing coats the same colours as the walls. They are in a hurry, concentrating. Focused on something that is nothing to do with me. They don't see me. They walk fast and disappear behind doors, and muted voices come through the walls, sometimes a groan, a scream, or a fit of weeping.

I feel like a shadow. Even when I am sitting with her. In an empty room that I found without actually looking for it. The wall around us is green. There's a nail in it with a wooden crucifix hanging from the nail. A plastic plant on a side table. The bed and the covers are white. Medical equipment. Tubes, electronic apparatus. The technology looks curiously old. Much used, wearing out. The recurrent, soft humming note dies away in the silence, the way the notes of the piano died away back then after she had struck the keys.

The recurrent, soft humming note saying that she is alive.

Sleeping, waking.

It all happens so fast, that's why you have to write it down. To keep a record. So that you can remember it some other time.

All so fast, so fast, I must come back to it later.

The device keeping her alive flows into her hand, into her arm, and is easily removed, as if it were only a plaster on a cut.

I leave the room, go along the right-angled corridors.

Other people come towards me. Their shadows fall on the walls. Some of them are sitting on benches, and look up when a voice announces an emergency.

When I step out into the daylight, the autumn feels like summer, the sun is shining as it was back at that time, and for a few moments I feel that only seconds have passed since then.

7

When Joentaa woke in the morning, Larissa had already got up. He tasted the stale flavour of the sparkling wine on his tongue. The dizziness and headache weren't too bad, but he knew that they had arrived in the hours while he was asleep, and would stay with him for a while.

He got up and went through the living room into the kitchen. The house was quiet and empty. No splashing, rushing water in the shower. He felt an impulse to call her name, but then the word left his mouth like a croak. He cleared his throat and tried again. 'Larissa,' he said in a neutral voice, one that she couldn't have heard even if she had been there.

But she wasn't there. He went down to the cellar and opened the wooden door to the sauna, which lay silent in the cool of morning. The narrow window was open. They'd forgotten to close it. He stood in the small, square room and looked at the aftermath of the previous day. The stones were cold, the water to pour on them was a calm, smooth surface in the old grey bucket, and he thought he saw imprints on the bottom step of the wooden bench, imprints left by their bodies and perhaps their body fluids, souvenirs of the heated hour they had spent here. Before they went off to Nurmela's house and his unusual birthday party.

What's he like, then – August?

And what would that heated, passionate hour in the sauna cost him?

He went up again. Sat down at the kitchen table and thought that it was Saturday, and she didn't really work on Saturdays.

Maybe she'd gone for a walk. Or a swim. The telephone rang. He stopped and waited until the answerphone came on. He knew it wasn't Larissa. Larissa never phoned. It was Sundström asking him to call back.

He went into the living room and over to the window in the front wall. His eyes searched the water of the lake. It was another calm, smooth surface, like the water down in the sauna in the dented tin bucket that Sanna had bought, when she was still alive and everything was all right.

He sat on the sofa, never taking his eyes off the lake, and thought that Sanna was dead and Larissa had disappeared. And that there was nothing else to think about.

She'd come back. In the evening. Or tomorrow. In a few days' or weeks' time.

He'd go and water Sanna's grave.

He went into the kitchen, poured water into a glass, and raised it to his mouth. Pasi Laaksonen from the house next door came past. With his fishing rod. He waved, and Joentaa raised an arm to return the wave. As usual. As he had on the day when Sanna died, and so many other days afterwards.

When Pasi Laaksonen went fishing late in the morning at weekends, Joentaa was usually standing at the kitchen window. He watched Pasi disappear down in the hollow leading to the lake, and wondered whether it was really just chance, a recurrent coincidence, or something entirely different.

Pasi with his fishing rod, walking by, waving. A few hours after Sanna's death. Perhaps he stood at the kitchen window so that he could experience the scene again and again. Because watching Pasi walk down to the water always brought back the moment when Sanna had died – and the moment when she had still been alive.

The longer he thought about it, the more conclusive that idea appeared to him, and he wondered why it occurred to him only now, years later.

He was still thinking about it when the phone rang again. He moved away from the window and went to answer it, walking with swift, springy steps, although he knew it wouldn't be Larissa.

It was Petri Grönholm. He spoke clearly, if a little slowly. Joentaa thought of the moment, not so long ago, when Petri Grönholm had thrown up on Nurmela's carpet, and the moment long before that when Sanna had stopped breathing, and then he thought of the fact that Larissa had gone without saying goodbye. Larissa or whatever her name was, and he had difficulty concentrating on what Grönholm was saying at the other end of the line.

'Kimmo?'

'Yes?'

'Did you get all that?'

'Not entirely. At the hospital, you said . . .'

'Yes, Paavo Sundström is on his way, and Kari Niemi is already there with the forensics team. The woman was very sick anyway.'

Anyway, thought Joentaa.

'So it's kind of odd . . . when she'd probably have died of her own accord.'

'Ah,' said Joentaa.

'Never mind that. Anyway, Paavo said we were to park in the car park outside the main building, and then there's signposting to Intensive Care.'

Joentaa nodded. He knew the Intensive Care ward at Turku hospital.

'So . . . can you pick me up? In case of any residual alcohol in my bloodstream. I was pretty well pickled last night, so I don't want to . . .' said Grönholm.

'Yes . . . of course I can.'

'See you soon, then,' said Grönholm, ringing off.

Joentaa stood there for a while with the phone in his hand.

As he was putting on his coat, he finally remembered Nurmela's first name. Petri, just like Grönholm. He wasn't entirely sure, but yes, he did think he saw the name in his mind's eye. Petri Nurmela, chief of police.

Cover name August.

Wasting electricity, he thought, and he switched on all the lights in the house before leaving.

8

Lauri says I ought to write it all down. He says I'll want to remember it some time. Because another thing you have to think about is that everything happens so quickly, and after a while it's all past and forgotten, and then you'd like to remember it. Lauri says. I think Lauri is a bit of a nutcase, with his books and his clever sayings and the way he acts in general, but he's smart as well, you have to give him that, and besides, he's a real friend, I know he is, so I'm going to write it all down.

Starting today.

I want to, as well. Which is funny, because there's nothing I hate more than writing essays and dictations and all that stupid stuff. But I think Lauri's idea is a good one, even if just now I was nearly killing myself laughing at him, when he was trying to tell me that Matti Nykänen is bound to fall flat on his face some time, because there has to be more to life than flying through the air on two boards.

That's only logical, he says.

I asked him why he wanted to start on about Matti Nykänen when it's 30 degrees and we're dangling our feet in the water, and the sun is blazing down like it hasn't for a long time.

'You're right,' said Lauri. He often says that, although really he's usually the one who is right.

Sometimes I wonder why Lauri hangs out with me at all, because he's best at all school subjects and I'm worst at most of them, and by way of saying thanks I picked him first of all for my football team yesterday. I saw the jaws of all the others drop, and Lauri thought he'd heard wrong and didn't like to come over to me. I had to call his name out loud again, and then he came over slowly and gave me kind of an enquiring look. Then he played really well in defence, threw himself at the ball good and hard.

I guess Lauri also sometimes wonders why I hang out with him, and because we both ask ourselves the same question that makes the two of us a pretty good couple. And this is a lovely summer so far. Lauri said it's a summer that never ought to end, it's so good.

We let our feet dangle in the water. I'm quite brown from the sun, Lauri's wearing a T-shirt and has suncream on his arms, because he's terrified of sunburn.

He says I'll want to remember it some time, that's why I ought to write it all down. Not that I've told him anything at all yet. I only said I will, about the piano lessons. That's all. He gives me a funny look and says that I ought to write everything down, all that I remember, because I'll always want to remember that, about the piano lessons and of course about her too.

And also, he says, I must watch out, because there's no point falling in love with the wrong women.

Lauri of all people says that, Lauri Lemberg who's never kissed a girl because his smooching was useless when fat Satu Koivinen wanted to get up close and personal with him at the midsummer party.

It's a funny idea when you imagine it. Someone's smooching turning out useless. We'll see if I do want to remember it some time, but anyway I've written it down now. Dear diary. That's the way you put it, right? Dear diary. Hi, dear diary. I'll have to ask Lauri tomorrow if you really do put it that way.

9

Turku hospital. A large, white building with countless windows. Kimmo Joentaa had tried counting them once, on a sunny day before Sanna's death.

He had really meant to go home to look through his post and sleep for a few hours. But then he sat in the car instead, staring at the big, solid building, trying to pinpoint the window behind which Sanna was lying. And sleeping. Or dying.

Then he had begun to count, gave up at 174, got out of the car and went back along all the corridors to Sanna's room. That was quick, she had said, wearily and in a husky voice, and he had sat down beside her bed and tried to smile.

The car park still looked the same. Sun too warm for autumn, as it had been then. Grönholm, beside him, got out of the car. Joentaa followed and overtook him. He suddenly felt that he had to get all this over with quickly. He walked purposefully; he knew the way. Right-angled walls, arrows to wherever you were going. There was a uniformed woman officer outside the broad swing doors with the words *Intensive Care* above them. Joentaa took his ID out of his coat pocket and returned her nod before going on. Behind him he heard Petri Grönholm's slower footsteps.

Inside, white-clad forensics officers and a curious silence. Nurses both male and female were leaning against the walls, behind a glazed partition. Sundström was standing at the end of the corridor, deep in conversation with a man whom Joentaa knew.

Rintanen. The medical director of the hospital, who had

looked after Sanna during the last days of her life. The doctor who made it possible for him to be with her day and night, although the hospital regulations didn't really allow for that. One of the nurses had told him at the time that it wasn't usual, and he would only make himself ill if he didn't sleep and eat. Joentaa had nodded, and said nothing, and wondered why someone who didn't understand anything about death was working in a hospital.

He went over to Sundström and to Rintanen, who stood very upright but not tense, with his head slightly bent. He used to stand like that before. Joentaa passed the room where Sanna had been lying; he remembered the number, the snow-white paint. The door was closed. His legs began to tremble, and he had to go on a little further before uttering a greeting that came out of his mouth as a croak.

'Kimmo, my old mate,' said Sundström, imperturbably humorous. 'And Mr Grönholm in person. Good work.'

Joentaa nodded to Sundström and offered Rintanen his hand. 'Hello. We've . . . we've met before.'

Rintanen looked at him for a few seconds, and then memory kicked in. 'Oh, yes . . . that's to say . . . yes, your wife, a few years ago.'

'I'm glad to see you,' said Joentaa, on impulse.

'How are you?' asked Rintanen.

Joentaa gave him a nod. Sundström cleared his throat.

'I'm all right,' said Joentaa.

Kari Niemi, head of Forensics, passed them, his eyes fixed on something wrapped in transparent film. Niemi, who had given him a hug in the days after Sanna's death. He wondered if he was just imagining it, whether it was a product of his imagination, inspired by these surroundings, or if he really did still feel Niemi's hug.

Sundström, Rintanen and Grönholm were discussing the question of how to keep the normal business of the hospital going while a murder investigation was conducted at the same time.

Joentaa moved away from them and went over to the room where most of the scene-of-crime officers were working. One of them gave him gloves and an overall. A large room with only one bed in it. Because people on their way to meet death had the privilege of privacy.

He went into the room, trying to control the unsteadiness of his legs. The woman was lying on her back on the bed. Salomon Hietalahti, the forensic pathologist, was sitting at the window on a visitor's chair, making notes.

'Murdering a dead woman,' said Sundström behind him.

Joentaa turned round.

'She was in a coma, from time to time a waking coma. Persistent vegetative state, or apallic syndrome as our medical friend Rintanen out there calls it. In his opinion she had no prospect of recovery.'

Joentaa nodded.

No prospect of recovery, he thought.

'But here's the best of it – we don't know who she is. We don't even know her name.'

'How on earth . . . ?' said Grönholm.

Don't even know her name, thought Joentaa.

'Because the poor soul was found lying at the side of the road with traumatic brain injury. And without any personal details on her.'

Call Larissa.

'I think I remember that case. It was in the papers for quite a while, wasn't it?'

On the occasional table next to the telephone. Was he imagining it? He must go home, he must check.

'No idea,' said Sundström.

'Yes, it was. The unknown woman, unconscious and without any memory. Didn't you read about her?'

He must check up on it. He must go home. Grönholm and Sundström were talking about the woman lying a few feet away on a bed like the one where Sanna had lain. In a room that looked like the room where she had died.

'Though if she was unconscious, how would she have any memory anyway?' said Grönholm, and Joentaa wondered whether it was the residual alcohol still in his bloodstream that made him sound so stupid. He thought of Sanna. And of what was on the occasional table next to the telephone. His glance had fallen on it . . . but he wasn't sure. He must leave, he must go home.

'Kimmo?'

'The giraffe,' he said.

'What?' asked Sundström.

'I must leave,' said Joentaa.

'What?'

'Back very soon. I forgot something.'

'Kimmo? Hey, hang on a minute!'

Sundström's voice in the distance. He walked along the corridors fast, the way he had walked along them on the night when Sanna's pulse stopped beating.

'Kimmo, for God's sake!' cried Sundström, and he was out in the open air, running to the car, driving away.

He thought that he didn't even know her name.

And that he mustn't lose her.

IO

The light was on. It was difficult to spot that, because the sun was shining almost as brightly as the electric lights inside the house, but Joentaa saw that it was on.

The light was still on. Larissa wasn't there.

Of course not. For a moment he wondered if she ever had been.

As he opened the door and went into the hall, he thought of the occasional table with the telephone on it. Then he was standing in front of it, looking at the key.

The second key to the house. Larissa had left it behind. For the first time. Whenever she went away for an unspecified time, she'd always taken her key with her, so that when she did come back days or weeks later, she could unlock the door, put the light out, and sit in the living room in the dark.

The key hung from an ungainly wooden giraffe that had amused her enormously when they came upon it recently, as they strolled around a flea market down by Naantali harbour. She had gone back there that same day. To buy the giraffe pendant. And now she'd left the same ungainly giraffe behind for him, along with the key and her false name.

His mobile hummed its usual tune. He didn't reply. The landline telephone rang. Sundström, speaking in urgent tones, was leaving a message. Joentaa heard the voice but didn't take in what it was saying. He must find Larissa. Not just look for her, find her. Now, at once. He must be with her now, put his arms round her, hold her close and ask the questions that he'd forgotten to ask. And the other questions that she had left hanging in the air as she smiled, or said nothing, or vaguely shook her head.

He must ask questions, get answers.

Now, immediately.

He took his mobile out of his jacket pocket and called her number. The number where he could never reach her. The familiar anonymous voice spoke. The person he had called was not available. A new text. Nothing in his mailbox. His hands were beginning to shake. He went into the kitchen, poured a glass of water and sipped it.

Then he hurried downstairs to the room that had been Sanna's studio in another life. Before she fell ill, and stopped working for the firm of architects that had sent one of the most expensive wreaths on the day of her funeral. With a card signed by all the staff members.

He sat down at the desk and started up his laptop. Went into his email and opened it. Two new messages. He had won a lottery that he'd never played. The second message was from his colleague Tuomas Heinonen. He felt a pang. He must visit Tuomas in the hospital where he had checked himself in a few weeks ago, when his gambling addiction came back. Heinonen had been off work for months. He hadn't gone for treatment until he had gambled away the proceeds from the three-room apartment that he had inherited and sold, without telling his wife Paulina anything about it. Joentaa decided that he would call Paulina, and then he would go to the hospital with her and her little twin daughters and visit Tuomas, and then everything would be cleared up and all right again. He'd do that soon.

No message from Larissa.

He typed in her address: <u>veryhotlarissa@pagemails.fi</u>.
He wrote:

Dear Larissa,

I hope you're well. I'm rather worried. The key is still here. Did you forget it? I'll leave it in the grass under the apple tree, and then you can get in any time, even if I'm out.

Love from
Kimmo

He looked at the message, and wondered why he hadn't asked those important questions. Why he hadn't insisted on the answers?

He sent the message, and waited a few minutes for any feeling that someone was beginning to read it at the other end.

Then he went upstairs, found a piece of paper and a pen, and wondered what he was going to write. His eyes lingered on the photograph of Sanna standing on the shelf beside Larissa's stack of books. He had once talked to Larissa about Sanna. And about that photo. They had been lying on the sofa, and as a city exploded on the TV screen Larissa had got up to go over to the photograph.

A photo of Sanna on cross-country skis, leaning back and laughing her clear laugh, taken when she was still healthy, in the winter before her death.

Larissa had looked intently at the photograph, as if she were seeing it for the first time, and then she had said, 'Sanna was really wonderful.'

On the screen, the hero of the film had fallen into the sea from a great height without dying, and Joentaa had talked about Sanna. Probably for quite a long time, because when his voice died away the film was over, and Larissa had been sitting there very upright, clumsily stroking his leg, and their eyes met.

'I didn't want to make you . . .' he had begun to say, and she had laughed, but she was still crying, and she had said, 'Oh, Kimmo, I cry every day.'

II

He drove back to the hospital. As the car went down the street he tried to count the years, months and days that had passed since Sanna's death.

He got muddled up, and thought that it would be better to count the hours, or the minutes. The seconds. The moments that had passed by since that one moment that wouldn't ever pass by.

He had left the giraffe under the apple tree.

He sat in the car when he reached the car park, stopped counting minutes and began counting the windows again. That was certainly simpler. The police car had been left in a No Parking area. The forensic team's minibus was parked in the sun.

He got out of his car and retraced his earlier footsteps. Faded arrows in assorted colours pointed different ways. Blue arrows for Intensive Care, green for the nearby Surgical Ward. Yellow for Maternity. White for the cafeteria.

He followed the right angles and the blue arrows.

The room where Sanna had lain.

Kari Niemi, smiling as if everything were all right, showed him an item wrapped in transparent film and said something that Joentaa couldn't make out, because waves swallowed up the words before they reached him.

Sundström, red in the face, came towards him, and Joentaa thought of the giraffe under the tree.

'For God's sake, Kimmo!'

'I'm back,' said Joentaa.

'What got into you?'

'Nothing.'

'Kimmo!'

Joentaa passed him and stopped in the doorway. The woman was still lying on the bed at one side of the room, like an empty shell, surrounded by apparatus that now looked unimportant.

'The great unknown,' murmured Sundström beside him.

'Yes,' said Joentaa.

'We're using the cafeteria for interrogations,' said Sundström, turning away.

Joentaa nodded.

'Come on, damn it!' cried Sundström.

They followed the white arrows. The cafeteria too looked the same as ever. Large, bright pictures on the walls. Joentaa remembered them only when he saw them again. A view through the big window of the garden, the fountain, the benches grouped around it. Rice pies with egg butter under transparent plastic on the counter. He thought of Sanna carefully spreading egg butter on a roll a few days before her death, and saying that she felt better.

Members of the hospital staff were sitting at the tables in their medical coats, waiting to make statements. The discreet background noise of whispering.

Petri Grönholm was sitting at one of the tables bent over a laptop, and nodding to a young man who kept shaking his head apologetically.

'It looks as if no one noticed anything,' said Sundström, and Joentaa listened in vain for the familiar sarcasm in his voice. 'We have a dead woman no one knows, and a murderer no one saw.'

Joentaa nodded, and Sundström made his way to an empty table at the side of the big room. They sat down, and Sundström took some notes out of his shabby briefcase and put them down on the table like a newsreader about to begin his bulletin.

'Well then . . . to get into the ward you really have to enter a number code, but it seems that the door wasn't locked. No one knows why not.'

'I know,' said Joentaa.

'What?' asked Sundström.

'I mean I know about the number code,' said Joentaa. He even knew what it was, unless the code had been changed since then, because Rintanen had given it to him at the time so that he could come into the ward and leave it again when he liked. He had learned it by heart, and he still remembered it.

'I was talking to Rintanen the medical director . . .'

'Yes,' said Joentaa.

He had wanted to thank Rintanen, for everything. He'd catch up with that later.

'By the way, Kimmo, I heard that this is where your wife died . . .'

'Yes, it's a long time ago,' said Joentaa, wondering why he was talking such nonsense.

'Oh,' said Sundström.

'Quite a while ago,' said Joentaa.

Sundström scrutinised him for a few seconds. 'Rintanen says our woman sometimes had to be given artificial respiration. The murderer obviously cut off her oxygen supply. Simply switched the artificial respiration off.'

Joentaa nodded.

'She was found in a ditch beside the road in summer with severe traumatic brain injury, which was then diagnosed as . . . wait a moment . . . apallic syndrome.'

Joentaa nodded.

'In other words unconscious, in a coma. Then in a waking coma, a vegetative state. I didn't grasp what all that means in detail, but anyway, she wasn't really conscious at any point, she didn't know what was going on, and since being brought in here in summer she'd been kept alive only with the help of medical technology.'

Kept alive, thought Joentaa.

'The cause isn't entirely clear,' said Sundström. 'The woman was very badly injured. Maybe a hit-and-run driver knocked her down, or more likely someone not in a car hit her, struck her down and left her in the ditch. Rintanen also thinks it's possible that she suffered a stroke or a heart attack.'

Joentaa nodded.

'Inquiries by our colleagues about hit-and-run accidents haven't come up with any results. The woman was just found lying there.'

'Just found lying there,' said Joentaa.

'Yes. Fully clothed, and that's the point. No papers, no money, no one who knew her has reported her missing, although her photo was in the papers for several days.'

Several days, thought Joentaa.

A woman without a name.

'Maybe her name's Larissa,' he said without thinking.

'What?'

Joentaa saw Sundström's baffled face, and couldn't help laughing. A brief, slightly hoarse laugh. 'Forget it,' he said.

He closed his eyes and took a deep breath.

'Ah,' said Sundström.

Two women without names. A giraffe. August.

Sundström was looking at the printed sheets of paper.

'What are you reading?' asked Joentaa.

'Various stuff,' murmured Sundström, without raising his head. 'I don't understand why no one knows the woman.

Obviously the only people who called in when the photo was in the papers were nutcases.'

Maybe I should write everything down, thought Joentaa.

'Then we'll publish the photo again, how about that?'

Everything he didn't know.

12

But when there's no more to write down, then what?

There are some people you lose for ever.

There are some people who are easy to find.

Kalevi Forsman, for instance. Software solutions adviser. Or something like that. The company's Internet site is attractive and user-friendly. Forsman is niftily dressed, black suit, white shirt. Black and white. Features curiously soft, as if more work had been done on them after they were first formed.

Not a trace in his eyes of what I remember there – the sudden avidity, the way he froze at the end.

13

That afternoon, the idea had struck him as far-fetched and ridiculous, but in the evening Kimmo Joentaa did indeed begin to write.

He sat at the low table in the living room with a cup of camomile tea, in front of a sheet of white paper, and had the impression that both of them calmed him down a little.

Larissa had not come back. The giraffe was still lying under the apple tree.

The sheet of paper gradually filled up with words. *Larissa: likes playing ice hockey; eats a lot of chocolate; enjoys films with shootouts in them; bought a moped in the summer, she goes to work on it, and she's probably out and about on it at the moment. She used to go on the bus, or she was picked up by her colleague Jennifer – where does she work? She said things about herself now and then, but then she always added that whatever she says is a lie – must think about what could have been true. Find Jennifer.*

He stared at the paper. The letters written in a hand that wasn't really his own, so tidy, so neat, so clearly formed.

Suddenly he sat up straight and turned on the TV set. The late news bulletin was on. The presenter looked grave and composed. The unknown dead woman was one of the headline items. A TV correspondent outside the hospital, frowning. Carefully phrasing his remarks to hide the fact that he hadn't the faintest idea about any of it. How would he? Then the police chief suddenly appeared, Nurmela, facing forward, very upright in the sunlight, in front of those countless windows. August, thought Joentaa, and he thought that he must talk to Nurmela. If you judged the case by what Nurmela was saying, the criminal investigation team had everything under control.

The photo of the unknown woman came on-screen. The one that had already been published soon after she was found, in the hope of tracing family members. Now that the woman was dead, it might arouse a little more attention. Joentaa looked at the picture and tried to memorise it as the news presenter turned to other subjects. A beautiful woman, he thought. But a woman . . . a woman who somehow seemed faceless. A clear, pure, unrecognisable face.

He went on staring at the TV set for a while, neither seeing the pictures nor taking in the words, then stood up and, without stopping to think, called Tuomas Heinonen's mobile number. Heinonen answered after a few seconds.

'Hello, Tuomas, Kimmo here,' said Joentaa.

'Kimmo,' said Heinonen. As if he hadn't linked the name to a face yet.

'I just wanted to . . .'

'Nice of you to call,' murmured Heinonen.

'. . . wanted to call again,' said Joentaa. 'How are you doing?'

'I'm in hospital,' said Heinonen.

'Yes, I know. I could come and see you again.'

'Yes.'

'How are you doing, then?' Joentaa repeated.

'Hm?'

'Tuomas?'

'Sorry . . . I was just . . .'

'What is it?' asked Joentaa.

'Nothing, I was only . . . sorry. How's things with you? Say hi to the others for me.'

'Yes, I will. We had . . . I had a funny sort of day today. Do you remember Larissa?'

'The woman standing naked in your bedroom doorway last Christmas when I told you about the stuff I'd lost gambling?'

'That's right,' said Joentaa.

'How could I forget her?'

'Exactly,' said Joentaa.

'That was kind of a nice Christmas Eve,' said Heinonen. 'In spite of everything.'

Joentaa nodded, and a smile instinctively spread over his face as he thought of that crazy Christmas Eve. First Larissa or whatever she was really called had appeared on his doorstep, then a totally confused, deeply upset Heinonen had arrived in a Santa Claus costume – Heinonen who was always self-controlled, sober, reserved – telling him about the disastrous present-giving at home, and how he was busy gambling his family's money away betting on football matches in the English Premier League.

Almost a year ago, thought Joentaa.

'I only saw her that once. Are you two . . . are you still together?'

Together, thought Joentaa.

'I don't know. She's gone,' he said.

'Gone?'

'Yes, she often goes away, she often stays away, but this is the first time she's left the giraffe behind.'

'Ah. Okay,' said Heinonen. 'Giraffe?'

Joentaa heard a pattering sound in the background, and Heinonen didn't seem to be listening to him very attentively.

'I mean the key to the house. It's on a giraffe pendant.'

'Mmph.'

'So of course I'm worried. Because it's something new. I mean, for her to leave the key here.'

'Hmm? Yes. Yes, that figures,' said Heinonen.

'Well, tell me how you are,' said Joentaa.

'Me . . . fine, I'm fine,' said Heinonen. 'Doing this and that. Tomorrow it's a family therapy session.'

'A what?'

'Some therapeutic method. Depth psychology, I think that's it.'

'Sounds like . . .' said Joentaa, but then he didn't know what it sounded like.

'I did it once before when I was . . . at my first stay here, and it was okay,' said Heinonen.

'What's all that pattering in the background? Is it something on the line?'

'Hm?'

'There's a kind of pattering sound at your end.'

'Oh, that's from the laptop.'

'Ah,' said Joentaa, and Heinonen suddenly began giggling.

'Sorry, Kimmo, I won't lie to you, I'm so glad you called.'

'Yes.'

'It really . . . it means a lot to me. No one but you ever calls. Except for Paulina, of course.'

'Of course,' said Joentaa.

'I've just been placing a few bets,' said Heinonen.

A moment of silence.

'Aha,' said Joentaa.

'There's an ATP major on in the States,' said Heinonen.

'Aha,' said Joentaa.

'Tennis,' Heinonen explained. 'The tournament's showing live on Eurosport, so I can watch it all happen and see the results of the matches.'

Joentaa nodded, looking at the screen of the muted TV set, where a woman clad entirely in red was soundlessly forecasting sunny weather.

'I know it's ridiculous,' said Heinonen.

'I'll come and see you,' said Joentaa. 'When would be best?'

'An evening would be good. It's all . . . all very open

here. We can go out any time and get a drink down by the lake.'

'Let's do that,' said Joentaa.

'With the weather staying so fine.'

'Yes . . . well, better go to sleep now, Tuomas. And do stop . . . stop placing bets of any kind.'

'Okay.'

'And if there's anything I can do, call me any time.'

'Thanks.'

'See you soon.'

'Yes, see you soon. And tell Larissa hello from me when she comes back.'

'I'll do that.'

'If she remembers me, that is.'

'I'm sure she does. I'll just tell her hello from Santa Claus.'

It was a moment before Heinonen laughed. 'That's right . . . that stupid costume I was still wearing.'

'Sleep well, Tuomas,' said Joentaa. 'And no more tennis tonight.'

'Night,' said Heinonen.

Then Joentaa sat in the silence, watching with only half his attention as the bald man on the screen stood on the edge of a swimming pool in the sun, shooting people down with an outsize gun.

Late-evening entertainment.

He stood up, turned the TV off, and went to fetch his laptop.

He sat on the sofa, started the computer, and waited.

He had no new messages.

He sat there with the computer on his lap, and thought of Tuomas Heinonen sitting on his bed in his small room, also with a computer on his lap, watching tennis.

14

Dear diary,

People really do say that, Lauri told me, and he should know. I asked him if I could give him all this to read some time, but he raised his hands and said oh no, that would never do, then it wouldn't be a diary any more, no one's allowed to read it except me. That surprised me, because I'm sure I'd be interested to read Lauri's diary if he wrote one, specially if Saara was in it. The other boys, I mean Pekka and Aulis, have dropped out. I think I'm the only boy going to piano lessons now. I get some remarks at school, they call me a model student and all that, but I don't care. In fact I even laugh at it, and that feels good.

When I arrived this afternoon Anita-Liisa Koponen had just been plunking away on the piano, it almost made me feel ill. She can't play at all, but Saara still said she was doing well, which kind of made me angry, because that's what she always says to me too, and I hope she doesn't say it to everyone, or at least that she means it seriously when she says it to me.

I'd never have thought I'd play the piano of my own accord, but I even like it. Today we played some kind of classical piece as a duet, I mean I only played the bass notes, but it sounded lovely, and Saara asked if I could sense that. That it sounded lovely, I mean. I said yes.

Saara was wearing that dress, that very light, airy dress. As if she had just that dress on and nothing else.

Seeing that no one but me can read this diary, I'll be completely honest: when she opened the door to me in that dress, and I followed her into the living room, and saw her back where the dress was cut low, I got a hard-on. I had to bend over a bit and make funny distorted movements so that she wouldn't notice. She laughed. Such a nice, clear laugh, I couldn't feel bad about it.

Later her boyfriend Risto came along, and he and I played football a bit in the garden. I was in goal, and Risto shot low into the corners, so I had to throw myself full length.

When I got home there was trouble, because my mother thought I'd skipped the piano lesson on account of my dirty trousers, and she even phoned Saara to ask. I think it was Risto who answered, because after a while my mother laughed the way women only laugh when they're talking to men.

Anyway, then she came and put her hand on my head and apologised and even said she was proud of me. Probably because I play the piano.

Dear diary.

And not because of the e-rec-tion.

15

In the morning information began coming in. A number of people were sure they knew the dead woman. A number of people said they thought they knew her. A number of people weren't sure, but wanted to tell the police that the woman looked familiar to them. She had lived in Helsinki. In Seinäjoki. In Tampere and Joensuu. In Kotka, Savonlinna, Hämeenlinna. She had been unmarried, lived a secluded life, was gregarious, married, the mother of sons and daughters, a professor at the university, head bookkeeper for an insurance company, a cleaner in a department store.

The officers who took the phone calls and emails reported no definite leads, and other officers went out to check the most plausible stories.

Sundström had left his office door open, so that Grönholm and Joentaa could see him setting up one of his Excel spreadsheets. He typed names and times in with two fingers, jobs done and to be done, questions asked and to be asked; he cursed to himself when his computer crashed and closed his eyes as it rebooted.

'You want to save now and then,' muttered Petri Grönholm without looking up from his notes, and Joentaa leaned in the doorway unable to take his eyes off Sundström; it was going to take him quite a while to get the spreadsheet up and running again. But in the end it would be a smooth, white, symmetrical document made up of words without a single grammatical mistake, and it would indeed give some structure to the investigating team's work for the first time.

'I'll have it in a minute,' said Sundström.

'Easy does it, we still have ten minutes before the meeting,' called Grönholm from the next room.

Then the printer was running, and Joentaa jumped when Sundström said, 'We'll find her.'

He thought of his empty house in the morning. And in the night, part of which he had spent lying awake, in a drowsy state between dream and reality.

'We'll find her,' said Sundström.

Find a dead woman, thought Joentaa.

Then they went along the corridor to the conference room, from which came the sound of the other officers' conversation as they waited for them. Murmurs, suppressed laughter, some voices loud and clearly articulated, others softer, hesitant. They all fell silent when Sundström pushed open the door and entered the room, which was flooded with autumnal light.

'Morning, men,' he said, and Joentaa thought that he had the gift of injecting force and confidence into his voice, casually and without effort. They all sat down at the snow-white table, and Sundström had the spreadsheet handed round until they all had a copy in front of them.

Grönholm reported on what they knew, which was practically nothing. A dead woman. Name unknown. Origin unknown. Age unknown, estimated at between fifty and sixty. There had been nothing on her except the clothes she was wearing. No one had asked after her. No one had visited her in hospital. Reports of missing persons over the last few months had not uncovered any trail so far.

'This is still work in progress, of course,' said Grönholm. 'We'll start from the day when she was found and keep working our way forward and back. Chronologically, I mean. It could take us some time.'

Chronologically, thought Joentaa.

Sundström nodded, and Nurmela came into the room. With a spring in his step, as usual. He stood in the doorway for a moment, then carefully closed the door, turned to those present and asked Sundström not to let him disturb them. 'Just carry on,' he said, staying at the side of the room.

August, thought Joentaa.

And he thought that he must soon speak to August.

'Well . . .' said Grönholm.

'The picture in the newspaper,' said one of the uniformed officers.

'Yes?' asked Sundström.

'Well . . . I think maybe we ought to publish a better one.'

'A better one?'

'No one's recognised her. She looks like everyone and no one.'

Several officers nodded, and it occurred to Joentaa that his had been the same impression. A woman with a face from which all expression had been lost.

'Er . . . suppose we publish one with her eyes open?' asked the young officer. Sundström looked at him for a long time, and seemed to be waiting for the young man to look away.

In the end it was Sundström who looked away. 'The fact is, we don't have a picture of the woman with her eyes open,' he said.

'Oh,' said the young officer.

'That's right,' said Sundström.

'But I thought patients in a waking coma . . . I mean, usually their eyes are open.'

'I didn't say the woman kept her eyes closed all the time, I only said we don't have a photo of her with her eyes open.'

'Ah. I get it.'

'The photo we do have was taken on the day she was found in the ditch at the side of the road. At that point she was unconscious.'

'Okay,' said the young officer.

'Although that's definitely a relevant aspect,' said Grönholm. 'Kimmo talked to Rintanen, the doctor treating her at the university hospital. About the medical details, so to speak.'

Silence filled the room, and when Joentaa finally began to speak his tongue felt coated. 'Yes, that's right,' he agreed.

The phone call to Rintanen, the doctor, at the end of a sleepless night that had felt like the night, years ago, when Sanna died. Rintanen, who had stroked Sanna's shoulder and asked him if he would like to be alone with her for a little while. It had been hard for him to concentrate on what Rintanen was saying on the phone.

He had made the phone call from home before leaving. Had looked out at the lake where Larissa had played ice hockey and where Sanna used to swim. Had listened to Rintanen patiently and gently explaining the difference between a coma and a waking coma, and why it was likely that a severe traumatic brain injury, taking immediate effect, had caused first the coma and then the waking coma into which the unknown patient had fallen in the course of her time in the hospital.

'That's right,' Joentaa repeated, and he cleared his throat. 'What happened is that the woman came out of the coma after a few weeks, but she was still in what they call a waking coma or persistent vegetative state, meaning she was living in a rhythm of sleeping and waking, but was unable to react to her surroundings . . .' He cleared his throat again, and wondered why he sounded so stilted. 'Rintanen can't say for certain what event was the root cause of . . . I mean, what prompted the coma. An accident can lead to a coma, of course, but as we know, when the woman was found in summer our colleagues couldn't find anything to indicate that she'd been in an accident.'

'So we don't know who the woman is or what really happened to her,' said Sundström, getting to his feet, as if this summing-up was something they could live with. 'Some of the information coming in has already been checked. Questioning will continue at nine in the hospital. You will see who's assigned to what job from the—'

'Sorry to bother you,' said Kari Niemi, appearing in the doorway.

'Kari,' said Sundström. 'Cheer us up with the findings of forensic science, will you?'

'We actually do have something,' said Niemi. 'Whatever it may mean.'

'Yes?' asked Sundström.

'Lysozyme,' said Niemi.

'What?' asked Sundström.

'We found quite large amounts of a fluid on the sheet and the blanket under which the dead woman was lying. And a first analysis shows that this fluid contains lysozyme as well as . . .'

'Lysowhat?' asked Sundström.

'. . . as well as a large amount of water, along with mineral substances and salts, indicating that . . .'

Sitting on her bed, thought Joentaa.

'Hm?' asked Sundström.

Smoothing out the sheet. Stroking the cold, soft blanket with his hands until he touches her shoulder and her face, very lightly so as not to wake her.

'Lacrimal fluid,' said Niemi. 'We established that quite large quantities of lacrimal fluid were present on the sheet and the blanket.'

'Ah,' said Nurmela, who was leaning against the window wall in the sunshine.

'And what does that tell us?' asked Sundström.

Niemi shrugged his shoulders. Niemi, whose hug he still

remembered very well, although it was so long ago. The day after Sanna's death.

'A murderer who was shedding tears,' said Kimmo Joentaa in the ensuing silence.

16

Kalevi Forsman examined the name on the business card again. And the design, which had been on his mind all this time. So plain yet so effective. The lines curving harmoniously, the colours seeming to flow gently into each other.

He couldn't remember ever seeing such an attractive business card before.

He crossed the lobby and went up in the lift. The man was as good as his word. A picturesque view of the city and the bathing beach to the west of Helsinki, in the distance several of the huge ferries lying in the water like optical illusions. Women from the hotel or the catering service, in black dresses and white tops, setting up a buffet with drinks, coffee and cakes. He watched them for a while, then turned back to the window and stared out at the sunny sky. The steps behind him sounded soft and springy.

'How do you do?' said the man, already holding out his hand and smiling as he turned round.

'Hello,' replied Forsman.

'Come along,' said the man, going briskly ahead.

'Er, where to?'

'Out,' said the man, walking on.

'Where are the others, then?'

'You're the first,' said the man, opening a door that led out to the roof terrace. In the background the clatter and clink of crockery and the soft, quiet women's voices could be heard.

'I'm the first?' asked Kalevi Forsman.

'You are,' said the man.

'I see.'

'I think your program is interesting. I really do,' said the man.

'Good,' said Forsman.

'It's not . . . not polished, it lacks a certain finesse, but one could look at it the other way around and describe it as absolutely reliable. Your program gives the user a sense of always being on the safe side. Being in control. Do you see what I mean?'

'I think so, yes,' said Forsman. 'Indeed, that's the basic idea of our differential system.'

'Exactly. Well put. After all, that's what we all want. To be safe from danger. Even if it's only the danger of shares losing their value.'

'Which is not the least of life's dangers,' said Forsman.

The man looked at him enquiringly, and smiled.

'I mean . . . well, lives depend on that sort of thing,' said Forsman.

'Yes, indeed.'

'No, with our system you can calculate the value of your fund at any time, literally in real time. You can access it within seconds.'

'Yes, indeed,' said the man.

They were standing in the gentle wind; from time to time a dull thumping could be heard. Ocean-going steamers were probably being loaded up.

Forsman wondered what to say next, and the man said, 'There's something wrong with the weather.'

Forsman nodded, and followed the direction of his gaze out to sea.

'I . . . of course I'm glad to hear that you are thinking of acquiring our software,' he said, as the pause dragged on. His mobile vibrated in his trouser pocket.

'Oh, yes, yes, we are,' said the man. 'You're on our short-list.'

'Excuse me.' Forsman took the mobile out of his pocket and looked at the number on the display. Jussilainen. Couldn't wait patiently. Presumably wanted to ask how things were going.

The man never stopped smiling.

'Nothing important,' said Forsman. 'Well. When . . . when will the others be arriving?'

He felt hungry; he would like a biscuit. One of the chocolate biscuits that a lady from catering had put on the conference table below.

The man said nothing, and Forsman felt the smooth surface of the business card against his hand as he put the mobile away in his jacket pocket. He took the card out, with a feeling that it was something he could hold on to. Although the name was very unusual. Norwegian maybe, or Latvian, although the man spoke Finnish without any foreign accent.

'Do you like it?'

'Hmm? Yes, I do. Plain but attractive. We do a little in the way of design ourselves, especially my partner . . .'

'You could almost call this a one-off,' said the man, taking the card from his hand.

Forsman looked at him with a question in his eyes, and the man looked over his shoulder as if there were something important there.

'Do you remember Saara?' asked the man.

'Sorry?' said Forsman.

The man looked past him, with great concentration, and Forsman turned round. The hotel employees were sitting on chairs at the edge of the buffet area, laughing and deep in conversation, and on the conference table there were black and yellow bottles of drinks and plates of the kind of biscuits he liked and hadn't eaten for a long time.

'Saara. I asked you about Saara,' said the man with the strange name, and just before Forsman was lifted above the balustrade and fell to the depths below there was an answer on the tip of his tongue.

17

Joentaa drove to the hospital with Grönholm. The bed that the dead woman had occupied was empty and made up with clean sheets. The number of forensics officers around the place had been considerably reduced.

Grönholm, deep in conversation with Rintanen, was drinking coffee, and Joentaa went to the cafeteria to look for the police officer who was coordinating interviews with the hospital staff. He couldn't find him.

Rice pies with egg butter under the plastic covers. Coloured pictures on the walls. Pictures that Sanna had mentioned a few days before her death, but he couldn't remember her exact words. Turku lay in the sun beyond the glass wall, and the woman behind the counter asked what he would like.

He asked for a camomile tea, closed his hands round the hot cup and sat down at one side of the room. His mobile vibrated in his jacket pocket. Sundström's number. He waited until Sundström gave up, and put the phone on the table in front of him. He closed his eyes and tried to think, but failed because he didn't know where to begin.

Then he picked up his mobile and wrote an email to Tuomas Heinonen:

Dear Tuomas, hope you slept well. Please don't forget what I said about the tennis. Will come and see you at the weekend.

He sent the message and then stared for a while at the text of it. Then he tapped in Larissa's number and quickly wrote:

Dear Larissa, hope you slept well, how about ice hockey or doing something else nice this evening?

He sent the message, and waited to hear back that it could not be delivered. He looked at the message telling him that the recipient was not known, and he should check his details.

Recipient not known. Check the details.

Ice hockey in summer. But it was really autumn.

He drank his camomile tea and followed the arrows pointing the way to Intensive Care. Grönholm was still deep in conversation, but with someone else this time. Kari Niemi, head of Forensics, smiled at him, and Joentaa asked Grönholm whether his mobile had Internet access.

'Yes, sure, why?' said Grönholm.

'I have to look for something,' said Joentaa.

'I see.' Grönholm took the phone out of his trouser pocket and handed it to him.

'Thanks,' said Joentaa, and he went down the corridor, following the arrows to the exit. When he was in the car he began looking for the pictures that he had found online. He needed only a few minutes.

Larissa's face was unrecognisable in the photos, but everything else was on view. Her naked body in assorted unnatural positions. The tattoo on her upper arm. Some kind of fabulous creature, she had said. Behind the disguised eyes and the disguised face, he guessed at the trace of a smile. He tried to imagine the person behind the camera getting her to give that smile. *Larissa, teens, dream body, top service. 84 Satamakatu. Ring bell for Nieminen.*

He closed the Internet browser and dialled Grönholm's number. It took him a while to realise that he was holding Grönholm's phone in his hands. Then he started out. The police car had a satnav system. He tapped in the address and was reminded of the arrows in the hospital as a soft, strange female voice guided him to his destination. He parked the car and looked in vain for her moped as he went up to the house. Nieminen, whoever that was, lived right at the top. He rang the bell.

'Hello,' said a woman's voice.

'Hello,' said Joentaa.

'Up at the top, sixth floor,' said the woman.

Joentaa took the stairs. The building was in a good state of repair, inside as well as out; the white paint on the walls looked fresh. The door on the sixth floor was not locked. He waited for a while, and then it was pushed open. In the doorway stood a red-haired woman wearing a white bathrobe.

'Come in, darling,' she said, beckoning him in.

Joentaa nodded, and stepped into the corridor, lit by a faint lilac-tinted light.

'Been to see us before, darling?'

'No.'

'Then I'll introduce the—'

'I'm looking for Larissa,' said Joentaa.

'Larissa . . .' said the woman.

'I saw the ad.'

'Oh,' said the woman. Joentaa got the impression that she had lost a good deal of her interest in him.

'The advertisement. On the Internet.'

'It's not right up to date,' said the woman. 'Larissa doesn't work here any more. But we have two lovely girls who are very like her—'

'I want to see Larissa,' said Joentaa.

'Like I said, she doesn't work with us these days.'

'Jennifer,' said Joentaa. Her colleague who sometimes came to pick her up in the morning, before Larissa got the moped.

'Jennifer's here,' said the woman, her tone a little friendlier again.

'Good,' said Joentaa.

Then he stood in a dark room waiting for Jennifer. He had spoken to her only a few times. Hello and goodbye. Jennifer usually gave a wry smile when she saw him. Supercilious. Ironic. Or insecure. He didn't know which, and it hadn't interested him. This time she didn't smile when she came into the room. She looked rather confused.

'Oh,' she said.

'Larissa has gone,' said Joentaa.

'Yes,' said Jennifer.

'Do you know where she is?'

'No idea,' said Jennifer. 'She hasn't been here for several days.'

'But you two are friends,' said Joentaa.

'Yes,' said Jennifer. 'Of course. Sort of.'

'Sort of,' said Joentaa. 'Of course.'

'I like her a lot,' said Jennifer.

'So do I,' said Joentaa. 'That's why I want to find her. As quickly as possible.'

Jennifer did not reply.

'What's her real name?'

'Whose?'

'Whose? Whose? Larissa's, of course.'

'You don't know?'

Joentaa waited. She spluttered with laughter. Then she fell silent again and looked at him for a long time.

'I don't know either. We probably none of us talk about ourselves much, but she's . . . she's rather peculiar,' she finally said.

Top body, thought Joentaa. Dream service. The tattoo on her arm, the mole on her breast. He felt dizzy, and Jennifer fidgeted with her panties as she thought.

'Yes, rather peculiar. She always had pay-as-you-go mobiles and never topped them up – she threw them away instead – and when I told her she ought to sign a proper agreement she said she never writes her name on forms of any sort, on principle.'

Recipient unknown. Check the details.

'But I know she really likes you. If that . . . if that's any help,' said Jennifer.

'Where could she be?' asked Joentaa.

Jennifer shifted her weight to her other leg and seemed to be thinking again. In the end she shrugged her shoulders. 'We sometimes went for a drink, or to a club. But if I had to look for her I'd probably begin with you.'

Joentaa nodded, and thought of the giraffe under the apple tree.

'Could you please call me if you hear anything from her?'

'Yes . . . I think so . . .'

'Yes?'

'Yes . . . of course. Why not? But you're a cop, you'll probably—'

'Good, then let's exchange phone numbers, okay?'

'Give me yours, that'll be enough,' she said.

The dizzy feeling grew as Joentaa scribbled his number on a supermarket receipt. Jennifer took the scrap of paper and seemed to be wondering where to put it.

'Thanks,' said Joentaa, going past her to the door.

'I'll show you out,' she said.

'Right,' he said.

'Good luck,' she said, giving him a wry smile before she closed the door. Ironic. Or insecure. He didn't know which.

The sun was on his back as he drove away.

He was thinking vaguely of August, and the broad white bed in the small dark room, and the note with his telephone number that Jennifer, or whatever her real name was, had after some thought stowed away in her panties.

18

M arko Westerberg suppressed a yawn and a vague sense of sadness.

He leaned over the balustrade and looked down at the dead man on the ground. Fourteenth floor, his young colleague from Forensics had said, with a gleam in his eyes that Westerberg didn't understand.

Kalevi Forsman had fallen fourteen floors down. From the roof terrace of a hotel with an extremely fine view of the sea.

A long queue of cars had formed in front of one of the big steamers. The passengers were now sitting in a café in the sun, or leaning against their cars drumming their fingers on the paintwork, waiting impatiently to get away from Helsinki at last. For whatever reason, and wherever they were going. The sun was a little cold, and Westerberg thought, with a satisfaction that he didn't entirely understand, that autumn would come after all.

He turned and saw his young colleague Seppo, still busy questioning the smartly dressed waitresses, although by now it had become clear that they had nothing to contribute apart from the little that had already been said. Westerberg was reminded of Hämäläinen, the talk-show presenter who had been stabbed not so long ago on the premises of a TV station, and not a soul had noticed.

Obviously violent death had a certain casual look to it these days. Nothing that would strike anyone as particularly unusual. And anyway, the TV show host had survived, and according to the ratings was now more popular than ever as a result. Kalevi Forsman the software adviser hadn't been so lucky.

Westerberg looked at the young women helplessly shaking their heads, and Seppo, patiently nodding and taking notes, and he wondered what a software adviser actually did. At some point he had missed out on this terminology. Software adviser, account manager, help-desk administrator. What the hell did all that guff mean?

A forensic officer in white was leaning over the conference table, apparently looking for the particle of dust that would identify the murderer. Seppo thanked the smart young ladies and walked briskly towards him, but only to say that nothing new had turned up. Westerberg nodded.

'But at least what we do have is a start,' said Seppo. 'Two men. One rather short, wearing a striking sky-blue bow tie and a crumpled suit. That was Forsman.'

Westerberg nodded.

'And a second man who was already here before Forsman arrived. Not tall, not short. Well, if anything quite tall. Between one metre eighty and one metre eighty-five – perhaps, because one of the waitresses thought he was taller than that.'

'So quite tall,' said Westerberg.

'Not fat, not thin. Just normal,' said Seppo.

'Didn't one of the ladies say he was wiry?'

Seppo nodded. 'Yes, but the others couldn't confirm it. Good-looking, they all said that. But in an everyday kind of way. And in all seriousness they mentioned three different hair colours.'

'Three?'

'Fair, brown, grey.'

'Oh,' said Westerberg.

'He even said a friendly good morning to them, all the ladies agree on that.'

Friendly, thought Westerberg.

'He was standing on the roof terrace and seemed to be enjoying the view while the women set up the buffet,' said Seppo. 'The waitresses assumed that he and Forsman both belonged to the company that had hired the conference room. A chain of fitness studios, or more precisely two fitness studios that could be merging.'

Fitness studios, thought Westerberg, and he noticed that Seppo said the word as if it were perfectly normal.

'Forsman is not on the list of participants, and as matters stood has not the slightest . . .'

'This is getting me down,' said Westerberg.

'. . . not the slightest thing to do with the studios,' said Seppo.

'This is getting me down. Fitness. Account. Software adviser. Flat-rate surfing.'

Seppo didn't seem to understand him.

'All that shit,' Westerberg specified more precisely.

Seppo nodded.

'Never mind. So Forsman has nothing to do with the conference. In all probability the murderer won't be on any list either, but of course we'll have to work through the names.'

'Interviews are already in progress,' said Seppo.

Westerberg was about to say something else, but stopped and watched the forensic officer lying on the floor and feeling the underside of the table.

'Yes,' said Seppo.

'What actually happened here?' asked Westerberg.

'Well . . .' said Seppo.

'A man calmly goes up to the fourteenth floor of a hotel, says good morning to the catering ladies – in a friendly way, of course – stands on the roof terrace and enjoys the view. Then a second man comes along, the two of them talk. Then one of them falls off the roof and the other goes home. The end.'

Seppo nodded to himself, but then raised his hand. 'Not quite,' he said.

'Not quite?'

'No, he said goodbye as well. To the women.'

'Right. He said goodbye. I forgot that bit. In a friendly way, I assume?'

Seppo nodded. 'We're getting each of the women to put together a picture of him,' he said. 'Independently of each other. Although they all said they didn't feel able to do that.'

'We'll see.'

'One of them asked if she had to paint it herself.'

Westerberg shook his head. 'I hope you told her that all that is done by *software* these days.' He emphasised the word *software*, but Seppo didn't seem to get the joke.

They heard a uniformed police guard at the door telling someone, 'You can't come in here.' Westerberg took several steps into the room and saw a muscleman standing by the lift.

'The conference is cancelled,' said Seppo.

'Why?' asked the muscleman.

'Please go to the breakfast lounge on the first floor and you will be interviewed there,' said Seppo.

'I'll be what?' asked the muscleman.

'Please go to the breakfast lounge,' said Seppo, and the man actually went.

'There,' said Seppo, who cut a small and slightly built figure, not without pride.

Breakfast lounge, thought Westerberg.

19

It's evening. Dear diary. Olli spreads the cards and shuffles them vigorously. His eyes sparkle as he tells me to throw the dice. I throw, and move my counter into the first square. Sunset outside. All an illusion that the sun is moving. The outcome of imagination and limited vision. The earth rotates. Olli and I are passing the border between day and night. Olli wins the game.

'Yes!' he cries triumphantly. And then, 'Another game!'

'Time to get some sleep, don't you think?' I say.

'Another game!' says Olli.

Leea scurries by like a shadow. Sometimes in one direction, sometimes in another. She is talking on the phone. Her voice is always there, sometimes near, sometimes far. Although I can hear only her and not the person at the other end of the line, that tells me what they're talking about.

Henna, Leea's best friend, is having a baby. Her first. Now, at this very minute. She's in the hospital – another hospital – and has been walking up and down for hours, waiting for her labour pains to get intense enough. When that moment comes the doctor is going to carry out a Caesarian at once.

Kalle, Henna's husband, is standing in the corridor outside the operating theatre, waiting to be let in and phoning Leea to calm himself down.

But now they are both agitated and in no condition to keep each other calm.

Olli throws the dice and comments on his move in the game.

At forty-two, Henna is quite old for a first-time mother.

The baby will be called Valtteri, always assuming that, as the doctor has told them, it is a boy.

Leea is on the phone, Olli is throwing the dice, Henna is bringing a baby into the world. I find it difficult to keep those events related to each other.

It's warm in this house.

'You're not paying attention,' says Olli.

'Sorry.'

'You're not playing properly,' says Olli.

I stroke his head, my hand passing over his hair. I feel how soft it is. Leea says nothing. She puts the phone back on its charger and looks at me.

'Your turn,' says Olli.

'Henna's baby is coming,' says Leea.

Kalevi Forsman. Adviser for software solutions.

'It's your turn,' says Olli.

I throw the dice.

A man dies, a boy begins to live.

20

I n the night, Kimmo Joentaa called Police Chief Nurmela. On the TV screen, a scantily clad presenter was in search of animals with the initial A, and Nurmela's voice seemed to surface from deep sleep.

'Kimmo here,' said Joentaa.

'Yes . . . Kimmo . . . just a moment . . .'

'Hello?' said Joentaa.

'Yes . . . is there . . . anything new?' mumbled Nurmela.

'I have to ask you something about Larissa,' said Joentaa. Nurmela did not reply.

'Hello?' asked Joentaa.

Nurmela still did not reply; there was a crackle on the line.

'Alligator. Alligator. That's not it, Ari-Pekka, that's not it,' said the TV presenter, gesticulating.

'Are you crazy?' said Nurmela.

'Thanks for calling in, Ari-Pekka.'

'What?' said Joentaa.

'Look, it's three in the morning. I'm asleep. My wife is asleep.'

'She's gone,' said Joentaa.

'Who?'

'Larissa.'

'Kimmo, I'm going to—'

'I have to find her,' said Joentaa. 'Do you know—'

'Stop going on about that damn woman.'

'I went to the house where she was working, but she isn't there any more, and I thought you might have another number or address where she . . .'

'No, darling, no, no, go back to sleep.'

'. . . where she worked.'

'Hamster, no, that's not it. No, the first letter of the name is A. The initial is A.'

'Yes . . . lie down, darling, I'll be right back.'

'Are you listening to me?' asked Joentaa.

There was more crackling on the line, and then Nurmela's whispering voice came through quite close. 'Now then, listen to me, Kimmo, you arsehole. I want to get some sleep. I don't know the woman, and she doesn't interest me either.'

'I have to find her as soon as possible,' said Joentaa.

Nurmela said nothing.

'Like now,' said Joentaa.

'Kimmo, I'm hanging up,' said Nurmela evenly.

'She left the key,' said Joentaa.

'Ape, no. Ape isn't the answer,' said the presenter, who had now lost her bra.

'She never did that before.'

Nurmela had hung up, and for a while Joentaa watched the TV presenter.

Then he rang the number flickering on the screen. He waited for the now familiar message that he had been hearing for hours when he tried it, to the effect that all the lines were in use, and advising him to try again a little later.

Instead, another voice informed him that he was in luck and would be put straight through.

He waited.

The woman on the screen bobbed up and down on tiptoe and asked him his name.

'Er, Kimmo,' he said.

'Kimmo, lovely to talk to you.'

'Thanks. The same to you.'

The woman on the screen laughed, and Joentaa bent forward and narrowed his eyes to see her better.

'Kimmo, dear, are you still on the line?'

'Yes.'

'You have a lovely voice.'

'Do I? Thanks.'

'What is the right answer?'

'Giraffe.'

The woman laughed, a sudden, shrill laugh. 'The initial is A, sweetie-pie. The name begins with A.'

'I'm right, all the same.'

'I'm inclined to think our friend Kimmo isn't totally sober.'

'Are you hanging up on me now?'

'Thanks for calling in, Kimmo.'

The sports channel was showing a tennis match. He sat on the floor, leaning back against the sofa, and followed a few rallies before his head fell to one side.

One of the players served an ace. Applause.

Just before darkness came down on him, he asked himself, with remarkable clarity, whether he was falling asleep or falling unconscious, and what the difference really was.

21

Dear diary,

Saara laughed because I played all the wrong notes. I hadn't practised the piece, but I didn't want to admit it. I think I sat there stiffly and tried to press the right keys, but it sounded terrible.

Saara laughed, and suddenly stroked my hair very lightly. It felt incredibly good. As if she was petting me. Then she said we'd better play something else, and I could choose the piece, and then Risto was standing in the doorway asking what there was to laugh about.

'Nothing,' said Saara, quick as a shot.

'Oh, nothing?'

Saara shook her head, and Risto asked what the idea of the boy was supposed to be. I think he meant me, and Saara didn't get round to answering because Risto took a couple of quick steps our way and hit her.

Just like that.

She sat there, and I think she started trembling.

Risto went away and came back after a while, and he said we could play football.

Saara looked at the floor and didn't move at all. She was breathing very fast.

Then we played football. I chased every ball as if I was running for my life. In the end Risto praised me and clapped me on the shoulder, and then he put his hand on the back of my neck.

Exerting pressure. It almost hurt. I can still feel it now, although it was quite a while ago, and then I got on my bike and went home.

Lauri rang, but I don't want to see him at the moment.

I'm going to have to cry now, I don't know exactly why.

22

Kimmo Joentaa woke early in the morning with a headache and thinking of Sanna, who used to make the pain better. She would massage his head for hours when he woke up at night and woke her too, because the tablets hadn't worked and the pain was unbearable.

That had been when he first joined the Turku police force and wasn't getting on with the police chief of the time, Ketola. With Ketola's aggressive and remote stance.

It was a long time since he'd had one of those severe headaches, and he wondered for a while why. Maybe it was because he now thought of Ketola as a friend whom he hadn't seen for a long time. Or maybe it was because Sanna was no longer alive, so his head had burst apart long ago. As a matter of course and without his noticing it.

So the headaches had come back – look at it that way, and everything was all right. His tongue felt coated and dry, there was football on the TV screen, a series of goals being scored. The morning sun stood bright and clear over the lake outside.

He took last night's leftovers into the kitchen, put everything on the counter top next to the sink, went back into the living room, turned off the TV and got out his laptop. Sitting on the sofa, he logged in and wrote a message to veryhotlarissa@pagemails.fi. He decided not to spend long thinking about the right words, because he had a feeling that no words would be right anyway. He quickly typed:

Dear Larissa,

I hope you're well. Please get in touch. I miss you, and I'm worried because you left the giraffe here. It's lying in the grass under the apple tree, and it will stay there until you come back.

Love from
Kimmo

He sent the message, took two painkillers, showered and thought of Sanna as he rubbed his scalp dry.

He switched the light on before he went out.

23

O nce again Marko Westerberg was standing far above the ground of Helsinki, in a penthouse with a roof terrace, thinking that in all probability Kalevi Forsman the software adviser had been a lonely man.

The apartment lay bright and empty in the sunlight. Empty except for a narrow bed, a silver TV set, a scarlet sofa and an elaborately equipped computer terminal, as well as a designer kitchen, and a broad, varnished wooden table in the middle of the living room.

'No chairs,' Seppo had remarked perceptively.

He was right, there was a distinct shortage of chairs. And of everything else that could have made the apartment look inviting. A broad, long table just right for a pleasant evening with friends, but no chairs. Cream for coffee and several boxes of chocolates in the fridge, along with a few slices of ham past their use-by date.

In daylight the whole place looked even more peculiar than the evening before, but Seppo, not to be deterred, kept informing him, unasked, that this was the way such people lived nowadays.

'Such people?' asked Westerberg.

'Software advisers. IT nerds. Too busy earning money to do any living.'

'Forsman had debts,' said Westerberg.

'That doesn't make it any different,' said Seppo.

Westerberg sat down on the only chair, the one at the computer terminal, and picked up the photograph of Kalevi

Forsman again. The photo on his company's home page. Well-pressed suit, neatly arranged tie, and a smile that Westerberg thought would last only fractions of a second after the camera flash went off.

'Politician,' said Seppo.

'Hmm?'

'Should have been a politician,' said Seppo, nodding in the direction of the photograph.

Westerberg looked at Kalevi Forsman's face and thought the really odd thing about it was that Kalevi Forsman *had* no face. He was forty-three years old, had studied at university and got a good degree, built up a firm, employed twelve people, made a lot of money and finally, after years of presumably meteoric progress, lost a lot of money when several of his most important customers went elsewhere. He had spent the last few months writing a new program or improving the old one. Westerberg didn't understand that in detail, but Samuli Jussilainen, Forsman's partner, kept on mentioning that angle when the question of what Forsman had made of his life arose.

He had written a program, he had acquired customers, he had travelled to various countries to sit in various banks negotiating with various other people. He had spent the working hours of the day saving his company, and before he did that he had spent the working hours of the day building it up.

When Westerberg had asked Forsman's partner whether he had any friends the answer had been: yes, me. His parents were long dead, he had a sister who lived in Hämeenlinna, and all that Forsman's partner could tell them about her was that he didn't know her and Forsman had lost touch with her.

Westerberg looked at the photograph, at the smile on Forsman's face, so obviously artificial as to be almost comic.

'It would have been his birthday in a week's time,' he said, looking up to meet Seppo's eyes, but Seppo wasn't there.

'Seppo?' he called. No answer.

He stood up, and found Seppo in the bedroom. He too was examining a photograph.

'Look at this,' he said.

'Hmm?'

Seppo handed him the picture. An old one, yellowed. It had been crumpled up, and then at some later date smoothed out again. A stain near the top right-hand corner, perhaps coffee. Westerberg wondered whether it was Kalevi Forsman who had crumpled up the picture and then smoothed it out. And why.

'Is that Forsman?' he asked.

'Who?'

'Here, the boy on this side of the group,' he said, pointing to a teenager who seemed to bear a distant resemblance to the software adviser.

'How would I know?' said Seppo.

The smile was different, a reserved but genuine smile. The boy was looking ahead of him, straight at the camera.

'I think it's him,' said Westerberg.

Seppo nodded vaguely.

The boy was in a group of people on a sandy beach in the sunlight, in front of a dark blue lake. A summer's day straight out of a picture-book. Beside Forsman, if the boy was Forsman, stood another boy of about the same age, sideways on as if caught in the act of turning away. Beside the boys stood two men, smiling rather awkwardly, as if they didn't like being photographed. They were all wearing outdated bathing trunks.

In the background of the picture, a woman in a swimsuit lay in the sun. She wore sunglasses, her face was turned up to the sky, and at the same time she was half-glancing at the men and the camera.

'Forsman's father died when he was five,' said Seppo.
Westerberg nodded.

'So neither of the two men can be his father.'

Westerberg nodded, and wondered what it was that he didn't like about the picture. Maybe that unnatural-looking summer.

'1985,' said Seppo.

Westerberg looked enquiringly at him.

'19 August 1985. It says so on the back.'

19 August 1985. We had a barbecue and a pasta bake. No one talked about what happened. She smiled at me. Everyone is the same as usual, and R. says I'm not to worry about it.

'Aha,' said Westerberg.

'The picture was under his mattress,' said Seppo.

24

Dear diary,

I couldn't sleep and I didn't want to go to school. But I did go, because I thought I might see her. However, she wasn't there. The music lesson was cancelled.

The headmaster said she's ill, but that's wrong. They all think she's ill, but I know she isn't. And the boy from the upper school who was there with us was absent too. In break I smoked behind the bicycle racks, and Lauri kept me company although he doesn't smoke. He kept looking round in case a teacher came along and caught me with the cigarette, and he told me something, but I couldn't concentrate. I kept thinking of Saara and the boy from the upper school, his name is Kalevi Forsman, and then I thought they aren't there, and perhaps they don't exist. If they don't exist then yesterday didn't happen. Specially because of Risto.

It would be a good thing if Risto didn't exist.

I keep thinking of his face, and the sweat. Risto came in just as we finished the piano lesson. She said I'd played well, and held my hand very lightly. Risto coughed, and Saara jumped.

And then something happened. It's difficult to explain. It happened fast, and I didn't know at first just what was happening. I was sitting on the stool at the piano. Risto took hold of Saara's head, he pulled her hair and went out of the room with her.

Then I sat on the stool for a little while longer, because I didn't know what to do. I didn't hear anything else either.

Then I thought I'd better go, and I stood up. There were two men in the corridor, and they gave me a funny kind of look. Sort of pale, as if they were afraid of something, but one of them laughed when he saw me and said, sounding nervous, that he supposed I must be the model student. And he looked at the other man as if that was funny, but the other man didn't laugh.

Then suddenly the door to the next room opened, and Risto came in, and I saw Saara lying on the bed, and the garden was all in flower outside, and I think her nose was bleeding. Yes. And she, she was looking up at the ceiling in a way that . . .

Okay, I'll tell the rest of it later.

25

The conference room was bathed in sunlight. Kimmo Joentaa thought vaguely of the lights switched on in his house, and Sundström's voice was lost in a sea of facts.

'Forty-five to fifty-five years old, one metre sixty-five tall, slender, weight in life about fifty-five kilograms, dark brown hair, blue eyes. Right earlobe pierced, older scars of unknown origin on her upper arms and forearms as well as her back, operation scar on her knee. Very good teeth, obviously prophylactic treatment against caries from childhood. Appendix presumably present. No pregnancy stretch marks, no Caesarian scar. Traces suggesting burn marks of older origin in the region of her torso and her wrists.'

He looked up from the text that he was reading aloud.

'Burn marks,' said Grönholm.

'Yes.'

'That's new.'

'Yes. The photo is attached, and then it all goes out to a wide range of disseminators referring to our website,' said Sundström.

'Scars,' said Grönholm.

Sundström nodded. 'Hietalahti says there's some indication of physical abuse, although long in the past. Probably years ago, can't be precisely dated. He found most such signs only on closer examination of the body.'

Scars of older origin, thought Joentaa.

'Her fingerprint scans have given us no results so far,' said Grönholm. 'No hits in the criminal records. And of course no luck with the Missing Persons files.'

Sundström nodded and lowered the sheet of paper.

'That's all,' he said, and it sounded final.

Kimmo Joentaa stood up and walked out.

'Kimmo?' Sundström's voice, some distance away.

He went through the entrance hall, past the cafeteria and through the early signs of autumn to the long, low building in which Forensics was accommodated. The silent green halls where Salomon Hietalahti went about his work.

He waited at reception. Hietalahti came along a few minutes later and led him through the cool passages to the unknown corpse; her refrigerated drawer bore the number 17. The woman herself was known by a reference number: 1108–11. Hietalahti carefully lifted the cloth from her face.

'I haven't done the internal examination yet,' said Hietalahti.

Joentaa looked at him.

'I mean . . . I haven't finished the autopsy.'

'No. I know,' said Joentaa.

He looked at the dead woman's face, and thought of the TV presenter with her lavish eye make-up last night, the woman who didn't realise that *giraffe* was the right solution. She had been rather lively – even late in the night. The first woman ever to call him sweetie-pie.

He thought of driving to Lenganiemi and the graveyard. To stand by Sanna's grave. And then go to see Ketola. Ask how he was doing. Visit Tuomas Heinonen in hospital at the weekend. And meet Larissa. Have an ice cream together. Perhaps she would tell him her real name, just drop it casually into the conversation. It would take him several seconds to understand.

'Do you know how many ice-cream parlours there are?'

'What?' asked Hietalahti.

'Here in Turku, I mean,' said Joentaa.

'In Turku?'

'No, sorry. I don't even know for certain . . . it's probably just one of those ice-cream kiosks that pop up all over the place in summer. Are they still around now?'

'Kimmo, what on earth are you talking about?'

'Sorry. A friend of mine works in an ice-cream parlour, but I don't know which one.'

'Mmm,' said Hietalahti, and Joentaa couldn't take his eyes off the woman's face, which had lost all expression. Out of the corner of his eye he saw the cloth covering her body, and he thought of the tears on the bedspread. Amazing what they could reconstruct. What they could sum up.

He said goodbye to Hietalahti and went back through the green corridors. A moped was standing outside in the sun, next to some bicycles. The colour was right but not the number plate.

Even the initial letter was wrong.

26

Markus Happonen, town councillor and the second mayor of the municipality of Auno near Tammisaari, carefully passed his hand over his hair, and felt that everything was all right, although in his haste he hadn't got around to showering that morning. He examined his face in the mirror and worked on giving his smile a determined yet at the same time relaxed expression.

His daughter Outi hadn't come home until morning, when she had gone to her room without comment. Ina had criticised his command of crisis management. Veinö had shed tears and shouted that something was too loud. Too loud, too loud, too loud.

He turned away from the mirror, washed his hands, and went back into the sunlight. The journalist was sitting with his beer in front of him, leaning back and looking up at the sky. All around him were the lively voices of people enjoying the warmest autumn in living memory. Laughter rose from the beach, waitresses were serving pizza.

From a distance he examined the journalist, who had closed his eyes. He wondered whether he was going to ask any rather more personal questions. Very likely.

Your wife? Wants nothing more to do with me.

Your daughter? Hates me.

Your son? A useless weakling.

Ah, thank you, I'm sure it will be an excellent portrait. I'll send you the text as soon as it's ready so that you can authorise it.

The journalist opened his eyes, raised his beer glass to his mouth, and waved to him. Markus Happonen walked past the tables back to the chair where he had been sitting.

'I've already had a sip or so,' said the journalist, raising his glass again. 'Down the hatch.'

'Cheers,' said Happonen, raising his own beer to his mouth. Ice-cold. Wonderful. The journalist was fiddling with his little recorder.

'This is always something of an adventure,' he said. 'You'd think that one of these days I'd get the idea of where to switch it on and where to switch it off again.' He wound the tape back and forth, and then Happonen heard his own voice, strange and unpleasant and tinny as it came out of the recorder. 'I didn't aim to get a mandate from the country as a whole, particularly with my family in mind . . . it would be bound to change some things but . . . believe me, if my party colleagues really insist, then naturally I feel . . . and it's to be hoped that the result of the election will be what we all want . . .'

Confused remarks coming out of his mouth.

'Excellent,' said the journalist. 'Yes, I got all that. Shall we go on?'

'Yes . . . yes, by all means,' said Happonen.

He heard himself talking. What he said sounded good. Promising. Successful family man. He talked about his shepherd dog Rötte. About fishing. About the peace and quiet he valued so much, about his son's football games. Yes, a goalie. He thought of Veinö in his bright yellow jersey. The goal that was far too big for him, the ball that he was always fishing out of the net to kick back, morosely, in the direction of the centre circle. Veinö's team was bottom of its table, and Veinö played in goal because he wasn't good enough to play anywhere else.

'A good lad,' he said, and the journalist nodded and seemed to be deep in thought.

On his third beer Happonen began to feel more confident, perhaps because of the slight intoxication that was slowly setting in, but mainly because the questions were beginning to cover familiar ground. His career, his ambitions. His lightning start fifteen years ago. The youngest holder of office ever in Tammisaari. Youngest ever. Why? How did it feel? And what had brought him to politics?

'This may sound funny,' he said, 'but it was because I wanted to take responsibility. To change something. Improve it.'

The remark did sound funny, because he had made it so often before. The journalist thanked him and searched in his bag. He brought out a camera.

'Now for a nice photo. Maybe down on the beach?' he suggested.

Markus Happonen nodded, and followed the journalist as he went along the path and down the slope to the beach. Once they were there, he searched around for the best view. 'We must have the sun behind you,' he said. He guided Happonen to various different positions near the edge of the water. Several girls giggled, presumably wondering who the man whose picture was being taken might be.

Markus Happonen tried to smile in a relaxed yet determined way, and concentrated on the sound of cries and balls being struck on the mini-golf course. A group of young men were playing bare-chested; they seemed to be having a very good time. The journalist pressed the shutter release and took a picture. 'Wonderful, wonderful.'

Then he suggested taking another picture on the outskirts of the trees. He pointed in that direction. 'Maybe right on the shore, so that we have the trees occupying half the picture, and the expanse of water occupies the other half.' He seemed to like the idea. 'And you in the middle, of course.'

Markus Happonen nodded, and followed the journalist as he strode ahead.

'I'll just change the lens,' he said when they were in the pleasant shade of the trees.

'No problem,' said Happonen, and looked at the girls jumping into the water a little way off and the men laughing rather weakly, presumably because mini-golf was more difficult than they had expected. Happonen had opened the course a few years ago on a cold spring day.

'There's one thing that keeps going through my mind,' said the journalist.

'Yes?' asked Happonen.

'Your son. The goalie.'

'Veinö,' said Happonen.

'Why a goalie?' asked the journalist.

'Why?'

'Yes, why a goalie?'

'I think . . . I expect he thinks it's the most exciting posi-tion.'

The journalist nodded, and seemed to be thinking.

'Can you remember Saara?'

'Remember who?'

'Then you don't?'

'Sorry, remember who?'

'Well, another question, do you happen to know where Risto is?'

Happonen did not reply.

'Because I'm looking for him, haven't been able to find him yet.'

'I'm afraid I don't know anyone called Risto.'

'You're afraid, are you?' said the journalist in a curiously offhand tone, and went on searching in his camera bag.

'One for the road?' he enquired, and suddenly held out a bottle of whisky.

'What?'

'You didn't have one back then because you'd already left.'

'Didn't have one what?'

'One for the road,' said the journalist.

Happonen tried to dodge it, but the bottle broke on his left temple.

He was only vaguely aware of what happened next, or of the fact that his cries, which he hoped would reach the girls laughing in the background, were no louder than a whisper.

27

So, dear diary, I saw Saara lying on the bed, and Risto came out of the room, and her nose was bleeding. And she still had her dress on, but it was torn. She was lying on her back on the bed, looking up, and Risto said, 'Your turn now,' to one of the men standing in the corridor.

The man laughed in an odd kind of way, as if he felt embarrassed.

Then I saw that boy from the top form at school was standing in the bedroom with Saara. His name is Kalevi. Kalevi Forsman. I don't know him, but he was standing there with a wry look on his face. A wry smile, I mean.

The man Risto had spoken to went in and threw himself on top of Saara. Fumbled with his trousers and gasped while he was lying on her, and the bed squealed.

Forsman and another boy I know by sight, a tall, fat boy who's also in the top class and boasts a lot, I think his name is Happonen, were both standing beside the bed holding Saara's arms down, although she wasn't moving.

Then the man on top of her finished and Risto sent in the one standing beside me in the corridor. The man lay on top of Saara, and all the time Risto was chuckling to himself as if he wasn't all there, as if he'd gone crazy.

Saara just lay on the bed and didn't move at all.

I was standing in the corridor and I couldn't move either.

Then it was Forsman's turn, and then the other boy from the top class, Happonen, who talks so big, but he burst into tears and suddenly ran out of the room into the open air, with his trousers undone.

Risto called after him to stay, and he asked me if I wanted a go too. Well, little one, want a go too? That's what he said, and I think I shook my head, but maybe I didn't do anything because I couldn't move.

Then Forsman lay on top of her again, and then they all went into the living room, and Risto dropped on the sofa like a sack of potatoes and told one of the men to go and get something to drink. He was still fiddling around with his trousers, and Risto shouted at him again to go and get something to drink and five glasses.

Then it was the turn of one of the men I didn't know, at least not really; I know that one of them works at the supermarket, he goes all over the floors in the evening with a cleaning machine, and once he shouted at me for spitting out a piece of chewing gum.

But I don't know the other one at all, the one who was to fetch something to drink. He brought the glasses, and Risto stood up and filled them, and tried to give me one.

I think I shook my head, and Risto said something or other, that I could raise a glass with them or something like that. The others did drink something, I think, and Forsman's mouth was still wry in the middle of his face, and he kept pulling at his balls as if they hurt. Risto kept saying something to me, and suddenly he threw the spirits in his glass in my face and broke the glass on my head. Then he grabbed me by the throat and said that hadn't gone so well, and it was not for public consumption.

That's how he put it – not for public consumption.

Then he told the others to go away. They were holding their glasses and didn't know what to do, and then they all did go away when Risto shouted at them again to get out. There's nothing else to see here, he shouted. When the others had gone he fetched Saara, led her by the hand to the piano, and then he grabbed hold of me and told me to sit down beside her.

Then we were sitting side by side again, like before. Before all that happened. Saara in the blue-and-white summer dress.

It was all untidy and rucked up. There was that humming in my head, like bees or flies. Risto said Saara was to play something, and Saara looked at the floor. Then she raised her head and stared at the piano keys, concentrating on them. And then she pressed one key and it made a high sound. Then another key. High and somehow soft, but louder than the humming in my head. Yes, I wrote that down already. Like a kind of whispered scream.

Then Risto came back. Hauled me up and shoved me across the room, I don't know just how, but anyway his hand was on my throat all the time, and he kept on talking, and I felt kind of like I was going to die any moment.

He pushed me down on the lawn outside and said I was never to show my face here again. Never again. He kept saying that, never again, never again, never again.

He pushed me down until I was lying on the ground, and I saw the two wooden sticks we'd used last week to be the goalposts. I caught almost every ball that time, and in the end Risto was getting almost angry, but I think he didn't want to show it. Then he suddenly had the bottle in his hand, and he tipped the schnapps out all over me. It stung, and he said he'd kill me if I ever turned up there again. Then he went indoors and closed the door.

I rode home on my bike. I kept thinking of Saara all the time.

When I got home my mother asked how the piano lesson had gone, and I said it was okay, and then I went straight up to my room, because I didn't want her to smell the alcohol. I smelled of it, and it stung my eyes badly. I showered for a long time.

Today I saw Forsman at school. He was standing on the edge of a group, not saying much. Stood there looking quite normal, in a brightly coloured T-shirt, and he wasn't scratching his balls the whole time any more.

Saara wasn't at school again today.

Lauri kept on asking me if everything was all right, because I was acting in such a funny way. But I don't feel funny at all.

I just have to concentrate, because everything feels all mixed up.

I dreamed of Saara in the night, but I don't remember just what it was about, except that Risto was there too, like a huge shadow.

28

Marko Westerberg met the dead man's sister at Helsinki station. Kirsti Forsman had brought only a small case, and she was wheeling it along behind her as he led her through the concourse into the open air and over to the car. When he picked up the case to put it in the boot, he got the impression that there was either nothing in it or, at the most, a couple of bird's feathers.

She looked out of the passenger-seat window and only nodded as he threaded his way into the evening rush-hour traffic and explained the course of events. She was to make a statement. Give information about her brother. Go to the forensics department. Yes, that was no problem. No, she hadn't booked into a hotel, she was going to travel back that same evening.

Westerberg bit back his objection that it was already evening.

'Your . . . case?' he asked instead.

'Sorry?'

'I mean, you've brought a case with you.'

'Oh, I bought that in a shop at Hämeenlinna station.'

So much for the bird's feathers, thought Westerberg. And then he wondered why a woman would buy a case on the way to a city she intended to leave again at once.

In the mortuary she stood by the stretcher with her dead brother on it for a long time.

'Thank you,' she said at last.

Then she went along the corridor, walking with long, steady strides. Westerberg had difficulty keeping up with her. The evening sun was shining, both cool and warm. Kirsti Forsman lit a cigarette as they sat in the car, and Westerberg scraped the carriagework on another car's bumper as he backed out of his parking place.

He got out of the car to inspect the damage, and wrote a note giving Seppo's direct phone number and saying there was no need to report it to the police, they had already been there.

'Okay?' asked Kirsti Forsman as he restarted the car.

'Not too bad,' he said.

At police headquarters, Seppo was waiting with one of his catalogues of questions, which as a rule were logically constructed. Seppo's warm voice and Kirsti Forsman's clear, regular tones filled the room.

'You work as a lawyer in Hämeenlinna.'

'That's right. Mainly for Arsa, a dairy company.'

'Dairy.'

'Yes, milk. Yoghurt. Chocolate too in the north of the country. I draw up contracts and advise the company management on legal questions.'

'Yes,' said Seppo. 'Your brother. We need your help because he . . .'

'I don't know that I can help you there.'

'. . . seems to have been in touch with very few people.'

'I'm afraid we were hardly in touch at all ourselves.'

'Oh,' said Seppo, and Westerberg thought: so much for the catalogue of questions.

'We last saw each other at Christmas three years ago. I was thinking about that on the train,' said Kirsti Forsman.

'Where was that?'

'What do you mean?'

'Where exactly did you see each other then?'

'Oh, I see. At our house. We'd invited him. My husband and I. Well . . . my then husband. Kalevi came and spent the night. It was . . . really nice.'

'So the three of you celebrated Christmas together,' said Seppo.

She nodded.

'Three years ago?'

'Christmas three years ago.'

'Right, then . . .'

'That is, two years and nine months ago. Roughly.'

'Right. And since then . . .'

'We spoke on the phone now and then. I tried to reach him on his birthday last year, but I only got his answering machine.'

'Do you know anything about his lifestyle? I mean, we know he was in close contact with his business partner, but outside that did he have friends or . . . or a woman in his life?'

'A woman in his life . . . not as far as I know, no,' she said. 'The last was a few years ago, she was an employee of his company, but it didn't work out because he felt the two things couldn't be combined.'

'Couldn't be combined?'

'The private and professional spheres of life.'

'I see.'

'In fact we did talk about it this way and that at the time, and he called me more often for a while after he'd ended the relationship.'

'The relationship with this employee of the company?'

She nodded. 'And there were some legal aspects involved, because the woman wanted to hand in her notice.'

'I see,' said Seppo.

'But then she left of her own accord anyway.'

'I see. And there's been no woman in his life since then, so far as you know?'

'Not so far as I know. But as I said, we've not been in touch. We simply never had much in common. I'm a few years younger, I had a different circle of friends, different interests. A different life.'

'His firm was under pressure. Do you, by any chance, know of conflicts on a professional level that could give us somewhere to start investigating?'

She seemed to be thinking it over without coming to any conclusion. 'I don't think his firm was under more or less pressure than many others,' she said. 'He had to struggle, like everyone who sets up a company of his own. But I really do think his programs were good. When we last saw each other he'd just got a major new customer.'

'So that would have been about three years ago?'

'Yes, exactly . . . he talked about it that evening.'

'But it's quite a while ago.'

'Of course, but as I said, I can't confirm that his company was in difficulties. I just don't know what went on in his life.'

A different life, thought Westerberg, and said, 'We're asking only because he fell from the fourteenth floor of a hotel.'

The woman looked away from Seppo and turned her eyes on him.

'I understand that you didn't have much to do with your brother. It's certainly nothing unusual for brothers and sisters to lose sight of each other, but now he's dead, you know.'

She nodded, and he wondered whether she really did know. Whether it had sunk in.

'Do you know the people in this photograph?' asked Seppo. He showed her the picture he had found under the mattress in Forsman's bleak apartment.

She looked at the photo for a long time. Turned it over and examined the back of it as well.

'No,' she said at last.

'But your brother . . . you recognise him?'

'Yes, of course, this is Kalevi. But the others mean nothing to me. We had very different . . . relationships.'

Seppo nodded, and Westerberg thought about the word.
Relationships.

'It's quite an old picture anyway,' she said.

Westerberg drove her to the station. Her case was still light,
her handshake firm.

He waited, without knowing why, until the train began
moving, gathered speed, and some way off, on a long, gentle
slope, disappeared from his field of vision.

29

That evening Kimmo Joentaa went the rounds of the ice-cream parlours, from the marketplace to the cathedral and back, without meeting a single person who had seen a small woman of about twenty-five with light blonde hair selling ice cream in summer or autumn, and no one who had worked with her.

At the last place he visited he bought a scoop of vanilla and a scoop of tundra-berry ice cream in a cone. He sat on a bench beside the river, watched the sun setting, and tried to concentrate on the other, nameless woman.

Burn marks, scars, excellent teeth.

The internal examination had yet to be made. Or perhaps it was in progress at this moment, if Salomon Hietalahti in Forensics worked overtime.

Joentaa drove home and stayed sitting in his car for a little while, watching the light behind the windows.

Then he got out and said good evening to Pasi Laaksonen, who was watering the lawn in the garden next door. For whatever reason.

He went in, drank a glass of water, and started his laptop. Two new emails, one from a friend he hadn't seen for a long time, asking if he wouldn't like to go to handball again on Friday evening. Another from the lottery, which refused to desist from its attempts to make him rich.

He took his mobile out of his jacket pocket and called Tuomas Heinonen at the hospital. The answering system came on, Tuomas's good-humoured voice, presumably recorded either when he hadn't gambled his money away yet, or when he had just had a run of good luck.

'Hello, Tuomas, just thought I'd give you a call. I'll be in touch later,' said Joentaa.

He took out the piece of paper on which he had noted down what little he knew about Larissa, and added something to the scanty information. The registration number of the moped on which she rode around the place. It had taken a while, but after some thought he had managed to recall the letters and figures.

He smiled as he wrote. A little research that afternoon had come up with the fact that a few months ago the number plate had been removed from another, similar moped. The case was not high priority, and the number plate had never turned up.

Joentaa had refrained from telling his colleagues that he knew where it was. *On my girlfriend's moped, except that she's disappeared. What's her name? Well, that's a bit complicated . . .*

Joentaa looked at the letters and figures.

He pictured Larissa unscrewing the number plate.

Likes going for walks. Likes removing number plates from vehicles.

Presumably Pasi Laaksonen was watering his lawn to delay the onset of autumn.

Likes eating pasta bake and ice cream; her favourite flavours are tundra-berry and vanilla. Answers questions with a smile when she doesn't want to discuss them further. Her smile is aggressive and attractive at the same time.

He sent an email to veryhotlarissa. Not a new one; he re-sent the one that he had already written that morning.

The giraffe is lying in the grass under the apple tree. And it will stay there until you come back.

He switched the TV set on and watched tennis.

30

Dear diary,

After complaints about Silverman, the major bank, its shares have ended their profitable run on Wall Street and sent the Dow Jones plummeting. OMX Nordic closed at 902 with hardly any change, OMX Helsinki25 dropped 53 points to 2040. Shares in the Sampa Oy department store group have been under pressure since the parent firm made it known that it was ready to begin talks with potential investors about the future of the Galeria chain.

'What are you doing?' asks Olli. I take my eyes off the screen and see him in the doorway. In his pyjamas, blue bottoms and pale blue Superman top.

'I'm writing something,' I say.

'Writing what?' asks Olli.

I look at the text on the screen and wonder what to tell Olli. Market round-up, lighterage. Securities and quarterly figures. Weaker opening expected.

An email comes in. Koski wants to know when the article will be ready.

'Writing what?' Olli asks again.

'Oh, some sort of nonsense,' I say.

'Oh,' says Olli.

Soon, I type, and send the message.

Soon when? Koski replies, seconds later.

Soon soon, I reply.

'Can we play again tomorrow?' asks Olli.

'Sorry, I have to go away,' I say.

'Oh. Again?'

'Only for a couple of days,' I tell him.

Leea's voice in the background on the phone. Henna's baby has arrived. A boy, Valtteri. Henna and the baby have left the hospital, Henna's husband Kalle has been kept in for observation because he suffered a cardiovascular collapse during the Caesarian.

'The day after tomorrow, then,' says Olli.

'As soon as I'm back,' I tell him.

Markus Happonen, town councillor, then mayor of a place near Tammisaari.

'Go to bed, Olli!' calls Leea.

Olli groans and says, 'Goodnight.'

'Sleep well,' I say.

Round-up 2 – preview – weaker opening expected, send.

Thanks! Koski replies seconds later.

Town councillor, mayor. Markus Happonen's face was soft and round, just as it used to be. It always made me think of foam rubber, pink foam rubber. It didn't fit. Simply did not fit into the situation. A foreign body. A mystery in a mysterious situation. Face bright red, not pink. Lips pressed together. Running out of the room with his trousers undone. Nothing about it fits that man. A large, fat man talking big.

In his Internet photograph he looks different. The management team of the town council introduce themselves. Glasses have presumably been replaced by contact lenses. He looks satisfied. If I hadn't spoken to him, if I hadn't heard the effort in his voice, I'd have taken him for a happy man. Not a trace of the sweating, groaning boy who first hammered away at Saara with his little prick and then ran out of the room in tears. Forty-three years old, hobbies angling, cross-country skiing, his German shepherd dog. I expect the picture will still be on that homepage for some time to come, although the person it shows is no longer alive.

'Kalle's back at home,' says Leea, adding when I look enquiringly at her, 'after his cardiovascular collapse. He's back at home, and the baby is doing well too.'

Studied jurisprudence and political science. Once the youngest member of Tammisaari council. Married. Two children. Olli will soon be asleep. Leea's voice in the background. A recurrent, gentle, humming note in the silence.

It all happens so fast, that's why one has to write it down. To fix it on paper. And be able to remember it later.

'See you in the morning,' says Leea.

An empty space that I found without looking for it.

31

Kirsti Forsman arrived in Hämeenlinna at 22.46 hours. She walked through the pedestrian precinct at the end of which she lived, going over several messages that she had emailed or left by voicemail from her mobile as she went along.

Since the company had launched its new fruit yoghurt – with splinters of coconut and chocolate, sold in a Tetra Pak – legal questions about its manufacture and marketing had been accumulating.

She had a conversation of some length with the managing director, stopping from time to time in the warm lights of the shop windows to look at the displays. Clothes, shoes, delicatessen. The managing director seemed to take it for granted that he could bother her with clauses and their necessary rewording late in the evening.

At the end of the conversation he thanked her and asked her to turn up punctually for tomorrow's meeting although, unlike him, she was always punctual. It had turned cool.

Two excavators stood outside the last clapboard house at the end of the shopping arcade. Renovations to the gas mains, according to the letter put through all doors by the municipality. The works would be finished in two weeks' time, it said. Two weeks. Two weeks ago Kalevi had been alive, not that she had noticed it. Only now did it occur to her that his death left something missing, although she didn't know exactly what.

As she climbed the stairs and looked for the key to her

apartment, the idea formed in her mind: she was the last. The last of them still alive.

She had not been consciously aware of her father's death, and she knew him only from family stories. The death of her mother . . .

Her hand was trembling. The key didn't seem to fit the lock and fell on the floor. She picked it up and tried to calm herself as the trembling took over her whole body.

She concentrated on getting the key into the lock.

Her mother hadn't really died until yesterday.

Because now Kalevi too was dead.

At last.

She pushed the door open, went straight to the kitchen and opened the bottle of red wine that an over-attentive colleague in the law practice had given her on her birthday a few weeks ago. She drank, and thought that Kalevi hadn't called those few weeks ago to wish her a happy birthday.

She thought of the photograph. Kalevi had not looked the way she remembered him. Probably because she had no concrete memory left of Kalevi's appearance as a schoolboy. It was only the smile she had recognised, and it had looked as if Kalevi was pleased with himself. Although the date had been on the back of the photo: 19 August 1985. Pleased with himself and in a good temper.

She sensed memories coming back. Very specific memories. Things that had been said; she recalled them verbatim. Even the rising and falling of voices, the moments when her mother had begun shedding tears.

Kalevi's voice, which had lost its resonance. The murmuring and lamentations, all about something incomprehensible to her.

And then that photo. The normality of it. Kalevi smiling at the camera and noting, on the back of the photo, that he didn't have to worry about it. Because R. said so. That was the only indication of what might have been going on in his mind. The fact that he could no longer write the name out in full.

Risto. A name.

She picked up her glass and went into the living room. On the way she stopped several times because waves of feeling were running through her body. She went on.

When she was standing in the middle of the room the scream came out at last. It built up slowly and rose, until it finally broke out, too loud and too painful for her to hear it herself.

WINTER

32

When winter came the body of the unknown woman, reference number 1108–11, was buried.

Kimmo Joentaa, representing the investigating team, and Salomon Hietalahti, the forensic pathologist, were the only people who came to the funeral. Four employees of the cemetery carried the coffin; the pastor officiating said a few words that seemed to be lost before they could reach anyone listening.

It was cold, but not snowing yet. When the funeral was over, Kimmo Joentaa spent a few more minutes standing at the side of the grave, thinking that there must be people alive somewhere who missed this woman. People who laughed and suffered with her. And thinking that there would have been hundreds at the funeral, hundreds of strangers, if the date had been publicly announced. Fortunately it had not.

Most of the methods and opportunities known to forensic medicine had been tried with the unknown woman, but they had not provided any decisive clues as to her identity. An isotope analysis had shown that she was of northern European and probably Finnish origin.

'A Finnish woman. A perfectly normal Finnish woman,' Sundström had said, putting into words what they were all thinking – if, in that case, the dead woman had spent most of her life in Finland, then the absence of any useful clues was particularly annoying.

The number of people calling the police about the unknown woman had fallen, and her photograph appeared in the media only when the press office deliberately placed it there, to keep the stream of further information from drying up entirely.

There would presumably be a revival of interest at the end of the month, when the unsolved murder was one of the incidents mentioned in the Turku university hospital's retrospective survey of the year. A private broadcasting station had already asked Police Chief Nurmela for an interview, and he had said he was inclined to accept.

Nurmela had drawn Kimmo Joentaa aside several times in the corridor or the cafeteria to ask about Larissa in a whisper, with an almost comic conspiratorial expression on his face. Was she back? Had he heard anything of her?

Kimmo Joentaa had said no, and Nurmela had nodded in silence. Once Joentaa had plucked up courage, or simply obeyed an impulse, and asked the question that was of no significance, yet was still on his mind.

Why August?

Nurmela had stared at him, and in those seconds of silence Joentaa had wondered what devil had impelled him to ask.

But then Nurmela just uttered a brief, dry laugh and said, 'Well, no idea.'

'Probably a silly question,' Joentaa had said.

'Hmm? No, not at all. A good question. Wait a moment.'

Nurmela had gone to the drinks dispenser, fetched himself a coffee, and then sat down at the table again.

'Although there are one or two things that would interest me,' he said. 'For instance, how you came to know that woman. What were you thinking of?'

'What do you suppose I was thinking of?' Joentaa had replied.

'Kimmo, sometimes I seriously doubt whether—'

'I met her at Christmas last year. She simply turned up. I like her a lot. That's all.'

Nurmela had looked at him for some time.

'That's really nice, but the lady practises a profession that—'

'And by the way, she plays ice hockey really well. She's a goalie,' Joentaa had said.

Nurmela had leaned back to drink his coffee, and Kimmo Joentaa had thought about that remark of his. She simply turned up. I like her a lot. That's all. And really there wasn't much more to say. Except that he missed her.

Investigations of the case of the unknown murder victim concentrated on information that had come in, not all of which the team had yet looked at, although the number of new calls had died down. Day after day Joentaa, Grönholm, Sundström and three more detectives who had been assigned to the core group interviewed people who claimed to have known the woman in the photograph, but it turned out that none of them did.

They also interviewed those who asked after missing persons. Several cases that had been put on ice some time ago had been solved that way in the last few months. An elderly married couple from Paimio had been reunited with their daughter after many years. She had gone abroad and entirely forgot to tell her parents about it.

On the evening of 12 December, the first snow fell. It had covered the giraffe under the tree when Joentaa came home.

33

Dear diary,

OMX Nordic stands at 945 points, OMX Helsinki25 at 2,057 points.

Koski wished me a nice weekend and a good holiday.

I have now found them all except for one.

Kalevi Forsman, forty-three, software adviser.

Markus Happonen, forty-three, second mayor, town councillor. Or something along those lines. It makes no difference now.

Lassi Anttila, fifty-seven, cleaner and store detective in a shopping centre in Raisio near Naantali. Another interesting combination. He was hard to find . . . Nothing about him on the Internet, not listed in the phone book. Lives quietly and more or less alone.

Jarkko Miettinen, sixty-four, pensioner. Lives near Lappeenranta, in a care home specialising in the treatment of those with Parkinson's disease. They slow down, suffer from stiff muscles, tremors. The disease develops slowly. At first its progress is hardly perceptible.

There's one still missing. Risto.

When I got home Leea's friend Henna and her baby were visiting. Leea had baked a cake; it was very good. The baby laughed at me, and Henna was so pleased that she gave me a hug before they left.

Olli is in a phase where he gets cross when he loses. He had terrible luck throwing the dice all evening.

It's snowing outside, big flakes.

I bought the costume today. It looks convincing, presumably because it's real. Or at least, so the boy behind the counter claimed. He seemed almost proud of it.

Leea stands in the doorway and says she's going to bed.

'The velocity of its fall is about 4 kilometres per hour,' I say, without taking my eyes off the window.

'Velocity of what fall?' she asks.

'The falling snow. A speed of about 4 kph.'

She says nothing for a few seconds, and then asks how I'm feeling.

'I'm going away,' I say.

She asks where to.

'Only for a few days,' I tell her.

34

In the night he switched on his laptop, put it on the sofa and wrote to <u>veryhotlarissa</u>.

Dear Larissa

It snowed for the first time today. Did it snow with you? Where are you? You're not getting in touch, so I can tell you what's up here. At the moment we're trying to explain the death of a woman who hasn't yet been identified. Maybe you've heard or read about it. It's as if she didn't live anywhere. As if she'd fallen from the sky and straight into a coma. Sorry, what I'm writing is nonsense, but I'll send it anyway.

See you soon.
Love from Kimmo

He sent the message, put the laptop on the table, opened the glass door and ran down the slope to the lake where Larissa had played ice hockey and Sanna used to swim.

In the last weeks of her life, before he had to take her to the hospital, she would sit on the landing stage wrapped in rugs. She had told him not to worry when he asked if she hadn't better come into the warm house.

He remembered that. And his absurd hope that the illness would go away because he wanted it to. And the clumsy prayers he had sent up to a God in whom he couldn't believe.

He decided to visit Sanna's grave and call her parents. It was a long time since he had heard from them. Some while ago Merja, Sanna's mother, had spoken to his answering machine and asked how he was. Her voice had sounded clear and calm, stronger than the last time. He had been glad of that. And maybe it was the reason that he hadn't called back. He didn't want to find out that he had only imagined Merja's strength.

He went a few steps out on the ice and thought it seemed fragile. Although the children had been playing ice hockey on it that evening; he had watched them for a while. They had been shooting at an empty goal. As if they were waiting for the woman who had parried their shots last winter, protected by a cycling helmet.

The goal was still standing on the ice, with a pair of gloves and a forgotten stick. Kimmo Joentaa sat down in the goal and thought that he was seeing what Larissa had seen. Only the pucks flying around her ears were missing.

In the distance, he saw someone slowly moving towards him, running over the snow-covered grass, the snow-covered sand and the frozen water. Joentaa felt a pang, and thought for long seconds that it was Larissa.

Then he saw the boy coming closer. Roope, from one of the neighbouring houses. Roope slowed down and suddenly looked uncertain of himself, presumably seeing a shadow in front of the goal.

'It's me,' called Joentaa. 'Kimmo.'

'Oh,' said Roope.

'Sorry if I startled you,' said Joentaa.

'No, nonsense, not a problem. I just . . . I forgot my stick and my gloves.'

Joentaa picked up those items and handed them to Roope, who came hesitantly closer.

'Thanks,' he said. 'I don't know what I was doing, leaving all my gear here.'

Joentaa nodded.

'That stick is brand new,' said Roope.

'Looks like a good one,' said Joentaa.

'Yes, Jokinen plays with that make,' said Roope. 'And the whole national team, they're the main sponsors. I mean, they play with sticks like that and the same tape . . . and so on.'

Joentaa nodded.

'Where's Larissa?' asked Roope.

Joentaa looked at Roope, the boy from a nearby house. He had shot up in height. He thought of a day some years ago when a much smaller Roope had sat at his kitchen table drinking hot cocoa.

'I don't know for sure,' he said.

'Oh,' said Roope.

'You missed her today playing ice hockey.'

'Yup. It'd be . . . cool if she would play with us again.'

'I'll tell her that as soon as I see her,' said Joentaa.

'Okay,' said Roope, and after a few seconds' hesitation he turned away.

'See you soon,' said Joentaa.

'Yes, see you. And . . . and tell her good wishes from me too, will you? From Roope.'

'I'll do that,' said Joentaa.

'Okay, goodnight, then,' said Roope.

'Sleep well,' said Joentaa.

He watched the lanky figure of Roope walking away, pulling his stick along behind him, going over the ice and up the slope.

For a few minutes he tried to find the strength he needed to stand up. Then he went back the same way as he had come.

The house was empty. The laptop was purring like a cat. A robot cat, thought Joentaa vaguely, and it was time to get some sleep.

He bent down, pressed a key and then another, and for a

while he looked at the screen. There was a message from Larissa flickering on it. He stayed in the same position, bending over, and stared at the words.

From: veryhotlarissa@pagemails.fi
To: kimmojoentaa@turunpoliisilaitos.fi

Your unidentified dead woman. It's to do with male violence.

He sat down on the sofa, without taking his eyes off the screen.

He sat there for several minutes without moving. Then he leaned forward and began to write.

From: kimmojoentaa@turunpoliisilaitos.fi
To: veryhotlarissa@pagemails.fi

Dear Larissa

Lovely to hear from you. It's good that you're still around.
    I was talking to Roope just now, he asked if you'd be back to play ice hockey with him and his friends again.

See you soon.
Kimmo

He sent the email, feeling a relief that made his throat tighten.

He switched off the computer, took the woollen rug off the old armchair and lay down on the sofa. He thought vaguely of the words in Larissa's message. Of the unknown dead woman whose name had been replaced by a reference number.

Names don't matter, he thought.

Then he fell asleep, and slept deeply, calmly, without dreams.

35

Dear diary,

I went there today.

At last I went back there.

I was trembling all the time and I couldn't think straight. But I simply had to go there, and all the time I had the thought of seeing her in my head.

And telling her how much I like her.

And that I'll always be there for her and I can help her.

But it didn't happen like that.

I got off the bike quite early, where the path narrowed and the last row of houses began. I'd never been that far before. I'd kept going as far as the narrow road and then I always turned back, because I didn't know how I could avoid him if he came driving towards me in his great fat car. It was snowing hard.

I hid the bike in the wood, and went round the long way, along the field as far as the hill. From there you can get a good view of the house and the whole property, and you'd only have to walk through the wood for a few minutes to reach it; the garden leads straight to the little field and into the wood.

Risto's garden. Risto's field. Risto's wood.

It seemed to me that it all belongs to him, although that's not true. Nothing belongs to him.

Nothing and everything.

I couldn't help thinking of Anita-Liisa Koponen who looked at me in such a funny way at school today, and asked if I knew what the matter with Saara was. Because Anita-Liisa Koponen has been having piano lessons from Saara too. I only said no, I didn't know what was wrong with Saara. And I tried to act as if everything was normal.

I lay on the hill, keeping low down among the trees so that no one could see me. I was thinking that it all belongs to Risto and here I was in the middle of it. And that Risto would kill me if he found me there.

And Saara too. He'd kill her then as well.

I couldn't stop trembling, because I was cold too, but the cold came from inside me. I lay there feeling stupid and staring at the house, and I began crying because she wasn't there.

Which I ought to have realised, because no one goes out in the garden in weather like that, and I couldn't see into the house, it was too far away, and the windowpanes shone like mirrors.

Darkness fell quickly, and all the time I was just thinking that I couldn't tell her all I wanted to tell her. Then a light was switched on in the house, and I went closer. I thought it was dark enough, but I was also terrified, it's difficult to describe how bad that was. When I saw Risto's face at the window I fell down or I threw myself on the ground, I don't know which for certain, but anyway I was lying on the ground and I couldn't breathe properly. I got back into taller grass and lay flat there, waiting for him to come out. I was sure he would come out, but I was trying to persuade myself all the time that he couldn't have seen me.

Then, funnily enough, I wondered how he would kill me. And what he would do with me when I was dead.

I think I was talking out loud to myself, and I stared at the house and waited for him to come through the garden towards me. But he didn't.

I did see Saara for a moment, she appeared at an upstairs window like a ghost.

I thought of that as I rode home.

I thought of Saara being a ghost.

And Risto killing me and hiding me away so that no one would ever find me.

36

The team in Helsinki who had been investigating the case of the murdered software adviser Kalevi Forsman over the last few months had concentrated on the dead man's firm, and any progress they made simply led them into a blind alley.

Marko Westerberg was sitting at his desk on the morning of 13 December, studying the file summing up the case so far. All sorts of salient points, no solution.

Forsman had forged balance sheets, thus incurring the righteous wrath of several employees and getting two major customers into great business difficulties, because there had been an error lurking in what he boasted was his infallible system.

He had spent the days just before his death covering up for this error instead of eliminating the problem.

In other words, Forsman was finished; he had steered his firm straight into a brick wall, and soon Forsman's partner Samuli Jussilainen found himself the focal point of the investigations again. At first he offered no alibi and then he gave a dubious one, assuring the investigators that he knew nothing about the full extent of the bankruptcy threatening the firm and the demands of angry customers.

Marko Westerberg was leafing through the records and reports, feeling tired and uninspired, when Seppo came into the room, striding out with verve as usual, a mug in each hand and balancing his briefcase so that he was holding it steady in his mouth.

Seppo mumbled something incomprehensible, presumably because of the briefcase between his teeth, and Westerberg replied, 'Yes, good morning.'

Seppo handed him one of the hot mugs of coffee and immediately went into dynamic mode, switching on his computer and drumming his fingers on the table while the system came up.

'Seppo?' said Westerberg.

'Hmm?'

Westerberg sipped his coffee and mentally composed a scenario. 'Maybe we ought to consider those fitness studio guys.'

'Hmm?'

'You know, those two fitness studios that were planning to merge. The conference in the hotel when Forsman fell off the roof terrace.'

'Yes,' said Seppo.

'Maybe Forsman had done deals with both fitness centres, I mean sold them his software at an inflated price, so they finished him off.'

Seppo stopped drumming his fingers and frowned. 'Why would fitness studios want software meant for bankers and fund managers?'

Westerberg sighed. 'It was a joke, Seppo.'

'Oh, I see.'

'A joke,' Westerberg repeated.

'Yes, okay, I get it.'

Seppo went back to drumming his fingers, while the fax machine squealed and rattled in the background. Seppo typed on his keyboard, and then jumped up to collect the fax.

'Ah,' he said as he took the paper out of the machine. 'Mhm. Aha.'

'Something important?' asked Westerberg.

'The list,' said Seppo.

'Oh, yes, the list.'

'The list I asked for. From Karjasaari and the school that Forsman went to.'

'Ah,' said Westerberg.

'On account of that photograph. We still can't identify the other people in the picture that Forsman kept.'

'The one that was under the mattress,' murmured Westerberg.

'Exactly,' said Seppo, and Westerberg, who had been suffering from leaden exhaustion all morning, felt something else stir in him. An idea forming. He remembered the conversations that had got them nowhere at an early stage of the investigations – with Forsman's sister and with the headmaster of the school, who was far too young to have known Forsman as a pupil there. Their colleagues in Karjasaari, Forsman's home town, had sent various items of useless information. Forsman's parental home had been occupied for some time by a young family who had not known the dead man.

'Let me have a look at that, please,' he said.

'Just a moment,' said Seppo, without taking his eyes off the sheets of paper. He chuckled. 'There they go, sending us a list of a hundred and twenty-seven names without any comments.'

'Seppo, please give me that list.'

'Yes, in a moment . . . now that's a . . . a kind of funny coincidence . . .'

'Seppo.'

' . . . or not, as the case may be,' said Seppo.

'What is?'

'Markus Happonen.'

'What?'

'Quite an ordinary sort of name, I guess,' said Seppo.

'What are you talking about?'

'Markus Happonen, the local politician. The case was quite high-profile because he was standing for office of some kind.'

Westerberg nodded. Their colleagues from Tammisaari had circulated an email asking for cooperation. Which was something of an illusion, because every police force had to see to its own business. But the dead man had been a fairly prominent figure. And the circumstances of his death were a little . . . bizarre. Westerberg had skimmed the newspaper reports as well as the email from Tammisaari. Struck down by massive blows inflicted by three bottles of whisky, the first of which had probably been fatal. On the beach in broad daylight . . . In a hotel in broad daylight. Falling fourteen floors. In both cases people had been in the immediate vicinity and had failed to notice anything.

'Yes,' said Seppo. 'He's on this list. A Markus Happonen went to school with our murder victim Forsman.'

37

Kimmo Joentaa spent the morning in the shadowy domain of Päivi Holmquist, the friendly archivist.

He looked at the carefully stacked file folders, and vaguely heard the voices of Päivi and her young colleague Antti Laapenranta in the background. Päivi laughed, and Antti chuckled. Joentaa hadn't caught the joke.

He was trying to summon up an inclination to begin, but something deterred him. Maybe the number of files in which the leads provided in the last few months had been stored. He had half-heartedly begun to read, and stopped after a few pages because he had a feeling that he wasn't ready to tackle the job yet.

'Getting on all right?' asked Päivi behind him.

He raised his eyes and looked at her. She was smiling, and as always there was an aura of calm around her. He thought about that, and came to the conclusion that he had really never known Päivi Holmquist to be anything but calm. Always calm and smiling.

'I think so,' he said.

'There's not so much coming in now, but all in all it's a huge amount,' she said. 'I don't think we've ever had more feedback in such a short time.'

Joentaa nodded. A huge amount of information. And not the faintest trail leading anywhere.

'There are 2,711 files,' said Antti Laapenranta, who had come up to the table. He put a bottle of Coca-Cola to his mouth, and Joentaa thought of the first time he had seen

Antti at the reception desk of the archives. The shy, insecure trainee Antti, who had long ago become an able and self-assured colleague.

For a moment his memory went back to his own early days in this building, the cold manner of his boss at the time, Ketola, and once again he thought he would go and see Ketola soon.

Maybe he could talk to Ketola about Tuomas Heinonen, maybe Ketola would know how to help Tuomas. On the other hand, Tuomas had of course told him about his addiction to gambling in confidence, and Joentaa would have to ask him before passing it on to anyone else. But how was he going to help Tuomas if he couldn't ask anyone's advice? The number mentioned just now was echoing in his mind.

'How many did you say?' he asked.

'2,711,' said Antti Laapenranta.

Joentaa nodded.

2,711 leads. 2,711 people who said they had known the dead woman. And 2,711 people who were wrong. Probably.

He nodded again, and began leafing through the files and reading. He wondered what Larissa had been trying to tell him when she said it was male violence.

2,711 leads, male violence.

Larissa who wasn't really called Larissa.

A dead woman who wasn't telling anyone her name.

'Like a Coke too?' asked Antti.

'Hmm? Yes . . . thanks,' said Joentaa.

He looked down at the first file, a statement taken in the autumn on the day the photograph had first been published in the media. It was made by a girl of twelve who had recognised the dead woman as her mother. The transcript of the interview presented the girl's conviction, her refusal to admit that she could be wrong, and had a note in bold added by the officer recording it to the effect that 'the mother in question, first, was a good deal younger than the unknown woman, and second died in 2003'.

Antti brought the Coke.

Another 2,710 to go, thought Joentaa, hoping as he leafed on through them that the girl had a strong, loving father.

38

In Helsinki, Westerberg and Seppo were busily making phone calls. Westerberg deliberately kept pausing for effect in his remarks, because he knew from experience that at moments when the investigation of a case took a new turn, it might focus on something forgotten that was the crux of the matter, enabling them to make a breakthrough.

He kept yawning, as he always did when he was nervous, which irritated Seppo, who was young and hadn't worked with him for very long.

'Not bored, are you?' he asked.

'What? No, not at all,' said Westerberg.

'Glad to hear it,' said Seppo.

'Quite the contrary, in fact,' said Westerberg.

Seppo went on phoning, and Westerberg tried to concentrate on that crux.

Kalevi Forsman, software adviser. Markus Happonen, politician. Both murdered, both in daylight, both in a relatively bizarre manner with a short interval between the two murders. As if committed casually, thought Westerberg, and the word haunted his mind as he rang another number and tried to get a sensible conversation going with his agitated colleague at the other end of the line in Tammisaari.

'Yes, yes, Kalevi Forsman, I get that. But surely he has nothing at all to do with what we're investigating in the case of our politician?' said the officer in Tammisaari, and Westerberg thought. Casually. Falling fourteen floors. A bottle of whisky smashed against a head. No, not one. One, two, three bottles. Accurate blows, he thought. The murderer was well prepared.

Murders committed casually by a murderer who was well prepared.

'Not a bad idea once you think of it,' he murmured.

'What?' asked his colleague from Tammisaari at the other end of the line.

'A bottle of whisky as a murder weapon. In fact three, just to make sure.'

'Three what?'

'Bottles of whisky. The murder weapons.'

'When is that photo of your man Forsman coming through?' asked his colleague.

'Ought to be with you by now,' said Westerberg, but he was only half-listening.

He ended the conversation with his colleague, and searched for a contact number for Forsman's sister. A mobile number. He rang it, waited, and heard Kirsti Forsman's voice on a recorded message. Curiously stilted, giving her full legal qualifications.

He saw her in his mind's eye, in the pale blazer that she had worn when, stooping slightly but then standing upright, she had looked at her brother's body in Forensics. He broke the connection without leaving a message.

'Over in Tammisaari they're asking when they'll get Forsman's photo and our data on him,' said Seppo. 'Surely it ought to be there by now.'

'Yes, sure,' said Westerberg.

'Well, it's not waiting on the mail server, and everything from Tammisaari gets through,' said Seppo, handing him a pile of printed-out data files. On top was a photo of the dead politician, which immediately rang a bell with Westerberg. It had been in the media for several days, but Westerberg had paid it no special attention.

'Are you thinking what I'm thinking?' asked Seppo.

'What?'

Three bottles, fourteen floors, thought Westerberg. And the photo under the mattress. Forsman's sister who had turned the picture this way and that, only to say finally that she didn't know anything about it.

Seppo put the photograph on his desk, the picture that had been under Forsman's mattress. For how many years?

'I think he could be this other boy,' said Seppo, putting the photo on Westerberg's desk.

A radiant blue summer's day. The boy on whom Seppo's finger was resting stood turning away, in a clumsy, defensive attitude, and seemed to be looking out of the picture into a distance that he hoped to reach. But he was also smiling, faintly, indecisively.

'If you ask me, that could be our Markus Happonen,' said Seppo again.

Our Happonen, thought Westerberg, nodding.

Our Happonen, our Forsman.

A young woman officer was standing in the doorway with a stack of paper which looked heavy for her to carry. 'The records from Tammisaari,' she said.

'Fine, put it all down here,' said Seppo, making a sweeping movement in the direction of his desk.

'This is only the start,' she said. 'They're sending it all through as PDF files, and our system is getting kind of overloaded.'

The server, thought Westerberg. Our server, our PDF files.

'I'll be back with more soon. Järvi and Koskela are looking through it as well,' said the young officer, leaving. Seppo stood in front of the carefully stacked and stapled sheets of paper, smiling, and Westerberg wondered what there was about it to please him.

Seppo divided the stack carefully in two, and put half of the documents on Westerberg's desk.

'Or should we sort them according to content first?' he asked.

'Hm? No, better just start.'

Seppo nodded, and began leafing through the papers.

Westerberg sat there in silence for a while, deep in thoughts that he couldn't quite pin down. Then he looked at the first printout. He read for a few minutes, then looked up.

'What does PDF stand for?' he asked.

'Portable Document Format,' said Seppo.

Westerberg leaned back. 'You just thought that up, didn't you?'

Seppo didn't seem to be listening. 'What did you say?' he muttered.

'Oh, nothing,' said Westerberg, concentrating on the file in front of him again. The interview with the dead politician's wife had brought nothing to light, except that the interviewee had suffered what was presumably a nervous collapse.

39

In the afternoon Kimmo Joentaa went to the conference room with empty hands and a brain full of information. Sundström and Grönholm were already there; the other members of the core group of investigators were being brought in for an exchange of opinions only once a week now.

Joentaa sat down and interrupted Sundström, who was about to embark on a stocktaking statement.

'I'm doing something new,' he said.

'Oh . . . you are?' said Sundström.

Joentaa nodded.

'Doing what?' asked Grönholm.

'Going through all the leads again,' he said.

'Okay,' said Sundström.

'I'll have done it by this evening.'

'The old leads,' said Grönholm.

'Yes, all 2,711 of them. I've already read through nearly a thousand, and I'll be going on soon.'

'Okay,' said Sundström. '2,711 statements. And . . . what do you expect to come of that?'

'I expect to—'

'You know we've followed up every single one of them, and checked most of them ages ago, don't you?' said Sundström.

Joentaa nodded. 'I'd just like to . . . look through it all in a different way, from another point of view.'

'What point of view, for instance?' asked Sundström.

Joentaa thought about that and couldn't come up with an answer.

'Kimmo?'

'Male violence,' he said finally.

Sundström and Grönholm looked at him.

'Violence,' said Joentaa. 'On the quiet. So that at first it's not seen for what it is.'

He returned their gaze, and thought that he couldn't really express what he meant.

'See you later,' he said, leaving them.

40

In Rantaniemi near Laapeenranta this afternoon. I sit in the hotel, leaning against the bedstead, and I can see the sky through the window, the snow and the shopping centre that stands in the middle of this small town of clapboard houses like a gigantic ferry. A large green ferry run aground.

The costume fitted as if made for me, and the young nurse who took me through the bright nursing home, past tubs of flowers and paintings, gave me a smile and seemed to think it was a good thing that I came today, not the young woman who usually comes.Jarkko Miettinen seldom has visitors. Only relations and close friends are let in to see him, and the woman pastor who comes to encourage him and prepare him for death. As I am not a friend or relation, I went in the character of a pastor, a week earlier than the real pastor who, if the nurse is to be believed, is too young for this job anyway and always seems to be bored and unfriendly.

The nurse smiles at me before closing the door. Jarkko Miettinen is sitting in a wheelchair by the window, and doesn't take his eyes off the winter whiteness. He doesn't seem to have noticed me coming into the room. I take a chair and sit down beside him. Black coffee shines in a white cup on a white table.

I don't know how long it goes on. Miettinen is looking out of the window, and memories condense into concrete images, but they are still hard to grasp. Time stands still, but at the same time it is racing along a rail, forward and back, no stopping it, from image to image, until at last the old man slowly turns his face to me. My thoughts come to rest in those dead eyes.

I feel a little uncomfortable in my costume. Uncomfortable but at the same time protected. The boy in the shop made much of the fact that it's genuine, whatever he meant by that. Jarkko Miettinen can't see me, but he nods to me. I think I see his eyes light up as I open the box and give him the piece of quiche. Cream, salt, rye dough, cheese, salami sausage.

As he holds the piece of quiche and looks at it as if it were something strange but familiar, the images come back. A younger Miettinen, tanned and kneeling in a sea of coloured flowers in the sunlight. My mother beside him, praising his work. Miettinen turns to my mother and thanks her, smiling, and I see his face as I try keeping a football in the air so that it won't fall on the lawn. The lawn that Miettinen has just been mowing.

I don't know how long this memory lasts. Maybe only seconds, seeming to last longer because I need them to reconcile Miettinen, the landscape gardener giving our garden a makeover, with the other and yet identical Miettinen lying gasping and groaning on top of Saara.

That day is a long time ago, and the image is both loosely and firmly rooted in my mind. Miettinen – landscape gardener and rapist. I myself – a child.

My mother, who is dead now, stands in the picture, a strange and unsuspecting figure. To her, Miettinen is only a landscape gardener, no more.

She praises him again as I run indoors, shivering, and go up to my room. I remember how cold I felt.

Later Miettinen and my mother sit out on the terrace, and I hear them talking through the open door of my room. Miettinen is enjoying the quiche she has baked. Cream, salt, rye dough, cheese, salami sausage, mushrooms.

My mother praises Miettinen; Miettinen praises my mother's quiche.

Now, many years later, Miettinen raises his cup and then the piece of quiche to his mouth.

He eats patiently, and turns back to the window when he has finished.

I ask him whether he can remember Saara, but there is no reply. He sits there motionless; only his hand trembles, as mine did a few weeks after that dreadful day when I saw him standing in a flower bed in our garden wearing a straw hat and green overalls.

I ask him again. No reply.

For the sake of doing the thing thoroughly I show him the business card, but he won't look at it.

I ask him whether he knows where Risto is. No reply.

Perhaps his trembling gets worse, but I may be imagining that.

I stand up and walk out of the room. I carefully close the door after me. The young nurse, who is coming along the corridor towards me, says goodbye with a smile.

Miettinen's death is a matter of simple arithmetic. A sum of the probabilities that, to my mind, work out conclusively. Because of his age and weak constitution, it's possible that the amatoxin syndrome is already setting in. Vomiting, watery diarrhoea, stomach pains. But it will take some time. I shall not be here when he dies.

Outside, evening is falling fast. I look at the shopping centre, the ferry run aground, which begins to sway before my eyes, and after a few minutes merges with the black sky.

41

Westerberg and Seppo drove to Karjasaari. To the little town where the dead men had grown up and attended school together, about three hundred kilometres from Helsinki.

The most talkative person in the car was the lady telling them which way to go. Her directions were gentle and perfectly clear, and Westerberg slowly dozed off and fleetingly dreamed that the gentle voice became a loving, seductive one, and its owner was no longer leading him along roads to a strange place but by familiar paths to the bright room where she was hiding.

He felt humiliated by his dream, and tried to make his way back to reality, but didn't manage it until Seppo's voice broke through the images. Seppo was saying something that he couldn't make out.

'What?' he asked, opening his eyes and sitting abruptly upright.

'Oh, sorry,' said Seppo.

'What?'

'Sorry I woke you, I didn't notice that you . . .'

'Doesn't matter,' said Westerberg.

Seppo took the exit recommended by the friendly lady, whose voice now sounded tinny and strange again.

'Did you just say something?' asked Westerberg.

'Hmm?'

'Did you say something? Some kind of word I didn't . . . or else I was dreaming it.'

'Oh, yes. Xing?'

Westerberg turned to Seppo and wondered for a moment whether he was still dreaming. But Seppo looked perfectly real, sitting at the wheel of the police car.

'What?'

'Xing. I said I've put my profile on Xing.'

'Oh, yes?' said Westerberg.

'It's a career portal.'

Westerberg nodded.

'A networking site,' said Seppo. The voice recommended them to turn off after 200 metres, and Seppo met his eye.

'Not that I'm thinking of changing my job,' he said, 'but I'd kind of like to remain open to . . . to something new.'

Something new, thought Westerberg. He hadn't the faintest idea what Seppo was talking about. But Seppo seemed to have said all he had to say, and the woman's directions were now confined to the road to their destination.

'Is there a Pling too?' asked Westerberg.

'Hmm?' asked Seppo.

'I wouldn't mind signing up to Pling.'

'To what?'

'Or Zong.'

Seppo looked at him. 'Are you taking the mickey?'

'Just joking,' said Westerberg.

Then Seppo concentrated on the road again, and Westerberg pursued a hard-to-define chain of thought until Seppo said he suspected there might be a fault in the satnav system.

'Hmm?' said Westerberg.

'We're going to drive into the water any moment now. Take a look.'

They were surrounded by an enormous lake, and Seppo was steering the car over the only firm terrain visible for far around, a bridge.

'Oh,' said Westerberg.

'Yes,' said Seppo.

'Remarkable,' said Westerberg.

After a few minutes, however, land came in sight and they turned off along a fork in the road. A few minutes more, and the tinny female voice announced that they had reached their destination.

Karjasaari. Clapboard houses in the wintry evening sunlight. Pale pastel colours. Snow clung to the trees like candyfloss. The street lamps were already on; it would soon be dark.

The school building passed by, and Westerberg recalled his fruitless conversations at an earlier stage of the investigation with the young headmaster, and with teachers long retired who had only the vaguest recollections of Kalevi Forsman as a school student.

He thought again of Forsman's sister Kirsti, who had come to Helsinki in the evening and left again that same evening, and in the brief interim had said goodbye to her brother, with whom she must have lost any real contact some time earlier. Considerably earlier.

She had gone back to Hämeenlinna, and the investigation had gone off in a direction which, he hoped, brought them closer to the dead man than his long-forgotten childhood.

Seppo drove the car towards a building with gigantic letters fixed to its roof. Karjanhovi, the hotel into which Seppo had booked them, probably the only one in the little town.

It was only a feeling that he had, but it was an intense one, and it could be summed up in a simple sentence.

'I think we've come to the right place,' said Westerberg.

42

The lead that Kimmo Joentaa was looking for was hidden in just a few lines, and he overlooked it at first, before going back minutes later to the transcript entered in the extensive records under the number 1,324.

He read the text again. One of their colleagues who had been looking after the hotline at the time had written it down after the conversation.

Anita-Liisa Koponen, born in Mikkeli on 14 May 1973, thinks she recognises the unidentified dead woman as her piano teacher from her home town of Karjasaari. On being asked whether she could be certain of that, Koponen replies that the unknown woman played Sibelius like an angel; on being asked whether she could give us the dead woman's name, she replies that she can't remember it. On being asked why not, she replies that angels have no names; on being asked when she last saw the dead woman, she replies: in another life. On being asked whether she can provide any facts that would be useful to the police investigation, she replies that the unknown woman fell victim to the Devil. On being asked what she means by that, she replies that angels are always victims of the Devil, that's the way of the world; finally the lady ends the phone call. It came in on 30 September, was passed on to P. Grönholm for examination and evaluation.

Kimmo Joentaa read this text several times, until the letters began to blur in front of his eyes. He tried to find a plausible answer to the question of why he had returned to this lead.

Why he had first leafed through the files past it, only to go back on his tracks.

He recognised Petri Grönholm's handwriting on the yellow note added to the sheet of paper with the number 1,324 on it. He looked at Grönholm's note and read that, too, several times:

Incidentally, this lady suffers from severe bipolar disorder, is living at present in an institution for the psychologically sick in Ristiina.

Under it, Grönholm had written the address of the hospital. The thought of Tuomas Heinonen briefly came back to Joentaa's mind. He tried to imagine this phone call that had involved a police officer in Turku and a woman in Ristiina in a curious conversation lasting several minutes and hovering somewhere between bureaucracy and transcendentalism. And somewhere in the process it had been sent off to end up in the file for those contributions from the public that could safely be ignored.

Joentaa closed his eyes and massaged his temples.

Angels, devils, in another life. A piano teacher.

Passed on for examination and evaluation.

'Kimmo, we're going now,' said Päivi Holmquist behind him.

He turned round and nodded. 'Yes, of course. Have a nice evening.'

'Did you get anywhere?' asked Antti Laapenranta.

'I don't know. Maybe,' said Joentaa.

'You did?' asked Päivi.

'Perhaps. Listen to this,' he said, taking the sheet of paper out of the folder. He read aloud the transcript of the phone call, and then looked at two faces so baffled that he couldn't help laughing.

'Okay,' said Antti Laapenranta.

'It sounds . . .' Päivi began, and then stopped.

' . . . a little peculiar,' said Joentaa.

'Just a little,' said Antti.

Joentaa nodded and filed the record of the phone call away again. Didn't want anything disturbing the neatly kept sequence of files.

'I'll go on for a while, okay?' he said.

'Of course, Kimmo,' said Päivi. 'See you in the morning.'

'See you in the morning,' said Antti too, and Joentaa waved to the two of them until they were in the lift.

He drew the keyboard towards him and logged into the Internet. A little later the email address of veryhotlarissa appeared. As his fingers were moving over the keys, it occurred to him that he was probably committing some kind of offence. Passing on the results of police investigations to third parties. Or something along those lines.

Does this give you any ideas? he wrote, and sent the complete record of the whole conversation to the woman whose name he didn't know.

He sat there in front of the screen for several minutes, waiting for an answer that didn't come. Then he got out his mobile and called Grönholm, who sounded breathless when he replied.

'Petri?' said Joentaa. 'Kimmo here.'

'Hi, Kimmo,' said Grönholm.

'Are you still there?' asked Joentaa.

'What do you mean, there?' asked Grönholm.

'Well, at the office,' said Joentaa.

'At the office. Er, no.'

'You're not?'

'Kimmo, it's quite late, past eleven.'

'Oh.'

'Do you play tennis?'

'Tennis?'

'Yes, I'm having a game with some friends at the moment,

and I thought you could play with us too some time. If you like.'

'Sure. Actually I've never played tennis.'

'Never mind, we're not all of us very good,' said Grönholm.

'I see.'

'Okay, Kimmo, see you in the morning,' said Grönholm.

'Yes . . . Petri, just one moment . . .'

'They want me for the third set. Can it wait until tomorrow?'

'Ah . . . yes, of course.'

'Thanks. And say hi to the night porter for me,' said Grönholm, ending the call.

43

Again and again, Kirsti Forsman's eyes were drawn to the huge Viking ship on the wall. It looked different, more menacing but at the same time more menaced, because it seemed to be capsizing in a strong swell, but all the same she kept thinking of the TV series she used to watch as a child: *Vicky and the Strong Men*.

The waitresses, wearing costumes suggestive of the Middle Ages, were serving delicious dishes, and Tapio Takala, the managing director of the company she worked for, had been talking to her for what felt like an eternity, because a new Tetra Pak guideline threatened to restrict the means of distribution. She nodded, and clung to her glass of red wine, and at some point Takala had begun addressing her as 'My love'.

'My love, I'm sure you understand that we need an idea here. I'm counting on you,' he said.

She nodded. Her thoughts were moving in an area where Takala and his fruit yoghurt with chocolate and coconut chips occupied a comparatively small space.

Vicky and the strong men were more important.

And the calls to her mobile.

Westerberg the Helsinki police officer had left no messages, but she had recognised his number. She had looked at his business card often enough, and although she never called the number she knew it by heart.

She looked at the ship, thought of Vicky, let Takala's torrent of talk flow past her and wondered why Westerberg had tried to reach her three times. In the morning, in the afternoon, in the evening.

And soon night would fall, and Takala was still talking non-stop, and the waitress brought dessert, mango cream with pineapple slices, which seemed to have little to do with Vicky, the strong men and the Viking ship on the wall.

Takala had more red wine poured, and when at last there was a sudden silence, Kirsti Forsman wondered whether he had really just wanted to discuss Tetra Paks and guidelines with her or whether he had something else in mind, something that he hadn't achieved yet.

She smiled at him and felt slightly tipsy, a feeling that wouldn't turn to nausea until later that night or in the morning.

Takala raised a hand and ordered two espressos.

Her iPhone buzzed. Like a swarm of bees.

Westerberg.

She stared at the number on the display, and waited for the swarm of bees to move on. When the phone fell silent Takala did what she had really wanted to do, breathed audibly out.

'Nothing important?' he said, and Kirsti Forsman had the impression that there were other words mingled with those, something like: What could be more important than me, my love?

She smiled and shook her head. Nothing important.

She thought of Kalevi. Of that summer's day in the distant past. The humming of bees and flies. Kalevi telling their mother something in a wavering, breaking voice, like a small child. Their mother's eyes. The horror in them, the sadness, the fear that couldn't be put into words, and all the words in the world would not have been up to the story that Kalevi had told.

Kalevi, who was crying like a child.

Her mother, who had no more tears to shed after several days.

And she herself, who had shut that day away as if in a room to which she would never return. She had thrown away the key. She had met Kalevi now and then. The last time at Christmas nearly three years ago. Kalevi upstairs in the guest room. His soft snoring behind the closed door against which she had leaned her head for a few minutes.

Takala seemed euphoric, challenged her to a duel with their mobiles converted to laser swords.

She ate the dessert fast and greedily, the fruity mango cream, and emptied the last glass of wine in a single draught.

Takala was playing the flute on his mobile, elegiac notes that even added up to a tune.

'Lovely,' she said, and Takala looked pleased and insisted on escorting her home.

Outside the front door he lost his nerve, perhaps because she hadn't laughed at any of his jokes on the way, and when he was about to embark on a hesitant 'Goodnight' she asked if he wouldn't like to come in.

The surprise in his face finally made her laugh, and a few minutes later, while she was lying under him on the squeaking bed and smelled his sweat, she imagined herself lying in the arms of Westerberg, whom she had somehow liked, even though he had found the key that she had been trying to lose all her life.

44

Kimmo Joentaa drove down a long, narrow road that night. The dazzle of headlights came towards him less often, and the lakes hidden behind the snow-laden trees to left and right drew in on the road, until at last it became a long bridge leading over the water.

Soon after that, early in the morning, he arrived in Ristiina and parked the car outside the hospital from which the interview with the reference number 1,324 had come.

He was feeling tired, and knew at the same time that he wouldn't be able to sleep if he tried to now. He had often felt like that in the first weeks and months after Sanna's death.

The hospital lay in the dark, surrounded by a large garden. A massive building like a villa, it seemed to consist of a main house and several subsidiary structures. Lights were on here and there. Behind one of the windows Kimmo Joentaa saw a young woman and a young man. The woman was sitting at a desk in front of a computer screen, the man was talking and didn't seem to notice that the woman wasn't listening to him.

Within minutes, a sharp breath of cold air filled the interior of the car, and Joentaa reached for the file lying on the passenger seat.

Anita-Liisa Koponen. Believes she recognises the unidentified dead woman as her piano teacher. Can't remember her name. Played Sibelius like an angel.

He leaned back and thought of Larissa. Tried to imagine where she was. Probably asleep. Breathing, dreaming, weeping.

She wouldn't be able to remember her dream when she woke up.

The woman on the other side of the window began to laugh, and the man shook his head and went over to the computer. The woman pointed to the screen and laughed again, and once more the man shook his head, presumably to show that he couldn't share the woman's amusement.

Joentaa watched the two of them engaged in their silent dialogue. How far away from him they were, although only a few metres separated them. A low wall, part of the garden, a windowpane.

He looked down at the file without reading it. Angels have no names. His thoughts began circling round memories that faded before he could grasp them. Only to come back again. Sanna swimming in the lake and laughing, although she was mortally ill. Larissa trudging through the woods ahead of him, telling stories from the novels she read or the films she saw, or about the children with whom she played ice hockey.

He closed his eyes and felt sleep approaching after all. For a while he imagined letters emerging from all the stories, all the words he had heard, single letters that began to form a name.

Just as he was thinking he could read the name, a repeated knocking brought him back to reality. He was looking at the face of a bearded man who was knocking on the window of the driver's door.

'Excuse me,' he called through the glass.

'Yes?'

'Are you all right?'

'Yes. Yes, I'm fine.'

The man nodded, turned up his thumb and went towards the hospital building. The cold inside the car had spread, and the darkness was giving way to a touch of daylight. Cars drew up and parked near his own, people climbed out, ran stooping past a porter's lodge into the courtyard beyond and disappeared into the main building. Room after room was flooded with electric light, and the snowfall setting in made the morning look brighter than it was. The room where a young woman and a young man had been bending over a computer screen some time earlier was empty.

Kimmo Joentaa put the file, which had slipped down between the seats, back on the passenger seat and waited to feel the impulse to get out. His mobile, lying beside the file folder, was blinking at him. He picked it up. A call that had come in at 5.30. He imagined hearing Larissa's voice as he tapped in the number to bring up his mailbox.

Then he heard the tired, distant voice of Tuomas Heinonen. 'Kimmo, Tuomas here. Call me, please . . . when you have time. I have . . . a few difficulties.'

Joentaa lowered his mobile and thought of Tuomas, sitting in a room in another hospital. Tennis, he thought. Good quota, wrong tip. He almost felt as if he could hear the rhythmic sound of a rally in the background, behind Tuomas Heinonen's soft voice.

He ought to call Paulina and ask her how it was possible for her husband, during a stay in hospital to cure his gambling addiction, to bet on tennis matches. And first he would call Tuomas and tell him he really must stop all that nonsense at once.

He slipped the mobile into his coat pocket and got out of the car, leaning forward as he ran to take the edge off the cold. He showed his ID to the porter, who was sitting upright behind his little window, and explained that he urgently wanted to talk to Anita-Liisa Koponen.

'On what business?' asked the porter.

'On what what?'

'On what business?' repeated the porter.

'Oh, I see. Angels,' said Joentaa.

The porter gawped at him, and seemed to have another question ready, but Joentaa didn't let him get it in.

'Angels, devils. Life, death. Summer, winter, fire, water. The usual thing, you know what I mean.'

The porter nodded, and hesitated briefly. Then he rang a number, had a conversation on the phone, and told him – it sounded rather ambiguous to Kimmo Joentaa – that one of the hospital staff would be along right away to take care of him.

45

The breakfast buffet in the Karjanhovi Hotel was surprisingly lavish. Apart from a very old man who was stoically reading a newspaper at the side of the room without ever turning the page, Westerberg and Seppo were the only guests there. Seppo ate a hearty breakfast: scrambled eggs, sausages, cheese, salmon, and he finished with some curiously multi-coloured muesli flakes.

Career portal, thought Westerberg as his young colleague shovelled the colourful muesli and milk into his mouth like a child.

'Looks delicious,' he said.

'Absolutely. Have some yourself,' said Seppo.

'Tomorrow, maybe,' said Westerberg.

Seppo nodded, pushed his dish aside, and went on from where he had left off before the muesli. 'Right, about Happonen, the dead man in Tammisaari . . .'

'Mhm,' said Westerberg.

'What I don't understand is that neither we nor the Tammisaari investigators have managed to get hold of a usable picture of that man . . . I mean the journalist who, of course, wasn't a journalist at all.'

Westerberg nodded, and raised his coffee cup to his mouth. He thought of Kirsti Forsman, the software adviser's sister, who hadn't rung back. When he tried to reach her again this morning it had gone straight to voicemail.

'Tammisaari,' said Seppo. 'A man saying he's a journalist arranges a meeting over the phone with Markus Happonen, a local politician, pegging it to Happonen's ambition to make a career nationwide.'

Westerberg nodded.

'Helsinki,' said Seppo. 'A man arranges a meeting with Kalevi Forsman and speaks to him during a computer fair on the pretext of being interested in buying one of his software systems.'

Westerberg nodded.

'In both cases the man suggests a meeting place that is publicly accessible, at a time when there will certainly be people on the spot.'

Westerberg nodded.

'In both cases, despite the public nature of those meetings, no one is able to sketch a picture of the man afterwards that tells us anything about him, and in both cases no one registers the moment when the crime is committed.'

'Perhaps that's why,' said Westerberg.

'What?'

'Perhaps the fact that it was done so publicly, all out in the open, covered up particularly well for the crime,' said Westerberg, feeling rather philosophical.

'Hm, yes, if you look at it that way,' said Seppo.

'Because no one is expecting it, no one notices it,' said Westerberg.

Seppo looked at him for a long time, but seemed to be pursuing his own train of thought. 'All the same . . .' he said.

'Yes?'

'I don't understand how it can have been so easy,' said Seppo.

'It was easy because the man succeeded in making it look easy,' said Westerberg, and as soon as he had spoken those words he stood up, suddenly feeling they had been tossing words back and forth long enough. 'What's more, we still don't know whether all this really hangs together.'

'Two murder victims who both went to school in the same dump in the back of beyond and took their school-leaving exams in the same year,' said Seppo.

'How would I know if that's it? You have that date at the Town Hall at ten, and I'm going to the neighbouring village to see Happonen's parents.'

Seppo nodded, and Westerberg stood waiting for a while, hoping that Seppo would finally get to his feet. But he was sitting there lost in thought.

'Seppo?' asked Westerberg.

'Hmm? Oh, yes, sorry. Quarter to ten in the lobby?'

'Right. See you then.'

Westerberg walked across the room, and turned round before getting into the lift, stood there for a moment, and watched Seppo pouring milk and more coloured flakes into a glass dish. Tomorrow, he decided, he would try that multi-coloured muesli himself.

46

The young woman who collected him outside the porter's lodge was the one who had been looking at a computer screen early in the morning, laughing heartily at something.

She wasn't laughing now, but looked at him with a neutral expression, introduced herself as Arja Ekström and asked what this was about.

Arja Ekström, nice name, thought Joentaa.

'You must be freezing,' he said.

'What?'

'Sorry, I just thought . . . in this cold . . . with only your white coat on . . .'

The woman laughed at that, but only briefly, and Joentaa got the impression that she felt embarrassed by losing control.

'Why don't we go in and discuss it in peace?' suggested Joentaa.

'Of course,' she said, going ahead. He followed her across the courtyard and over to the main entrance. Warm air met him as they went in.

The woman walked purposefully down a corridor lined with potted plants, and finally knocked on the door of an office at the end of the long passage.

Joentaa heard the muted call for them to come in, and he recognised the man who rose from behind a broad desk and came towards them – the tall, bearded man who had knocked on his car window and asked whether he was all right.

'We have a visitor,' said the young woman. 'Police. Mr . . .'

'Joentaa. Kimmo Joentaa,' said Joentaa.

The woman nodded, and introduced the bearded man as the director of the hospital, Stefan Holmgren.

'Good morning,' said Joentaa.

'Police . . .' said Holmgren, and Joentaa had the impression that he was lost in thought, fitting the face he saw before him into this morning's situation. Possibly the way Joentaa had been lounging in his car didn't match the psychologist's idea of a police officer.

'I'm from Turku, and I'd like to speak to one of your patients, a woman,' said Joentaa. 'It's in connection with our inquiries.'

'From Turku,' said Arja Ekström. 'That's a very long drive.'

'Turku. That rings a bell with me,' said Holmgren.

'It's about Anita-Liisa Koponen. Is she still being treated here with you?'

Holmgren nodded. 'Yes. I remember that case myself . . . she thought she recognised the dead woman who couldn't be identified.'

Joentaa nodded.

'I spoke to one of your colleagues about it,' said Holmgren.

'I know,' said Joentaa. 'The lead she gave us was checked, and initially classed as not very important. But now I would very much like to speak to Ms Koponen again.'

'Yes . . . of course,' said Holmgren. 'If it seems necessary to you. Do you ascribe any . . . real significance to what she said, then?'

'I'd like to talk to Ms Koponen, and then I'd be able to assess that better.'

'Yes.' Holmgren nodded to himself, and seemed to be thinking, as if he wanted to formulate some distinct idea. 'And you drove here . . . from Turku? At night?'

Joentaa nodded.

'Without arranging an appointment, and without knowing whether Ms Kaponen is still having treatment here?'

At that Joentaa laughed. 'Does that tell you something about my psyche?' he asked.

'Yes, to some extent,' said Holmgren, 'but don't worry. Not everything that's significant can be interpreted immediately. I'm sure that's much the same in your profession as in ours.'

Joentaa wondered how he could have given a rational explanation of his impulsive decision to take to the road at once, just like that. Probably by saying: I couldn't sleep anyway, so why not drive to Ristiina? Or something like that.

Holmgren looked at Joentaa and seemed to choose his words carefully for what he said next. 'Anita-Liisa Koponen has been with us about seven months, with a few short breaks. But she kept coming back because she – well, she can't get her bearings in everyday life. She suffers from bipolar disorder, accompanied and possibly set off by the consumption of drugs that in the long run alter the personality.'

'Yes,' said Joentaa.

'So if you are asking our opinion of the credibility of—'

'I'd really like to speak to Ms Koponen first,' said Joentaa.

Holmgren looked at him for a long time. Then he nodded. 'Of course,' he said. He picked up the phone, tapped in a number and had a short conversation. 'Arja will bring her here,' he said when he had hung up. He turned to his young colleague. 'I think the ergotherapy room is free.'

Then Joentaa was following the purposeful Arja Ekström again, fighting off an impulse to ask her what she had been laughing at this morning.

She led him into a large, bare room that smelled of lemon. The snow was coming down harder beyond its windows. A lavishly made-up, red-haired woman and a corpulent young man were waiting for them.

'Thank you, Tarmo,' said Arja Ekström, and the young man stood up and shuffled away. Joentaa looked at the woman, who was sitting very upright at a long table against the background of the winter landscape, and looked lost.

He went up to her, offering her his hand. 'I'm Kimmo Joentaa,' he said. 'From the police in Turku.'

The woman's hand lay softly in his. 'It's good that you're here,' she said.

'Yes,' said Joentaa, and he turned to Arja Ekström. 'Thanks,' he said. 'I'll look in on you again before I leave.'

Arja Ekström stood there for a little while in silence, then she nodded and went away. Joentaa sat down opposite the woman.

'Ms Koponen, I'd like to talk to you about a lead you gave us some time ago. It's about the body of a woman whom we hadn't been able to identify yet . . .'

'I know,' she said.

'You told a colleague of mine that you recognised the woman in the photograph.'

'Of course,' she said. 'She was our music teacher at school. And I also . . . I had piano lessons with her. One summer.'

'One summer?'

She nodded.

'Do you know what summer that was? What year?'

'She offered to do it. She was there for only that one summer, as a supply teacher, because Irmeli Nikola was so ill.'

'Do you remember what summer that was?' asked Joentaa again.

'I've been thinking of that,' she said.

Joentaa waited.

'I didn't really want to play the piano at all. But I went . . . because my parents were so keen for me to be able to play something. Because they'd bought the piano, and my brother couldn't play it.'

'Can you remember the year?' asked Joentaa.

'And I liked going to the lessons because she was so nice. A really nice person.'

'Can you remember her name?' asked Joentaa.

'It was in 1985,' she said.

'1985 . . .' said Joentaa.

'Because after that everything was different.'

Joentaa waited.

'Different from before,' she said.

'What happened then?' asked Joentaa.

'She was ill too,' she said.

'The piano teacher?'

'Just like Irmeli Nikola. But Irmeli Nikola had cancer, and she . . . I mean the other teacher, after a while she didn't come any more. No one ever said why.'

'Can you remember the woman's name?'

Anita-Liisa Koponen said nothing, and looked at him as if she didn't understand the question. Behind her, the snow and the morning sky were merging into an expanse of grey. The make-up that the woman in front of him was wearing began to run, and Joentaa thought what a strange contrast she presented – on the one hand the calm voice, the controlled gestures, on the other the mysterious tenor of her words. And a clear, regular face hidden behind a mask of make-up.

She said, 'Angels have no names.'

'That's what you told my colleague,' said Joentaa.

'Because that's how it is.'

'Can you tell me what happened at the time?'

'What do you mean?'

'I mean what happened then.'

She looked at him for a long time. 'Oh, that,' she said at last.

Joentaa waited.

'Do you really want to know?' she asked.

Joentaa nodded.

She picked up her handbag, took a handkerchief and a small mirror out of it, and examined her face for a few seconds before carefully wiping the handkerchief over it. Then she seemed to pull herself together, and smiled. 'You could have told me my make-up was running,' she said.

'Sorry,' said Joentaa.

'We played a duet, four hands on the keyboard. I don't remember what it was. And she played really well. I thought for the first time that it might be good to be able to do that . . . do you understand what I mean?'

'I think so, yes.'

'It was hot. All those days were very hot, the whole summer. Then the lesson was over, and I was about to go. I'd packed up my things. The book of music, and the thing that my parents had given me, that device for setting the time . . . do you know what it's called?'

Joentaa waited for her to go on, but she seemed to be expecting an answer.

'No,' he said.

'Well, we didn't use it. She just laughed when I took the thing out of my bag, but I had unpacked it, so I packed it up again at the end of the lesson.'

He tried to meet the woman's eyes, but as she spoke she was looking at the door through which Arja Ekström had disappeared a little while ago. She spoke thoughtfully, and seemed to be concentrating entirely on her memories.

'Then I went out, and I'd reached the front door, and just as I was going to open it that man came in from outside, her boyfriend. He smiled at me and said something, and pushed me ahead of him into the living room. Then everything happened very fast. I think it only lasted a few minutes. Maybe five.'

The woman turned her eyes away from the door and

looked at him, and for some reason Joentaa thought of
Christmas. Warm white light, parcels carefully done up with
ribbon bows which came undone when you pulled gently
at the ends.

'I remember going home. If I hadn't known what the man
had done to me I could have sworn it hadn't happened. It
was very quick because of the difference in strength between
us. And because it was such a surprise.'

She looked at him as if expecting confirmation.

Joentaa nodded.

'He'd pushed up my skirt and pulled my panties down. I
can't remember the feeling any more. I only know it happened.
What I always wondered later was, where was she?'

'Your . . . piano teacher?'

'Yes. She'd gone. She had been in the living room just a
moment before, and then she'd gone. I wonder where she
was. Do you understand?'

Joentaa nodded. Christmas, gift parcels, he thought.

'I couldn't ask her. I didn't go back for any more lessons,
and she didn't come back to the school. I once asked another
student who had lessons with her too, but he didn't know
anything . . . she just never came back . . .'

'Did you . . .'

'When he let go of me, I left. I ran out and went home.'

'Can you tell me . . .'

She smiled. 'I've never told anyone what happened before.'

'I—'

'I'd like to stop now,' she said.

'Right,' said Joentaa.

She stood up and held out her hand to him. 'My room is
just round the corner here.'

'I'll take you there if you like.'

She laughed. 'I can manage for myself.'

When Joentaa went out into the corridor, he went back the

same way as he had come, concentrating on taking the right turns. The word occurred to him. He hadn't been aware that he knew it.

Metronome.

The device that her parents had given her, with which Anita-Liisa Koponen had been expected to keep time.

47

The politician's parents lived in a house where Westerberg immediately felt at ease. And also ill at ease.

The rooms were large and light, although grey sleet was falling outside. Through the living-room window he saw a well-tended terrace, and a huge garden. The lawn was so neatly covered with snow that Westerberg wondered whether anyone had lent it a helping hand. Maybe these days, thanks to modern technology, you could not only mow lawns but smooth out a covering of snow when it lay on such surfaces.

He had called that morning to say he was coming, and formed a picture of the man at the other end of the line that was surprisingly close to the reality. Joosef Happonen's powerful voice belonged to a tall man with hair cut very short and a winning smile; you would never have thought that his son had recently met a violent death.

Joosef Happonen's wife, Suoma, was small and thin, and her voice sounded as if it came from a tape recorder when she asked if he wouldn't like to stay to lunch.

'No, thank you very much,' said Westerberg. 'I won't keep you long.'

'Really, it would be no trouble at all,' said Joosef Happonen.

'All the same, thanks but no,' said Westerberg.

'Then let's sit down,' said Suoma Happonen.

Westerberg nodded.

'I'll make us some coffee,' said Suoma Happonen, and disappeared into the kitchen while her husband sat opposite Westerberg on the second of the two low red sofas.

'Well, and how can we . . . help you?' he asked.

'As I told you on the telephone, I've come from Helsinki. In the course of an investigation, we came upon a cross-reference that brings us here to Karjasaari.'

'To Karjasaari?' asked Happonen.

Westerberg was about to go on, but then, in the echo after the word, he heard Happonen's voice falter when he said Karjasaari.

'Yes . . . Karjasaari, that's the name of this place, isn't it?' he asked.

'Of course,' said Happonen.

'What is it?' asked Suoma Happonen behind Westerberg. He turned and saw her standing in the middle of the room with a tray, and Happonen said, 'Nothing.'

She came closer, carefully put the tray on the coffee table, and sat down beside her husband.

'Nothing,' he said. 'Mr . . . Westerberg is talking about a cross-reference that brought him here.'

'That's right. We're investigating the case of a murdered company director . . . and we found a connection with Karjasaari and your son.'

Suoma Happonen nodded, and Joosef Happonen put an arm round her shoulders.

'Did you know a boy . . . a man of your son's age by the name of Kalevi Forsman?'

Happonen shook his head, barely perceptibly, and Suoma Happonen said, 'Of course.'

'He was at school with your son . . . so you remember him?'

'Yes, indeed,' said Suoma Happonen, and her husband said, 'No, I'm sorry . . . but there were . . . Markus had a lot of . . .'

'But you must remember Kalevi, they were very close friends for a time.'

'Do you remember when? At what age?' asked Westerberg.

'Yes . . . not long before they left school, I think . . . the two always went swimming together during that particularly hot summer.' She picked up the coffee pot, and sat like that for a few seconds. 'Yes, it was the summer of their last year at school. 1985.'

1985, thought Westerberg. *19 August 1985. We had a barbecue. No one talked about what happened. She smiled at me. Everyone is the same as usual, and R. says I'm not to worry about it.*

Happonen was sitting there as if turned to stone. His wife poured coffee.

'Milk and sugar?'

'Black, please,' said Westerberg.

She made as if to hand her husband a cup, but he did not react.

'Joosef?' she asked.

'Hm?'

'Coffee?'

'Thanks,' he said, taking the cup.

'I want to show you something,' said Westerberg.

'What is it?' asked Happonen.

'Just a moment.' Westerberg opened his bag, which he had put on the sofa beside him, and took out the photograph. Markus Happonen, Kalevi Forsman and two unknown men in the sun.

'Is that your son in the picture? With Kalevi Forsman?'

Suoma Happonen reached for the photograph, looked at it and nodded.

'Yes, that's Markus.'

'May I?' said Happonen, taking the picture.

'I recognise Kalevi as well,' she said.

'How about the other two?' asked Westerberg.

'No, to be honest, they don't mean anything to me. What about you, Joosef?'

Joosef Happonen looked at the picture. And at something behind it, Westerberg thought.

'Joosef?' she asked.

'No,' he said. 'I . . . don't recognise anyone in it. Not even Markus. Are you sure that's him?'

'Of course it is,' she said. 'I even still remember . . .'

'No, I'm sorry,' said Happonen.

'. . . I even remember his swimming trunks.'

Happonen laughed – a forced laugh – and gave the photo back to Westerberg.

'Thank you,' said Westerberg.

'Is it . . . is it important?' asked Happonen.

'It's the cross-reference,' said Westerberg.

'I see,' said Happonen.

'Is that . . . do you mean . . .' said Suoma Happonen.

'Kalevi Forsman is dead,' Happonen said. He seemed to be addressing neither Westerberg nor his wife nor himself. He was addressing no one in particular. He gave the information as a plain statement of fact.

Westerberg waited a few seconds. 'Yes, you're right. We found this photo in Kalevi Forsman's apartment. Under the mattress of his bed.'

'Under his bed?' said Suoma Happonen.

'The photograph . . .' said Happonen.

'Yes?'

'The photograph is rather old.'

Westerberg nodded. He looked at the wintry scene beyond the window, the summery scene in the photo, and thought of Kirsti Forsman, the dead software adviser's sister, who didn't answer the phone when he called her, and who had said exactly the same thing in another room a few months ago.

48

Dear diary,

Back in Helsinki, in time for my interview with the chart technician. The building where the Stock Exchange is housed is a grey block of masonry with banners on its flat roof waving in the wind.

We're sitting in a small, stuffy room. The chart technician is very young, he is smoking, he wears a blue suit and a yellow tie, his hair stands up in peaks, and from what he says I conclude that he seriously thinks he is some kind of scientist.

He talks about the past and the future, about geometry and statistics, and I make a few notes while he enjoys the sound of his own voice and assembles platitudes, speculation and the pseudo-intellect of business management to build up a whole.

Of all the joke characters working on the money markets, chart analysts are the most amusing. With their fingers on the pulse of the financial world. Or something of that nature.

The interesting thing is that a few weeks after the system crashes, no one can remember the crash any more. Sometimes I wonder if I could achieve some of that deeply internalised suppression of reality myself.

He explains that there is cause for concern in the banking sector, and he anticipates being obliged to lower target prices. Lower them considerably, he adds.

Finally I ask him, just by the way, about Sedigene stocks; in what current trend of the charts does he see them?

'Sedigene?' he asks. 'Biotechnology?'

'That's right,' I say.

He seems to be thinking – thinking, mainly, what answer that question is expected to elicit.

'Neutral,' he says at last. 'Why?'

I wave the question away, and a little later I set off for home. Evening is falling. Leea gives me a hug and goes into the kitchen to make coffee. Olli is pleased to see me and wants to play what at present is our favourite game.

'Get it all set up,' I tell him, and I go into my room.

An Internet search of the surprisingly up-to-date home page of Seudun Sanomat, the Rantaniemi local paper, tells me that an inmate of the care home for senior citizens was taken to hospital after a collapse of his cardiovascular system, and died there. According to this article, the initial suspicion that it might have been due to food poisoning has not been confirmed, since apart from the dead man no inmate of the care home has complained of stomach pains, and no more such cases are expected.

An interesting line of reasoning, leaving several variables out of account.

I join Olli in the living room. Olli is kneeling on the floor with the board and the cards lying carefully arranged in front of him.

'Off you go, then,' I say, and Olli picks up the dice. He waits for a moment, closes his eyes, concentrates, and throws.

49

Westerberg spent a considerable part of the evening with the poker machines in the hotel lobby.

Seppo sat bent over the files in the dimly lit, deserted breakfast area, muttering barely audibly from time to time that no one could win against the machines.

Westerberg fed another handful of coins into the machine, and Seppo murmured, 'It's an impossibility.'

'What?' asked Westerberg.

'An impossibility. Beating a machine.'

Westerberg concentrated on the cards fizzing up on the display. King, king, jack, jack. And an eight.

'Double pairs,' he said. 'With kings.'

'That's not much,' said Seppo.

Westerberg pressed a button to get rid of the unwanted eight of clubs. He thought of the dead politician's parents, of the moment when the father's voice had faltered, and Seppo said the question of the business card was bothering him a little.

'What?' asked Westerberg.

'The business card.'

Full house, thought Westerberg.

'I've got a full house,' he said.

'With kings?'

'With jacks.'

'Hmm.'

'What do you mean about the business card?'

'The lady at the Town Hall, Happonen's secretary . . .'

'Yes?'

'Well, former secretary would be more like it.'

'Yes, yes, Seppo. The business card . . .'

'She remembered that Happonen had had one of our man's business cards. He left it there after the preliminary conversation. It didn't turn up in the course of the investigations, which suggests that the murderer took it back, presumably after committing the crime.'

'Aha!' said Westerberg, as coins rattled out of the poker machine.

'Congratulations,' murmured Seppo. 'Unfortunately the lady didn't know any more.'

'It's not likely his own real name and address were on it,' said Westerberg.

'Exactly,' said Seppo.

Westerberg nodded. 'Why the card, then?'

'Exactly,' said Seppo.

'And what was on it, if not his real name?' said Westerberg.

'Exactly,' said Seppo.

Westerberg thought it over while he counted the coins. 'Twenty-three euros sixty cents,' he said.

'And how much did you put in the slot?' asked Seppo.

More than that, thought Westerberg. 'If the real name wasn't on it, then presumably . . .'

'. . . it gave a false one,' said Seppo.

'Hmm,' said Westerberg.

'Why risk it?' said Seppo. 'He must have reckoned with the possibility of not getting the card back.'

Lost in thought, Westerberg contemplated his next hand. Seven of clubs, nine of diamonds, queen of diamonds, ten of hearts, ten of clubs. He turned his eyes away from the flashing display and looked at Seppo, who was leafing through a file.

'You're looking for . . .'

'Mentions of a business card,' said Seppo.

'In connection with Forsman.'

'Exactly.' Seppo took out his mobile, tapped in a number and waited. Westerberg turned back to the screen and exchanged the seven, the nine and the queen for cards that improved his chances only slightly.

Seppo apologised to whoever was at the other end of the line for disturbing him so late, and assured him that it was important. Then he listened for a while, and finally asked several times why he hadn't been told about this before. He did not seem to get any sensible answer, and ended the conversation. 'Goodnight,' he said. 'Yes, I understand, yes, fine, thank you, goodnight.'

'Who was that?' asked Westerberg.

'Jussilainen,' said Seppo. 'Forsman's partner in the firm.'

'Yes?' said Westerberg.

'He thinks he remembers that Forsman had a business card – he even thinks he remembers holding it once himself – because Forsman liked the design.'

'The design,' said Westerberg.

'Yes, Forsman held the card in front of Jussilainen's face. Because of the design. And only now we hear about it.'

'Can Jussilainen remember the name?'

'No. Only that it was unusual in some way. And he didn't like the design himself.'

'Ah.'

'Jussilainen didn't like the colour combination. And he remembers that the name sounded funny, and the man's profession was given as adviser. In Happonen's case it just said journalist.'

'Adviser,' said Westerberg.

'Yes, the man said he planned to buy Forsman's software on behalf of a bank.'

'Yes,' said Westerberg.

'And no such business card turned up when we sifted through their contacts.'

Westerberg nodded, and watched the machine swallowing up his coins. A pair, then a double pair. Not enough, as Seppo so rightly said.

'Perhaps he simply wanted to make his cover story more plausible?' said Seppo.

Westerberg thought about that. 'Perhaps. But I'm thinking of something else.'

'Maybe, for some reason or other, he really did use his real name?' said Seppo.

Westerberg shook his head. 'He knows that, with a little luck, we could get our hands on the card.'

'But why this whole rigmarole? Why was it important to him to give Forsman and Happonen his false name?'

The machine made triumphant clanging sounds.

'Names don't matter,' said someone behind Westerberg's back. He turned, and thought he liked the look of the man before remembering that he knew him already.

There in the dim light was Kimmo Joentaa, the young policeman from Turku, with whom he had worked on a very curious case at Christmas a year ago.

50

Kimmo Joentaa stood there, feeling weak at the knees, and wondered if this really was Westerberg.

He had got the hospital to give him a few more names and addresses, relations of Anita-Liisa Koponen. Then he had driven to Karjasaari along the long, narrow road leading over the water.

He had found the house where Anita-Liisa Koponen's parents used to live; it stood looking well-tended but abandoned under a pale sun on the outskirts of the woods. After that he had driven to the school.

A friendly secretary had spent several minutes looking through files, and finally said she was afraid that it was difficult to find the name of a supply teacher who had spent only one summer at the school, when that summer was more than twenty years ago. But she had promised to let him know if she found anything or came across anyone who could help him further.

After that he had booked into the only hotel in the place, had spent some time sitting on the bed with his laptop open in front of him without getting any message from Larissa, had let Sundström know that he was investigating in Karjasaari – 'Where? What?' Sundström had responded – and finally went to sleep in the hotel room when it was nearly afternoon, seconds after his head hit the pillow at last. And now he wondered vaguely whether he was still dreaming.

'Kimmo,' said Westerberg.

'Marko,' said Joentaa. He was pleased to see him, a man

he hadn't thought of for a long time, but who was none the less familiar to him at once. He had been listening to the two of them, Westerberg and his colleague, for a while as they talked about names, false and real, and Westerberg had fed the poker machine with coins without concentrating on the game.

False names, real names. The number you have called is not available. While Westerberg introduced his young colleague Seppo, Joentaa realised why he had been so pleased to see Westerberg. Meeting someone you don't expect to meet. Who could have been anywhere, but who happened to be here in this dark hotel, playing that machine.

He thought of the key under the apple tree, the light in the windows.

He sat down at the table where Seppo was already sitting, which was covered with file folders just like the ones Joentaa had been leafing through the night before. 2,711 leads from the public. Angels. Devils.

'Good to see you,' said Westerberg.

'Same to you,' said Joentaa, and Seppo asked whether he would like some coffee, pointing to a white pot.

'Is there any tea?' asked Joentaa.

'Er . . .'

'I really came down to make myself a tea,' said Joentaa. He stood up, but Westerberg got in first.

'Coming in a minute,' he said. 'I'll make you one.'

'Camomile, please,' said Joentaa.

A few minutes later Westerberg came back, put the cup down carefully in front of Joentaa, a live band began playing a tango in the adjoining restaurant, and it was Seppo who, after a brief pause, asked the obvious question. 'Seeing that you're, well, a police officer too . . . ?' he began.

Joentaa nodded. The sound of the music was muted as it reached the large breakfast room where they were sitting, and

Joentaa felt a curiously gentle, almost pleasant pain behind his forehead.

'So what are we all actually doing here?' asked Seppo.

'Well,' said Westerberg.

'You're here on professional business?' said Seppo.

Joentaa nodded. He looked at the files that Seppo had pushed over to him. 'Can you two tell me what your case is about?' asked Joentaa.

Westerberg nodded to Seppo, and Seppo began telling the story. Joentaa listened intently, and only occasionally interrupted with a question. When Seppo finished, the music in the restaurant had also come to an end, and a few shadows passed by, almost inaudibly wishing each other goodnight.

Joentaa leaned back and drank the last cold dregs of camomile tea.

A dead company owner in Helsinki.

A dead politician in Tammisaari.

A confused woman, her mind clear as glass, in a hospital in Ristiina.

An unknown dead woman in the cemetery in Turku.

'Yes,' he said, and Seppo went to get some coffee. The fruit machine rattled a little way off, and Joentaa looked at Westerberg, who was always wide awake when he looked as tired as he did now, and he thought of what Seppo had said at the end of his story.

A false name on a finely designed business card.

A murderer passing the time of day in a friendly manner.

Seppo brought the coffee back, and Westerberg asked Joentaa, 'So what brings you here?'

'The unknown woman who died,' said Joentaa. 'You must have followed that case.'

'The coma patient in the hospital in Turku ...' said Westerberg.

Joentaa nodded.

'Oh,' said Seppo.

'What does she have to do with Karjasaari?' asked Westerberg.

'I don't know yet,' said Joentaa. 'But going through our leads I came upon a woman who said the dead woman had been her piano teacher.'

'Piano teacher,' said Westerberg.

'Yes, in the summer of 1985, here in Karjasaari.'

'Summer of 1985,' said Seppo.

'Karjasaari,' said Westerberg.

'The woman's statement didn't seem credible at first, since she's having psychiatric treatment. I met her in a hospital in Ristiina.'

'Then did she give you a name?'

Joentaa shook his head. 'She either doesn't know the name or doesn't want to give it. She described the woman as an angel.'

'Angel,' said Westerberg.

'1985,' said Seppo.

'I don't know exactly why I followed up the lead. A friend of mine . . . she said I should look for signs of violence in connection with the dead woman. And in fact the autopsy did come up with suggestions of the effects of violence in the distant past. The statement given by the witness, Anita-Liisa Koponen, is full of hints of that kind.'

'1985,' said Seppo again. 'Only then?'

'What do you mean?' asked Joentaa.

'You said the witness mentioned the year 1985.'

Joentaa nodded. 'Yes, that's right. She said the woman had been there only for that one summer, she was standing in for a teacher who was ill, and then she fell ill herself.'

'Summer of 1985,' said Seppo, looking at Westerberg.

'Got the photo there?' asked Westerberg.

Seppo nodded, took a photograph out of one of the folders

and pushed it Joentaa's way. 'August 1985,' said Seppo. 'That's Happonen on the extreme right, with Forsman next to him.'

Joentaa picked the photograph up. The sun in the picture was shining considerably more brightly than the dim light in the room where they were sitting. A bright sun long ago. Two boys in swimming trunks who were no longer alive. Two men he didn't know.

'Who are the other two?' he asked.

'We haven't been able to find out yet,' said Westerberg.

Joentaa turned the picture over and read the text on the other side.

19 August 1985. We had a barbecue. No one talked about what happened. She smiled at me. Everyone is the same as usual, and R. says I'm not to worry.

He looked up.

'Yes, well,' said Westerberg.

Joentaa held the photograph up to the dim light and concentrated on the woman in the background. She was propping her head on one hand. Her eyes were hidden behind her sunglasses.

'That woman?' he asked.

'We don't know,' said Seppo.

Summer of 1985, thought Joentaa.

'We're in the process of identifying the people in the picture, but it's difficult,' said Seppo.

'Neither Happonen's parents nor Forsman's sister recognise anyone in it,' said Westerberg. 'Happonen senior even said he didn't recognise his own son.'

Joentaa looked up.

'His wife was forthcoming, but the man's father . . . he sort of shut down on us when we asked about the photo. And about his son's younger days. It was the same with the sister of the other murdered man, Forsman.'

Joentaa thought of the woman in the hospital, with her clear face behind the heavy make-up. I can manage for myself, she had said before closing the door behind her.

'I'd like to speak to Happonen's parents,' he said.

Westerberg nodded. Seppo yawned, and passed his hand over his eyes. Westerberg began humming the last tune that the tango band had played.

'Right,' said Seppo. 'Forsman, Happonen, and the unknown woman in Turku, then. Yes, there does seem to be some connection, do we all agree?'

Westerberg stopped humming, but did not reply, and Joentaa thought of Roope, shooting at an empty goal because the goalie was missing.

'Hello?' said Seppo.

'Let's think some more tomorrow,' said Westerberg, standing up. 'Sleep well, both of you.' He went up to the poker machine again and gave it an enquiring look, as if he expected to get his money back. Then he turned away. 'Sleep well,' he repeated, and went out.

'Right, see you in the morning, then,' said Seppo.

'See you in the morning,' said Joentaa.

Seppo gathered up his files, and Joentaa said, 'Could you leave that photo with me?'

'Yes, sure,' said Seppo. He took the picture out of one of the folders and handed it to Joentaa.

'Thanks,' said Joentaa. He stayed sitting there alone for a few minutes longer, holding the photo up to the dim light. He concentrated on the woman in the background. Her sunglasses hid her eyes. She seemed to be turning to the sun, and at the same time glancing sideways at the men in the foreground. Her lips were compressed. The trace of a smile, as if she had instinctively reacted to the camera although her thoughts were far away. She seemed to be lying on her stomach in a relaxed position, her head propped on one hand. At the same time she looked tense. As if she had had difficulty in achieving her relaxed, casual manner.

Joentaa looked at the picture until he could no longer see it. He went up to his room and switched on his laptop. He had two messages. His new telephone bill, and an email from veryhotlarissa.

From: veryhotlarissa@pagemails.fi
To: kimmojoentaa@turunpoliisilaitos.fi

Yes.

Joentaa looked at the single word for a long time before he finally began to laugh. Yes. A wonderful word. He wrote:

Dear Larissa,

I suspect that by 'Yes' you mean that I ought to follow up the lead I sent you. The piano teacher, right? Lovely that you're there.

Love from
Kimmo

He sent the message and an answer came back within seconds:

From: veryhotlarissa@pagemails.fi
To: kimmojoentaa@turunpoliisilaitos.fi

Yes.

He laughed. A burst of hearty laughter, louder than he'd laughed for some time. Then he picked up the photograph, put it on the bed, and wrote:

'19 August 1985. We had a barbecue. No one talked about what happened. She smiled at me. Everyone's the same as usual, and R. says I'm not to worry.'

Does that say anything to you?

Oh yes, something else – did I tell you that the boys would like to play ice hockey with you again?
The giraffe and I are both waiting rather impatiently.

Yes.
See you soon, sleep well.

Kimmo

He waited a long time, but no new answer came. Instead, his mobile rang at two in the morning. It was Tuomas Heinonen to tell him that he'd won the jackpot.

'What do you mean?' asked Joentaa.

'The jackpot. I'm winning it all back. A tournament on the PGA tour. Woods played a round in sixty-five.'

'Oh.'

'Golf. The PGA tour. He did it. He really did it, and broke the record for the course. And I was betting on him.'

'I see.'

'It's just finished.'

'Tuomas, you know that I—'

'Sleep well, Kimmo, I just wanted to let you know.'

'Yes.'

'Wanted to share my pleasure.'

'Tuomas, you really must—' said Joentaa, but Tuomas Heinonen had already broken the connection.

Kimmo Joentaa put his phone on the bedside table, lay down on the bed and soon fell asleep.

He dreamed of a large, picturesque golf course with no one playing on it, although the stands were full of spectators.

51

In the morning, when Joentaa was sitting at breakfast watching Westerberg and Seppo shovelling multicoloured muesli flakes into their mouths, he had a curious phone call, from Holmgren. It took Joentaa a few seconds to work out who that was.

'What did you do to our patient?' asked the man who had introduced himself by that name.

'I . . .'

'She's screaming. Screaming and laughing.'

Holmgren. The bearded head psychiatrist at the Ristiina hospital.

'Anita-Liisa Koponen. You questioned her yesterday, and a little later she started screaming and laughing. And then she made pasta and tomato sauce for the patients and the staff.'

'I . . . I'm sorry.'

'Don't be sorry. This is a breakthrough. It gives us hope.'

'Oh.'

'But I have to know what she told you.'

'Hmm. Yes,' said Joentaa.

'Yes?'

'I . . . well, I don't know whether I can tell you.'

Holmgren did not reply.

'She said she'd never told anyone about it before. So I don't think I can tell you behind her back.'

Holmgren still said nothing.

'Do you understand?' asked Joentaa.

'Yes,' said Holmgren. 'Yes, I do understand.'

'You could ask her about it, see if she'll tell you too.'

'Yes,' said Holmgren. 'Several times in my career I've had to refer to my medical duty of patient confidentiality, although the other way around . . . but yes, I do understand. You're perfectly right.'

'I may have to speak to Ms Koponen again,' said Joentaa.

'Please do. Any time you like,' said Holmgren.

'And very good luck to you and Ms Koponen for now,' said Joentaa.

Holmgren laughed. 'The same to you,' he said and ended the conversation. Westerberg, coming up to the table with another bowl of muesli, asked, 'Anything important?'

'That was the doctor at the hospital in Ristiina,' he said. 'The psychiatrist treating my witness Anita-Liisa Koponen.'

'The one who recognised the dead woman as her piano teacher?'

'That's the one. It seems she's doing better. I don't exactly know why, but she told me something yesterday. An incident in the past . . .'

'Ah,' said Westerberg.

Violence, thought Joentaa. Casual brutality. A natural enough catastrophe, but Anita-Liisa Koponen hadn't seen it coming. It had been twenty-five years before she was able to talk about it for the first time. And then, at last, she had begun to scream.

He thought of what Westerberg had said. That the father of the dead politician refused to recognise his son in the photograph. And the same was true of the sister of the other dead man, Forsman.

'Are we going to see the politician's parents?' he asked.

Westerberg nodded. 'After breakfast. I said we'd be there at ten.'

'Good,' said Joentaa.

'And Kimmo, I'll need that photo back,' said Seppo. 'I want to show it around today.'

Joentaa nodded. 'I'll bring it right away,' he said. He went to his room and called Sundström, to bring him up to date with developments.

'Westerberg?' asked Sundström. 'You mean Marko Westerberg from Helsinki?'

'Yes,' said Joentaa.

'There in that dump? Karjasaari.'

'Yes.'

'Because of a double murder.'

'Presumably.'

'That's somehow connected to our dead woman.'

'I think so, yes,' said Joentaa.

'Because a nutcase thinks she recognises the woman as her piano teacher.'

'Yes,' said Joentaa.

'Whose name she doesn't know, she only knows she was an angel.'

'That's right,' said Joentaa.

He waited for Sundström to crack a joke and dismiss the subject of Karjasaari and all the rest of it, but as so often Sundström surprised him. 'Okay,' he said. 'If anything else comes of this it could get us further forward. Will you call again this evening and tell me what the prospects are?'

'I'll do that,' said Joentaa.

'And send me through the addresses of the nutcase's relations. We'll set about checking up with them. Maybe they'll be able to remember the piano teacher's name.'

The nutcase's relations, thought Joentaa.

He put his mobile on the bed, picked up his laptop and switched it on. No new messages had come in.

No news of a big win on the lottery.

No telephone bill.

Not even a 'Yes'.

52

Dear diary,

Saara isn't there any more. The house is empty. No one lives there now.

Anita-Liisa Koponen told me that today. She told me although I didn't ask her, and I never talk to her, but she came up to me at break and told me.

At midday I went there with Lauri, and the house really is empty. Risto's big car has gone, and so has Saara's little one. The curtains have gone. I didn't want to, but Lauri kept saying we ought to go into the garden and see what it looks like inside, and then I went with him, and when we were in the garden I suddenly thought that Risto might be there after all, and I began trembling. Trembling like mad. Lauri asked if everything was all right, and I said yes, yes, everything was fine.

This morning Lauri helped me a lot with the dictation, because I was sweating so much I almost burst into tears, because I couldn't concentrate and I couldn't keep up. It was all much too fast, and then Lauri took my exercise book and wrote the dictation out for me, and old Itkonen didn't notice because he never sees anything. Later Lauri even apologised to me because he made a couple of mistakes on account of doing it in such a hurry, my goodness. I didn't say so, but I couldn't care less whether I make ten mistakes or a hundred or a thousand. Nothing matters now, but no one would understand that.

So then we were in the garden and we looked through the

window. It was all empty inside. The sofa had gone. The big bed in the bedroom had gone. The piano had gone. I was trembling, and I thought I was going mad with fear or sadness or goodness knows what.

Lauri asked me what was so bad now.

Nothing, I said, but we're here.

Why are we here? Lauri asked, and he said none of this is logical, and he wants to understand it. And I ought to tell him what's going on.

Forget it, I said.

And that's just it. That's what I'd like to do.

At last. At last. At last.

Forget it.

53

'So here you are again,' said Joosef Happonen.

They were sitting opposite each other on the low red sofas that Westerberg had already described during the drive there. Joentaa understood what Westerberg had meant when he said he had felt both at ease and uneasy in the house. Suoma Happonen brought coffee, and Joosef Happonen repeated:

'Here you are again.'

'Yes,' said Westerberg.

'And of course we wonder . . . why. Forgive me, but what do you want from us?'

'Mr Happonen . . .' Westerberg began.

'We would like to have some peace at last.'

'We understand that.'

'Then . . . what is it?'

Everyone is the same as usual, thought Joentaa.

'Sugar?' asked Suoma Happonen. 'Milk?'

'No, thank you,' said Westerberg. 'Well . . .'

'For you?'

It took Joentaa a moment to realise that she meant him. 'No, no, thank you. Nothing for me,' he said.

Suoma Happonen poured coffee for Westerberg and sat down beside her husband. 'For you?' she asked him.

'What?' asked Happonen.

'Coffee?'

He waved it away.

'The piano teacher,' said Joentaa, following an impulse.

He saw the woman's enquiring glance. And the look in the man's eyes, which was extinguished when Joosef Happonen simply closed his eyes. As if he had been forcing himself to keep them open too long, just waiting until he could finally close them.

'The piano teacher?' asked Suoma Happonen.

Her husband took his arm from around her shoulders and let himself lean back. His eyes were still closed.

'What piano teacher?' asked Suoma Happonen.

'A woman who worked at the school that your son attended,' said Joentaa.

'That means nothing to me,' she said. 'Markus never had piano lessons. He did once play the violin, but only when he was small, after that he didn't want to. And of course we didn't make him go on. Although it would have been nice. But . . .'

'Perhaps she taught your son at school in the regular lessons on the timetable,' said Westerberg.

'Yes . . . of course that's possible. But why is that important?'

'Mr Happonen?' said Westerberg.

Happonen opened his eyes.

'Can you remember a woman – she'd have been young at the time – who taught your son? In the summer of 1985?'

Happonen looked at Westerberg, and did not reply.

'Mr Happonen?'

'Joosef? What's the matter?'

Kimmo Joentaa saw Joosef Happonen slowly slide off the sofa. He stood up and took a step towards him. Westerberg had also risen to his feet, but he stopped in mid-step, and Suoma Happonen too sat as if frozen as her husband collapsed on the floor, and after some vain attempts to catch himself up lay there on his back.

'I'll be all right in a moment,' he whispered.

'Joosef,' said Suoma Happonen tonelessly.

'I'll be all right in a moment. Don't worry.'

'What is it, Joosef?' asked his wife. 'Joosef?'

'Mr Happonen?' asked Westerberg, and Joentaa went to get a glass of water. He had no idea whether it would help, but he had drunk water in small sips the day after Sanna's death. When he came back Happonen was just sitting up. He handed him the glass. Happonen nodded and drank a little.

'Yes. Thanks,' he said.

'All right?' asked Westerberg.

'Yes, yes, I'm fine,' said Happonen, hauling himself back up on the sofa. 'Fine. I don't know what . . . I kind of . . . collapsed.'

'Joosef,' said Suoma Happonen.

'Not like me at all,' murmured Happonen. 'Hasn't ever . . . happened to me before.' He laughed. 'I'm all right. Where were we?'

'The . . . the piano teacher,' said Westerberg.

'Yes. Right. I'm sorry, I can only confirm what my wife said. Our son Markus never learned the piano, and I really don't remember his teachers at school now.' He cleared his throat and sat upright.

No one talked about what happened, thought Joentaa. *Everyone is the same as usual.*

'Well . . . anything else?' asked Happonen, and his briskly casual tone was in almost comic contrast to his collapse of only a few seconds earlier.

'Mr Happonen . . .' said Westerberg.

'No,' said Happonen.

'The fact is that—'

'No,' said Happonen. He got to his feet and walked across the room, taking long strides. 'I'd like you to go now. I must . . . we must have a little peace.'

'Of course,' said Westerberg.

They sat there for a little longer. Suoma Happonen was wringing her hands and shaking her head, presumably to show that she didn't know what was going on either.

Happonen was waiting for them by his front door.

'I'm sure you'll understand,' he said when Westerberg and Joentaa had joined him.

R. says I'm not to worry about it.

'Do you know a man known as R.?' asked Joentaa.

Happonen said nothing and stared at him.

'What?' he asked at last.

'R. A name. So far we know only the initial.'

'No. I'm sorry. Goodbye,' said Happonen.

R. says I'm not to worry about it.

She smiled at me.

'Good heavens,' said Westerberg wearily as they reached the car.

L. as in Larissa, thought Joentaa.

A. as in August.

54

Dear diary. 15 December. The hotel room is beige. The wall, the chairs, the bedspread, the cushion, all of them beige.

Lassi Anttila, fifty-seven, is a store detective and in the evening a cleaner at a shopping centre in Raisio, near Naantali.

I went there today.

A pleasing sensation.

Following a detective.

I assume it's something to do with control. Presumably everything I've done recently is to do with control. Losing control and getting it back.

The rituals, the diary, the business cards. At the end I even held a card under Miettinen's nose, although I knew he wouldn't be able to make anything of it.

Sitting at the computer, carefully adjusting the template to size, switching on the printer, printing out the card. A name that doesn't mean anything to anyone but me. Profession: adviser; journalist; pastor; security scout – no, none of that is normal.

I don't think there's any such thing as a security scout, but it will do for Lassi Anttila.

Keeping a diary at my age – that's not normal.

I called Leea.

Talking to Leea, about her friend Henna and the baby.

Helping Olli with his homework. Explaining why five divided by five is not zero, but five minus five is.

'I see,' he says when I've finished.

The thought of Olli growing larger and older. The boy becoming a man, with a profession, a life that will keep him away from what's important now. The games, throwing dice, that fill our time together, the joy and annoyance of them will become a memory. Diffuse, pale. Maybe – if I ask him later – he will narrow his eyes and nod his head to signal that yes, he has a picture before his eyes. But in reality there'll be nothing there, only my claim that there was something once.

You were a bad loser, I shall tell him.

In the end, only a bent crash barrier is left. A mark from braking that no one is looking for. A dead man whom no one misses. A dead woman whom no one knows.

I had an interesting conversation with Leea today about the question of why she always hopefully opens junk mail franked Infopost instead of simply throwing it away. Contrary to all expectations, she claims, there might be something interesting in it.

Shares in Sedigene, biotechnology, are classified neutral by analysts, and outside it is snowing. Ice crystals are hexagonal. They form angles of exactly 60 and 120 degrees. The resulting structure is a kind of perfection that can't be seen with the naked eye. A perfection that does not demand to be perceived.

Look at it that way, and perhaps Saara was a snow crystal. In a summer that was much too hot for her – and us – to survive it.

55

The daily paper that devoted a page to the little town of Karjasaari was published in the larger neighbouring town of Laappeenranta. The chief editor, who looked very young apart from his grey hair, received Seppo in his office with the ostentatious dynamism of a man who is short of time.

'Karjasaari, you say,' he said, wrinkling his brow.

'That's right,' said Seppo.

'You're taking an interest in Karjasaari in connection with police inquiries.'

Seppo nodded.

The chief editor also nodded. 'That's . . . well, surprising. To the best of my knowledge nothing of any possible interest to the police has happened in Karjasaari for the last hundred years.'

'We don't have to go back as far as that,' said Seppo. 'The case was twenty-five years ago.'

'What?' asked the chief editor.

'Twenty-five years,' said Seppo. 'We're trying to identify people in a photograph that was taken twenty-five years ago . . .'

'Oh.'

' . . . and we'd very much like to look at your archives, or to talk to people who were writing about Karjasaari at the time.'

'Oh,' said the chief editor again.

'Can you help us?'

'I don't know. There certainly won't be anyone on the paper

who was working here twenty-five years ago. Far from it . . . at the moment we're a young team here.'

'Do you have archives going back to the year 1985?'

'1985 . . . I'm afraid not. At the moment we're digitising the archives, but we go no further back than the year 2000.'

2000, thought Seppo. And before that? Before that the Flood, or what?

'We do have the paper editions for 1985 still available. But you'd have quite a time of it sorting through them . . . oh, I've just had another idea . . .'

'Yes?'

'I know there was a freelancer writing on Karjasaari for us, she met almost all her deadlines. Myself, I joined the paper only in 2004, but everyone said the lady had been working for us for ages . . . a rather eccentric character . . .'

'Where can I find her?' asked Seppo.

'Hm. Just a moment, I'll ask.' He picked up the phone and had a conversation of some length with one of the staff, presumably the editor responsible for the Karjasaari column. 'Okay,' he said at last. 'No, send it over to me, please, before we start spelling it out. Yes. Fine, *ciao*.'

Ciao, thought Seppo.

'We've got her,' said the chief editor. 'And the funniest thing about it is that she still works for us from time to time. She must be almost eighty.'

Seppo nodded.

'My colleague is sending me the contact details over.'

'Excellent,' said Seppo.

'I'm sure you'll understand that you've made me rather curious. What sort of a case is it you're working on?'

'I can't give you the details at the moment. There'll certainly be more information for the press very soon.'

The chief editor leaned back. 'Karjasaari. Now and then someone falls into Lake Saimaa. A drunk fell through the ice in winter a few years ago, the little town lies directly on the water. In fact, in autumn and winter there's a nice winter fair in the marketplace. But otherwise . . . well, a quiet country idyll, nothing for our local journalists to get their teeth into.'

'Yes, a pretty little town,' Seppo agreed.

The chief editor cleared his throat, swivelled his chair Seppo's way, and sat up ramrod straight. 'Although something did happen recently – I've just remembered. Happonen. Our editorial team really did have news about the place to occupy them for quite a while. But the man only spent his childhood and youth in these parts.'

'Right,' said Seppo.

'That case is still unsolved if I remember rightly . . .'

'You do, it's about Happonen. But with the best will in the world I can't tell you more at the moment.'

The chief editor looked at his screen for a while, and seemed to be formulating a question in his mind before he asked it. 'Could we agree that I'll be the first you inform when the case goes public? As soon as you can give more details?'

Who am I, Seppo thought, to decide on a thing like that? But he replied, 'Yes, I think so.'

'Great,' said the chief editor. He still hesitated slightly, and Seppo felt an impulse to tell him that, chief editor or not, he had no right to hold up the police in the course of their inquiries.

'Yes,' he said at last.

'Then I'll print you out the address and phone number of our oldest freelance contributor. Give her my regards.'

56

Joentaa and Westerberg had lunch in the hotel, and after that Westerberg went to his room to make some phone calls. Although not until he had entrusted a large amount of his small change to the machine eternally flashing away in the lobby.

Joentaa thought of Tuomas Heinonen. Maybe he'd tell him about Westerberg. And that you could still have fun gambling if all you lost was a handful of pennies.

His mobile hummed its tune. Joentaa looked at the unfamiliar number for a few seconds, and thought of Larissa. Of hearing her voice. Then he did in fact hear the voice of a woman, the helpful school secretary. She said she'd found something.

'You have?'

'Yes . . . but I don't know if it will get you much further.'

'We'll soon see. I'll be with you in ten minutes' time.'

'Right . . . you'll find me in the library,' she said, and then Joentaa broke the connection and ran to his car.

He drove to the school and parked outside the long, low, flat-roofed building. It was easy to find the library, which was in the basement, and instinctively Joentaa thought of the archives in the basement of the Turku police station, where stuff that had been forgotten for ages was kept.

The secretary was sitting with two men and bending over some papers. She waved him over when she saw him.

'Samuli Svensson, deputy head of the school, and our librarian Petteri Savo,' said the secretary.

Both men shook hands with him, Svensson firmly, Savo more softly. The deputy head had a crew cut and was a small man, while Savo was tall, with hair standing out in all directions.

'We hear that you're interested in our school,' said the deputy head. 'Mrs Rantanen and Mr Savo have looked out everything we have.' He pointed to the books and folders lying on the table.

Joentaa nodded, and went over to them.

'May we ask what this is really about?' asked Savo.

'A woman who taught here in 1985. Although only for a very short time, as a supply teacher.'

'Yes, yes, Mrs Rantanen has told us that already. But . . . why . . .'

'I assume that you were neither of you here in 1985,' said Joentaa. Or perhaps he was wrong. Savo must be nearly sixty.

'I'm afraid we weren't,' said Svensson. 'Mr Savo here is certainly our rock of ages, but even he didn't join the staff until 1989.'

Joentaa nodded, and examined the books and papers on the table.

'It looks like more than it is,' said the school secretary. 'We've drawn up yearbooks of all the school's activities and exhibitions since 1990, but there wasn't one yet in 1985.'

'And . . . what did you find?'

The secretary took a set of papers stapled together off the table, and handed it to him. It was a school magazine, its cover showing girls and boys standing in the sun outside the school building. Presumably a whole year's intake. Almost all of them were letting out silent shouts of glee; the photographer had probably encouraged them to make a noise. The title of the magazine was a plain one: *Upper School Magazine*.

Joentaa sat down at the table and opened the magazine at

the first page. 'You'll find the rankings at the end,' said the secretary.

He looked up enquiringly.

'Drawn up by the final-year students before the leaving exam,' said the secretary.

Joentaa leafed through the pages.

'Page eighty-seven,' said the secretary.

Joentaa opened the magazine at that page and ran his eyes over the names and numbers.

'I came upon something,' said the secretary in the background. 'Wait a minute, I'll show you.'

She leaned over him and pointed to a table, headed by the words *The Nicest*. It took him a little while to realise that the students were assessing their teachers on this page. They had had twelve years' experience of being marked by them, and now it was the other way around. *The Strictest. The Worst-Dressed. The Latest to Arrive.* But also *The Most Committed. The Most Easy-Going. The Nicest.* In first place for the nicest was a teacher called Harkonen. Second came one Mr Väsänen. Third was Ms Koivula. Joentaa read the report on her.

Unfortunately Ms Koivula was only here for the summer of 1985, but she didn't need any longer than that to turn the collective heads of the male half of our year. How she did it no one is quite sure, because she didn't seem to be trying to make them like her. But she certainly had the nicest smile you can imagine, and angelic patience. For instance, when Jani A. threw a tennis ball at her head during the lesson – by accident – she surprised the whole class by handing him back the ball and asking him not to throw it quite so hard another time. That's what she was like. When Ms Koivula left again after a few months and Mrs Niskala came back, some of the boys may even have failed their exams out

*of unrequited love, and with Mrs Niskala's return the usual
old boring music lessons came back as well.*

Joentaa's gaze lingered on the letters. He heard the secretary's voice in the distance. 'That could be her, don't you think? And earlier on there's another mention of her. Wait a minute.'

She picked up the magazine and leafed through it purposefully to find the page she was looking for.

'Here.'

Joentaa looked at the photograph she was pointing to.

Angelic patience, he thought.

Not to throw the ball quite so hard another time.

'The pictures of the students,' she said.

Joentaa looked at the picture of one boy. Appearing reserved and yet almost forthcoming, smiling uncertainly. He read:

In his last year here Kalevi F. underwent a strange transformation, from a shy hanger-on to a ladies' man who had several short but intense, we'd be inclined to say desperate, relationships with several of the girls in our year. There's a rumour that his sudden courage in approaching the opposite sex was the result of Kalevi's frustration, because he didn't get anywhere with the real lady of his heart, our supply teacher for music, Saara K., in the short time that she was with us this summer. Nor did any of the other boys in our year either.

Joentaa closed his eyes. He was trembling.

Kalevi F.

Saara K.

'Does that . . . get you any further?' asked the deputy head.

Supply teacher for music, Saara Koivula.

By accident. A nice smile.

'Yes . . . I think it does, yes.'

'We keep full records here,' said Savo the librarian.

'Is it . . . is it about Ms Koivula, then?' asked the deputy head.

'I think it is,' Joentaa repeated.

A strange transformation, he thought. Like Happonen's father, who slid off the sofa from one moment to the next, just like that.

Joentaa took the magazine and said goodbye to the school secretary, the deputy head and the librarian. As he went up to the ground floor and out into the open air, he tried to remember his own teachers at school. People he had seen all the time then, in his childhood and adolescence, and he had no idea what they were doing today or even if they were still alive.

Unfortunately she was only here for the summer of 1985, he thought as he got into the car. And he also thought that of course angels had names like anyone else.

57

The journalist Marlene Oksanen lived in a small clapboard house that vaguely reminded Seppo of the Moomin family's home. Sky-blue like the trolls' house, he thought, and then a woman who looked remarkably like a troll herself opened the door to him.

'Mrs Oksanen?' asked Seppo.

'And you're the policeman?'

'Er, yes. Seppo is my name,' he said.

'Come along in, please,' she said, and went ahead of him into the little living room. Two coffee cups were standing ready on the table, with a coffee pot and a cream cake decorated with grapes.

'You'll have some coffee?' asked Marlene Oksanen.

'Oh, yes, thanks,' said Seppo.

Marlene Oksanen poured coffee, and Seppo let his eyes wander over the walls, which were covered with framed photographs. Not of people but of landscapes. Lake landscapes; the theme always seemed to be the same.

'Lovely,' he said.

'Hmm? Oh, yes, that's Lake Saimaa, taken from the same place at different times of the year. I like the winter photo best.'

'Ah.' Seppo went closer to the four pictures and looked at the frozen lake glittering behind snow-covered trees. The autumn picture was in shades of pale red and yellow; spring seemed to have begun at the very moment when Marlene Oksanen pressed the shutter release. And the blue of the summer photo was so vivid that Seppo instinctively took a step back.

'Those are . . . really beautiful photos,' he said.

'Thank you. I was always more of a photographer than a journalist. I just wrote the texts to go with them, and of course I tried to do it all justice. It's always particularly important to get the names right.'

To get the names right, thought Seppo.

'When people are in the newspaper, naturally the first thing they look for is their names. And if you've spelt them wrong . . . well, that's bad.'

'That's exactly why I'm here,' said Seppo.

'Now, do have something to eat,' said the little woman, who was sitting bent over her own cake, carrying the cake fork to her mouth with quick but neatly controlled movements, which again made Seppo think of the trolls. A Moomintroll. A Hemulen, perhaps, the meticulous old troll, the collector.

'And I'm sure you also have a collection of photographs of the town . . . of Karjasaari.'

'Of course. Thousands of them. Never throw anything away.'

A Hemulen to the life, thought Seppo.

'It's possible that we might want to look at those photo-graphs,' said Seppo, and he almost swallowed his next mouthful of cake the wrong way because Marlene Oksanen said she had even taken a photo of the exhibitionist.

'Er . . . what?' said Seppo.

'The exhibitionist. The man who ran around in the forest undressing in front of little girls.'

'Mhm.'

'He really did wear just a coat, and he opened it wide if anyone was coming towards him. Exposed himself not just in front of little girls, in front of me too.'

'Oh,' said Seppo.

'It must have been in . . . yes, the nineties. I didn't

deliberately go looking for him, but I always kept my eyes open when I was driving through the forest. And there he suddenly was, and I had to brake sharply. He opened his coat, and I took the camera out of my bag and snapped him before he'd closed the coat again.'

Seppo nodded. The exhibitionist exhibited, he thought vaguely.

'He was so surprised that he didn't know what to say. Then he did say something, he said that I wasn't to publish the photograph and he had problems. And do you know what I told him?'

Seppo carefully raised his fork to his mouth and shook his head.

'I told him: We all have problems.'

Seppo waited, but the story was over. 'Yes . . . of course,' he said, and he really did find it surprisingly enlightening.

'Of course the photograph was never published. And the man was never seen in the forest again. Either with or without his coat.'

'Hm,' said Seppo.

'Would you like to see the photo? I'd show it to you.'

'Er . . . maybe later,' said Seppo. 'I'd really like to do the opposite and show you a photograph that I have here.'

'Yes?'

He took the photo out of his coat pocket. Removed it carefully from the transparent film into which he had put it, because by now he had come to think of it as the most significant lead they had.

Summer. Forsman, Happonen, two unknown men.

'It's about those two men in particular,' he said. 'Do you happen to recognise either of them?'

He pushed the picture across the table to Marlene Oksanen, who got to her feet, left the room, and came back with an oversized magnifying glass. The Hemulen, thought Seppo again, didn't the Hemulen go around with a magnifying glass just like that? Yes, he did, the Hemulen studied the mysteries of life on the ground with his magnifying glass.

Marlene Oksanen sat bending over the picture and murmuring to herself. 'It's taken beside Lake Saimaa. Down by the bathing beach. I recognise the place.'

Seppo nodded.

'That's little Happonen . . . well, not so little any more . . . and now he's . . . oh, that's bad.' She looked up. 'Is that why you're here? Because of little Happonen? Because he's dead?'

'Yes . . . that's part of it,' said Seppo.

'Terrible,' she said.

'Do you recognise the men?'

'Yes . . . of course.'

'Of course?'

'I must think a moment.'

Of course, he thought.

'I know who one of them is. This one. I once wrote something about him. Just a moment.' She went out again, and a few minutes passed by before she came back with a photograph album. *1983*, it said on the cover. 'It was to do with the refurbishment of the Town Hall.'

Seppo took the album and looked at the close-up of a neat and tidy flower bed. Beside it was a caption – *Town Hall Square Ablaze With the Beauty of Roses*.

'Aha,' said Seppo.

'The man in the picture, I mean your photo . . .'

'Yes?'

'He's the gardener, I'm sure he is.'

58

'The gardener?' asked Westerberg wearily, which meant he was wide awake.

They were sitting in the muted light of the breakfast area again. The poker machine was blinking. Music had begun to play in the background. Joentaa wasn't quite sure, but he thought he heard the same languid tango rhythms as the evening before.

'The gardener,' Seppo confirmed.

'The gardener, then,' said Westerberg. 'The gardener and a music teacher who only . . .'

' . . . danced together for one summer,' said Seppo.

'Seppo, I left that unsaid because it gives the wrong picture,' said Westerberg.

'Sorry,' said Seppo.

Joentaa leaned back and let the exchange of words pass him by. Those two seemed to make a good team. The clever, weary Westerberg, and Seppo, who always focused on the essentials.

He listened to the two of them for a little while, feeling remarkably comfortable. The soft and muted music coming through the walls of the restaurant next door seemed to him light as a feather, and the ideas in his head hovered as if on clouds, going round and round in circles.

A murderer shedding tears.

A woman whom he missed without really knowing her.

A dead woman who had a name at last.

A giraffe in the snow.

And a photo, a yellowing snapshot from the past that seemed to be coming closer and closer to the present. To this exact moment, to this second when Westerberg said, 'Yes, and what do we know so far about this gardener, this man . . .'

'Miettinen,' said Seppo. 'This is my turn.'

'This is your turn. Meaning?'

'Meaning I've been to the address – well, the address that the helpful lady, I mean that local journalist, gave me, but the nursery garden was closed.'

'Closed.'

'Until further notice. And no one reacted when I rang the bell of the house next to it.'

'Hmm,' said Westerberg.

'I'll try again.'

'Do that,' said Westerberg. He seemed to be, for him, unusually restless and edgy. Joentaa guessed why. While they were sitting here in the twilight, their colleagues in Helsinki, Turku and Tammisaari were beginning to go down the new paths that had opened up within a few hours. A full police search for the woman who had been called Saara Koivula was now in progress. By evening, several Saara Koivulas had been traced throughout the country, but there was one little problem.

They were still alive.

Early in the evening, Joentaa had phoned Sundström. 'So now we have her damn name but we still can't find her,' Sundström had said. Joentaa had not replied, and Sundström had added, 'Is she our dead woman anyway? On the basis of the photographs we published she's been recognised only by the witness in the nut-house.'

'The witness is credible,' Joentaa had said.

'Isn't there a photo of the teacher in that school magazine?'

Joentaa had said no. He had been through the magazine several times without finding a photograph of Saara Koivula.

'But there's a connection with the case that Marko Westerberg is working on. Kalevi Forsman. And a connection with the death of the politician Happonen.'

'Yes, yes, but what is it?'

Joentaa had given him the second name that Seppo had now told him. Miettinen, Jarkko. Landscape gardener.

'Aha,' Sundström had said. 'Landscape gardener, yes. But where the hell is the connection between all these . . . ?'

Dead people, Joentaa had thought. The connection between all those dead people, but Sundström had left his sentence unfinished, and they ended the conversation.

Now Joentaa saw that Seppo, sitting opposite him, was talking on the phone, and while an expression of surprise spread over Seppo's face, and the band in the restaurant switched musical style and changed to the blues, Joentaa had a feeling that the connection was that very thing.

'What's the latest?' asked Westerberg as Seppo sat there holding his mobile without telling them what he had heard.

'Seppo?' asked Westerberg.

'Miettinen,' said Seppo.

'Yes?'

'That was his son on the phone. Miettinen lives in a care home in Rantaniemi. He has dementia and Parkinson's disease.'

'Oh,' said Westerberg.

'I mean, lived in a care home,' said Seppo, and Joentaa thought yes, that was the connection. Death.

'What?' asked Westerberg.

'Lived there,' said Seppo. 'Jarkko Miettinen is dead. According to what is known at present, as a result of his poor state of health.'

'What?' said Westerberg again.

'In circumstances that have not yet been conclusively explained,' Seppo specified.

59

Westerberg and Joentaa drove to the nursing home for senior citizens in which Jarkko Miettinen the landscape gardener had lived and died. It had begun to snow, and Westerberg was humming a tune that sounded like a lullaby as he concentrated on driving the car along the narrow road.

The home stood in a large clearing in the woods, a pastel-coloured clapboard house in the darkness, illuminated by pale lanterns. They rang the bell, and a young woman opened the door.

'Police?' she asked.

'That's right,' said Westerberg. 'Was it you who spoke to my colleague Seppo on the phone?'

'Yes,' she said. 'I'm Laura Järvi, supervisor of nursing services here. We were expecting you. Come in.'

Joentaa followed the woman and Westerberg along a dimly lit corridor, seeing the vague figures of people sitting on chairs and sofas in the front hall. Motionless, like statues. He nodded to them with a murmured, 'Good evening.'

'It will soon be their bedtime,' said the nursing supervisor, as if she felt she had to explain the presence of the old people. When she switched it on the light in Laura Järvi's office was bright and all-embracing, and for several moments bathed the room in uncomfortable clarity.

'Yes . . .' she said. 'So it's about Mr Miettinen, who unfortunately has died.'

Westerberg nodded. 'We need all the information you can

give us. About Miettinen and most of all about the course of
. . . about the hours and days before his death.'

'Is there . . . is there anything wrong about his death, then?'
she asked, and Joentaa wondered whether there was such a
thing as a death with everything right about it.

'Yes, we have reason to suppose that there was indeed
something wrong with it,' said Westerberg.

'Well . . . it was a kind of sudden collapse. Mr Miettinen
suffered severe vomiting and diarrhoea, and of course he was
taken to hospital at once. As far as I know he died the next day.'

'What of?' asked Westerberg.

'That . . . that hasn't been fully established yet. But Mr
Miettinen was very ill anyway. It had been touch and go with
him for months.'

'Hmm,' said Westerberg. 'We'll have to speak to the doctor
who treated him.'

'Mr Miettinen died in the hospital. That's at the other end
of this town, on the hill and right beside the church.'

'Right. Can you please tell us, with as few gaps in his daily
life as possible, just how Mr Miettinen spent the days before
his death?'

She looked at him as if she didn't understand the question.

'Do you see what I mean?' asked Westerberg.

'That's a hard question to answer,' she said.

'Oh . . . why?'

'Well, Mr Miettinen's daily life was . . . was all a gap.'

'Oh?'

'Mr Miettinen didn't have many visitors. Now and then, as
I told your colleague, his son came, but not often. Of course
we cared for him. Got him to walk a few metres up and down.
To eat and drink. To sleep.'

'I see,' said Westerberg.

'He spent most of his time sitting in his room looking out
of the window.'

'Can we see the room?' asked Westerberg.

'Of course. Come with me.'

She put out the light, and then they went along the corridor again. The people sitting on sofas and chairs had disappeared. As if they had never been there, thought Joentaa.

The nursing supervisor opened the door to a room, pressed a switch, and it was flooded with light. An empty, freshly made-up bed. An empty chair, an empty table. You could guess at the snow outside the window, softly falling to the dark ground. A few photographs in film envelopes and a transparent plastic bag lay on the bedside table, along with a red Advent calendar. With a piece of chocolate behind each little door.

'These are the personal things that his son hasn't taken away yet.'

Westerberg went over to the window and concentrated on the scene outside, as if he had caught sight of the answer to important questions there, and Joentaa leaned on the edge of the bed to control the sense of vertigo that had suddenly come over him.

'The pastor came to see him,' said the woman.

'What did you say?' asked Westerberg, without taking his eyes off the window.

'The pastor. About once every two weeks Mr Miettinen liked to see a pastor, and this time . . . yes, in fact that was different.'

'What was different about it?' asked Westerberg.

'The pastor. Normally it's a young woman pastor who visits him, but this time someone else came instead, a man. A very . . . he seemed a very nice man.'

'Where can we find this pastor?' asked Westerberg.

'I don't know. I'd never seen him before.'

'You'd never seen him before?'

'No, as I said, he came instead of the usual woman pastor. And now that I come to think of it, he came out of turn.'

'Out of turn?'

'Yes, his colleague the woman pastor had been here only a week before, so it wasn't really time for the next visit yet.'

'How long did he spend with Mr Miettinen?' asked Westerberg.

'Not very long,' she said. 'Quarter of an hour, I'd say.'

'And that was the day when Mr Miettinen's symptoms set in?'

She thought for a moment. 'Yes,' she said. 'A few hours afterwards.'

'What did he look like?' asked Westerberg.

'The pastor?'

'Yes.'

'Tall, slim. Normal.'

Normal, thought Joentaa. Passes the time of day in a friendly manner after throwing a man off a balcony. Calmly has a beer with a politician in full view of the public before murdering him with three bottles of whisky.

'Any more details?' asked Westerberg.

'Mid-blond hair,' she said. 'And a thin face. He was smiling all the time, but not in a pushy way. It was . . . it was a completely natural smile.'

Westerberg nodded.

'To be honest, I can't imagine the pastor having anything to do with your investigations.'

'I'd like to speak to the woman pastor. Can you phone her?'

'What, now?'

'Yes, please.'

'All right. I have her number in the office.'

Joentaa was still standing by the bed, and noticed the slightly uneasy silence only after a little while.

'Kimmo?' asked Westerberg.

'Hmm? Oh, yes – you two go. I'll just stay here for a moment.'

'Well . . . all right,' said the nursing supervisor.

'See you in a moment,' said Joentaa.

Then he was alone, looking at the bag of photos lying on the bedside table. He thought of the day after Sanna's death. Of the nurse who had handed him a bag just like that, and the things inside it. The book that Sanna had been reading, with a bookmark in it between the last page she had reached and the other pages that she would never read now.

He looked at the square white table standing by the window, and the white chair. He tried to imagine Miettinen sitting at that table and looking out of the window. Day after day.

After a while Westerberg came back.

'No such man as that pastor,' he said.

Joentaa nodded.

'The local woman pastor had no idea what I was talking about, and the nursing supervisor's jaw dropped when she heard that,' said Westerberg.

'Funny, isn't it?' said Joentaa, more to himself than to Westerberg.

'Yes, and there's more to come. I called the hospital, and the doctor told me that it could have been poisoning. Poisonous mushrooms.'

'Mushrooms?'

'Liver failure. It was all very fast because the victim's constitution was already massively weakened. Possibly amanita mushrooms. In the circumstances they're going to carry out a post-mortem first thing tomorrow.'

Joentaa nodded.

A death-dealing pastor, he thought.

A gardener who will tend no more gardens.

A murderer who smiles.

And sheds tears.

60

When they got back to the hotel, Seppo was still sitting between the breakfast room and the lobby, on the same chair at the same table beside the flashing machine. He was on the phone.

'Yes, darling. Exactly. Here come my colleagues, I'll have to go. Yes, love you too. See you tomorrow.'

He broke the connection and looked expectantly at Westerberg.

'Seppo . . .' said Westerberg wearily.

'Yes?'

'Who on earth is willing to talk to you of all people at this witching hour of night?'

'Hmm? Oh, that was Marianna. My fiancée.'

Marianna. Nice name, thought Joentaa.

'Oh, I see. Your fiancée,' said Westerberg.

'Any news?' asked Seppo.

Westerberg seemed to be still deep in thought, presumably about Seppo's fiancée, but then dropped into one of the chairs and said, 'We went to the nursing home. And communicated with the hospital. Miettinen,' he added, 'was probably poisoned. We were only able to talk to the doctor on night duty, but they think it was food poisoning, probably with mushrooms.'

'Mushrooms,' said Seppo.

Westerberg nodded.

Mushrooms and bottles of whisky, thought Joentaa, sitting down himself.

'They're doing a post-mortem tomorrow,' said Westerberg. 'Have you heard anything from Helsinki?'

'Not much,' said Seppo. 'They've made multiple copies of our photograph, and the technical people are working on filtering out the fourth man. It will go out on the telex tomorrow.'

Westerberg nodded.

'With mention of the connection to Happonen,' said Seppo. 'Because of course the media need to be fed something, a titbit to induce them to place the photo prominently. No mention of Forsman and the music teacher for the time being.'

'Excellent,' said Westerberg.

Instinctively, Joentaa reached for the photo lying in the middle of the table. He looked at the two boys and two men, all bare-chested, and all united in the same forced cheerfulness. Three of the four were now dead. And the search was on for the fourth, using a clip from a photograph twenty-five years old.

'The question is whether the technical boffins can get a usable picture at all. Especially as the man must be much older now,' said Seppo, as if he had read Joentaa's thoughts.

Joentaa looked at the woman in sunglasses in the background, who seemed to be simultaneously looking at something outside the photo and in at the group it showed. He picked up the picture and held it up to the light. Tried to guess what her eyes were like behind the sunglasses.

'All clear?' asked Seppo.

Kalevi F. A strange transformation. From hanger-on to ladies' man. Short but intense relationships. We'd be inclined to call it the result of his desperation.

Joentaa shook his head, and Westerberg abruptly stood up. 'I'm going to get some sleep,' he said. 'You two had better do the same.'

'Okay,' said Seppo.

'I'll be up in a minute,' said Joentaa. 'Sweet dreams.'

He watched the other two go, and raised a hand to wave before they disappeared into the lift. A few minutes later he stood up himself, and took the photo off the table where Seppo had left it for him, presumably on purpose.

He took the lift upstairs, went along the dimly lit corridor and unlocked the door to his room.

He sat on the bed for a while in the dim light, looking out of the window and thinking of Jarkko Miettinen, who had been alive two days ago, and whose body would be lying on a dissecting table tomorrow. Probably in Laappeenranta, where the nearest Institute of Forensic Medicine was located.

Miettinen poisoned. Happonen battered to death. Forsman thrown off a balcony.

Attractively designed business cards.

Casual brutality.

And the brutality inflicted on Anita-Liisa Koponen had been casual as well. Casual and immediate. A natural and unforeseeable catastrophe. Anita-Liisa Koponen had been raped in the presence of Saara Koivula, her piano teacher. She had never gone to piano lessons again, and had not seen Saara Koivula again either. Decades later the piano teacher had been delivered to the Turku hospital in a comatose condition, without papers, without anything to identify her.

He took a piece of paper with the logo of the hotel on it off the bedside table, picked up the ballpoint pen lying beside it, and thought for a while about what he really wanted to write. Then he simply wrote the names.

Saara Koivula. Anita-Liisa Koponen. Markus Happonen, Kalevi Forsman, Jarkko Miettinen. What were two schoolboys, a gardener, and a fourth, still unknown, man doing in one and the same photograph?

We had a barbecue. No one talked about what happened.

In the background, a woman with her eyes hidden behind

a pair of sunglasses, and much too far away, maybe thirty metres from the camera, for anyone to have been able to use the photo for identification.

She smiled at me.

In spite of whatever had happened.

It had been something so monstrous that the schoolboy Kalevi Forsman didn't have the courage to put what it really was into words. Didn't have the courage to call it by its name. The woman a 'she'. The man an 'R.' But then they had a barbecue, and R. had said that there was nothing to worry about.

Casually. Everything fine. Nothing had happened.

Kalevi F. A strange transformation. From hanger-on to ladies' man. Short but intense relationships. We'd be inclined to call them the result of desperation.

Who had actually written those lines? Joentaa stood up and found the school magazine lying on the table near the darkened TV set. He looked at the last page, and found the details. Names of the contributors to the magazine; the chief editor was one Xaver Blom. Joentaa leafed through the magazine and found Xaver Blom among the biographies of the students.

This text must be one of the very few in our magazine not by Xaver Blom. Good old Xaver can hardly spill the beans about himself. However, not only has our budding writer created this terrific souvenir for us, he has impressed students and teachers alike with his sharp wit, which lets no one off the hook, and expert knowledge of the novels of Aleksis Kivi that would have done credit to university professors. And even if some of us found the way Xaver always knows best just a little annoying, we can honestly say: Xaver, we're proud of you and we expect great things of you. All the best!

Xaver Blom. Not exactly a common name. He picked up

his mobile, called directory enquiries, and found himself talking to a slightly irate female voice. 'You don't know where he lives?' she asked.

'No, but you could look countrywide. The first name isn't very common.'

'Look at it that way and it isn't,' said the woman at the other end of the line, and Joentaa pulled his laptop over to him and brought up the system.

'You're quite right,' said the woman.

'Yes?'

'Only one Xaver Blom in the whole of Finland.'

'Oh,' said Joentaa.

'Lives in Karjasaari, number eleven Saimankatu.'

We expect great things of you, thought Joentaa. And the fact that Xaver Blom was still living in the small town where he had spent his childhood somehow made him seem just a little more likeable.

The woman gave him the phone number, and Joentaa had himself put straight through to it. As he waited, it struck him that Xaver Blom might possibly be asleep.

The man who answered after some time did indeed seem to have been sleeping.

'Yes . . . Blom . . .' he murmured.

'Kimmo Joentaa, of the Turku police. I have a question to ask.'

' . . . hello . . .'

'Can you hear me?'

' . . . what did you say?'

'Kimmo Joentaa, of the Turku police. I have a question to ask.'

'Is that . . . what . . . you arsehole.'

Joentaa was about to say something else, but Blom had rung off. Our budding writer, thought Joentaa, and he wondered suddenly whether one reason he was getting the man out of bed was that his style of twenty-five years ago in those texts seemed to him rather too sarcastic. He rang the number again.

'Are you out of your mind?' asked Blom.

'Joentaa, Criminal Investigation Department. I must apologise, but I urgently need some information from you,' said Joentaa.

'What kind of damn information?'

'Were you the chief editor of the school magazine in your last year?'

A few seconds passed, and Joentaa wondered whether Blom had rung off again, but he was still there.

'What did you say?' he asked.

'The school magazine for the class in their last year before their final exams.'

'Is this some kind of a joke?'

'No,' said Joentaa.

'It's not?'

'No,' Joentaa confirmed.

'Oh . . . now I see what you're talking about. Yes, I put the magazine together.'

'And you wrote most of it?'

'Yes, practically all of it,' said Blom. 'No one else wanted to do it.'

'Good. I need your memory.'

'My memory?'

'Yes. I'd like you to tell me about Saara Koivula.'

'Saara Koivula,' said Blom, in a toneless voice.

'Yes, do you remember her?'

'I certainly do. Our music teacher. Unfortunately only for a few months.'

'For one summer,' said Joentaa.

'Right, exactly. From just after one holidays until just before the next holidays. Then she went away.'

'Tell me something about her. Anything that occurs to you.'

At the other end of the line, Blom laughed. And seemed to be thinking. For a long time.

'She was . . . special,' he said at last. 'She was quite young, good-looking . . .'

'And?'

'She was very nice. And at the same time somehow kind of . . . disreputable.'

'Disreputable?'

'Well, as if she'd be available. For schoolboys' fantasies.'

'To what extent?'

'No, disreputable is the wrong word. Available is more like the impression she gave. I think boys felt that . . .'

'Yes?'

'I mean, she was so nice you felt she wouldn't give you the brush-off.'

Wouldn't give you the brush-off, thought Joentaa.

'In the sense of a schoolboy fantasy, if you see what I mean? The feeling that you only had to tell her you loved her and you could do anything you liked to her.'

Do anything you liked to her, thought Joentaa.

'It really is difficult to explain. It was the total absence of anything . . . aggressive about her. I don't think she was stupid, far from it, but kind of . . . totally naive. Yes, I think that was it. As a schoolboy I had the feeling that she was more naive than me, and naturally by comparison with the other teachers that was very unusual.'

Disreputable, naive, thought Joentaa.

'And all that combined with the fact that she looked like . . . like a princess. And yes, there was something sad about her too.'

Sad, thought Joentaa.

'Incredible to find all this coming back to me now. After so many years,' said Blom.

'Markus Happonen,' said Joentaa. 'And Kalevi Forsman.'

Once again there was a brief silence, and then Blom said, 'Two other students in our class. Happonen was an arrogant character. Tall and rather overweight, but so self-confident that no one would ever have thought of teasing him about it. Forsman was rather unobtrusive, but he was friends with Happonen, I think, because they both lived in the same street and had known each other since their early childhood.'

'Was there anything going on between them and Saara Koivula? You wrote in the school magazine that Forsman had . . . liked her.'

'Yes, yes, they both did . . . but so did everyone. There was nothing serious about it.'

Nothing serious, thought Joentaa.

'I don't understand exactly what you mean,' Blom persisted. 'Logically, there wouldn't have been anything going on between a school student and the music teacher.'

'You say in the magazine that Forsman changed in his last year at school. From being a hanger-on to . . . a ladies' man.'

'Yes, I suppose he did. Now that you mention it. He was chasing girls quite a lot in his last year.'

'Out of desperation, you write.'

'Desperation?'

'Yes.'

'Ah. Well, if you say so. Kalevi really did change, but of course I exaggerated a bit in the magazine . . .'

'What about Happonen?'

'How do you mean?'

'Did he change as well? In his last year at school?'

Xaver Blom said nothing for a while, and then said, 'No. Not at all, as far as I remember. He was top of the class right to the end, and rather full of himself all along. And since we're talking like this in the middle of the night, I can tell you a little secret of my own . . .'

'Yes?'

'I didn't really like him, because I was only the second-best.'

'Hmm,' said Joentaa.

'Well, it's out now, after . . . after twenty-five years . . . ?'

'Twenty-five years,' Joentaa agreed.

'And you're sure that you . . .'

'Yes?'

'. . . that you really are a police detective?'

'I am,' said Joentaa.

'Mhm. Is it . . . is it about Markus, then? I mean, he died.'

'Yes,' said Joentaa. 'It's about him too.'

'Crazy . . . I mean that was a strange story,' said Blom. 'What happened to Markus.'

Indeed, thought Joentaa.

'But what does Kalevi have to do with it? And the music teacher?'

'Does the name Miettinen mean anything to you? Jarkko Miettinen?'

'No. Who's he?'

'A gardener living in Karjasaari.'

'Gardener?'

'Yes.'

'Means nothing to me at all.'

Joentaa nodded.

'You really do ask some abstruse questions.'

'I know,' said Joentaa. 'Thank you. Sleep well.'

'Was that it?' asked Blom.

'Almost. I'd like you to look at a photograph. I can send it through to you tomorrow if it's been digitised by then. What's your email address?'

Blom told him.

'Fine. And I'll be in touch if anything else occurs to me.'

'Right. Well . . . it's been a pleasure.'

'Oh, one more thing. What's your profession these days?'

'I run an auditors' office in Laappeenranta.'

'Thanks. I really am grateful, you've given me a great deal of help.'

'That's good, then,' said Blom.

Joentaa put his phone down and sat in the silence. He was trying to pin down ideas that seemed to be hovering in the air, unanchored. Disreputable, naive, desperate. And sad. And disreputable wasn't the right word. Yet in a way it was. Or how had Blom meant that? So nice that you thought she wouldn't give you the brush-off.

He logged into the Internet, and then sat motionless for several minutes, looking at the latest message from veryhotlarissa.

He read it, and thought:

The budding writer had become an auditor.

The boy who was top of the class had become a politician.

The politician's friend had become a software adviser.

A long-forgotten moment had become a photograph.

He thought of Westerberg, and the relish with which he always said: software adviser.

He read Larissa's message again.

From: veryhotlarissa@pagemails.fi

To: kimmojoentaa@turunpoliisilaitos.fi

Seven years ago I worked with a woman from the Czech Republic. She was eighteen years old, and her boyfriend always brought her to work. If I'd told her that the man was no friend of hers, she wouldn't have understood me. She worked from ten in the morning to two at night. After several months she had a kind of breakdown and was taken away from the house. I've just been looking for her on the Internet, and I saw that she is now working in Helsinki under the same name. The pictures are the same as well, although she's seven years older now. Presumably her boyfriend is still the same too. Oh well, I'm hardly telling you anything you don't know already about this trade.

I don't know why, but I thought of her when I read the message you sent me. 'We don't talk about what happened. Everything's the same as usual.' You want to find R., but I'm sure you know that already. You're a clever guy, dear Kimmo.

Kimmo Joentaa read the message. Then he read it again. And then again. After reading it five times he finally worked out what was subliminally occupying his mind, something to be read between the lines. A Czech girl of eighteen who was now seven years older. That meant that Larissa herself – and at least he knew that she had been twenty-six on 15 April – had been only eighteen when she had begun working in that trade . . . or even younger.

15 April. Larissa's birthday.

He looked at the last line. Should he read affection or irony into it?

Probably both.

He wrote a short answer, turned off the computer and then the light.

From: kimmojoentaa@turunpoliisilaitos.fi
To: veryhotlarissa@pagemails.fi

Dear Larissa,
I'm thinking of you.
If the giraffe has gone to sleep, wake it up.

61

On the morning of 16 December Lassi Anttila, store detective and cleaner in the big shopping centre, had a very odd experience, one which was to occupy his mind for the rest of his life.

Around ten o'clock he was sitting in the fast-food restaurant in the shopping centre, drinking a coffee, when he saw his own face on the TV screen hanging over the counter. The sound was turned down, so that Lassi Anttila couldn't hear the words accompanying the picture; all he saw was himself the way he must once have looked, an eternity ago.

He got up and moved closer to the TV screen, looking to the right and left of him at the bored, abstracted faces staring at the TV without identifying the man on the screen with the man standing right beside them.

'Something wrong?' asked Mervi, the thin young waitress behind the counter, and followed his gaze to the screen, which was still showing the photograph. Anttila wanted to ask her to turn the volume up, but he bit back the words. A memory was vaguely beginning to surface.

'Lassi, you look as if you'd seen a ghost,' said Mervi, turning away.

Hadn't she recognised him either? Obviously not, as she was now busy with the coffee machine, entirely unmoved.

He propped himself on the counter, and for a little while watched Mervi going about her work, which she accompanied with muttered curses, because it seemed that one of the levers wasn't functioning.

'Can I help?' asked Anttila. He heard his own voice faintly, as if it were coming from a distance. Mervi's reply, on the other hand, sounded unnaturally close.

'You, help? That'd be something new,' she said.

'What would?'

'You helping anyone. Of your own free will. Something new, like I said.'

He looked at Mervi, and thought of the photograph. A newsreader was now talking on-screen. The photo. Of course Mervi hadn't recognised him. He wouldn't have recognised himself if he hadn't known that he had once been that man. Sunburned, early thirties. They had trimmed the picture to leave out his bare chest. And the others who had been standing there with him. A hint of Lake Saimaa in the background, but it could be the sky. Maybe he had only seen Lake Saimaa in the background because he knew that it must be there.

He remembered that photo. He also remembered the day it had been taken.

'Hellooo, Laassii.'

He jumped.

'You were going to help? With the coffee machine?'

'What?'

'Don't you remember? You offered only a few seconds ago.'

'Oh, yes. S . . . sorry.'

He cast another glance at the screen as he went behind the counter. An American soap opera was being shown now. A big-busted blonde was wriggling out of the embrace of a man who looked like Barbie's boyfriend Ken. Had they really just shown his own face on TV?

'The lever's sticking,' said Mervi.

He put his hand on the lever and wondered whether he had imagined the whole thing. He had once heard that everyone suffered from hallucinations at least once in his life. A professor had said so in some documentary, and he ought to have known. Everything was in working order again behind the counter, and Mervi clapped her hands.

'That's great!' she said.

'What?'

'The lever. Working again.'

'Oh,' he said, and took his hand off the machine, which was making gurgling sounds.

'Thanks, Lassi.'

'You're welcome,' he murmured.

He went through the wide concourse, rode down the escalator and went into his office, which was really more of a small cubbyhole near the underground car park. He sat down at the table and for several moments watched the images flickering on both monitors. The labyrinthine gangway system of the big supermarket. The lingerie department of the women's fashions store. The large hall of the specialist electrical goods store, with light pulsing through it. All seen from a bird's-eye view.

He thought of the others. Of Happonen. He'd gone in for politics. And had been murdered. But that had nothing to do with him. They surely couldn't be looking for him in connection with little Happonen. Little Happonen, little Forsman, that's what they had called the two of them at the time, although they had been sixteen or seventeen years old. All the same. Little kids. Happonen had cried like . . . like a baby on the day when that bad thing happened.

But that wasn't why his picture was on TV now. It couldn't be possible that what happened in the dim and distant past . . .

He thought of Jarkko Miettinen. He'd really liked him, but after . . . what happened everything had somehow fallen apart, everything was cancelled out. It had taken some time for them to realise it, but then he had begun avoiding Jarkko, and the two kids were busy with very different things, and one day, in late autumn or early winter, Risto had dropped in to see him, stood in the doorway smiling, and said goodbye.

He remembered that now. The scene was vividly present to his mind's eye, although only an hour ago he hadn't known he had any memory of it at all.

'So long,' Risto had said, and he hadn't really known what he could say in reply. Then Risto had gone to his car, and in the light of the street lamp he had seen her on the passenger seat. Saara. She had been sitting upright without moving, and when Risto had started the engine and turned the car, she had seen him and raised her arm. As if to wave to him.

He had thought about that again and again, for several months, that raising of her arm. What she might have been trying to express by it. And then that last memory had faded too, and the next summer had been a very different one, and so had the summer after that.

Years ago, when he heard in passing of Jarkko Miettinen's illness, it had left him cold. And he had only recently discovered that the kid Happonen had become a politician, that was when the poor man was murdered for reasons that, frankly, interested him very little.

And as for the other kid . . . he could barely remember his name. Or could he? Kalevi. Kalevi So-and-So. That was all. Whatever Kalevi So-and-So was doing these days, it was of no importance to him whatsoever.

He looked at the hands of his watch moving forward for a few minutes. Then he got to his feet and took the escalator up, back into daylight. He made purposefully for the large electrical goods store.

There was ski jumping now on the TV screens, large and small. Quietly, but still audibly, he heard the commentator's voice, which was highly agitated because a Finn had just been disqualified for too wide an acceleration. A little later a presenter and a former Olympics medal-winner analysed the state of the contest after the first round, and when the break came the presenter said goodbye, smiling, and gave way to the news.

The newsreader was the same. The news was the same. The photo was the same.

Lassi Anttila stood in the centre of a huge room, surrounded by flickering screens showing himself.

He felt his legs beginning to give way, but he forced himself to stay standing, and stared at one of the many screens, a particularly wide, expensive one, while the newsreader read out the text that went with the picture showing him as a young man.

He closed his eyes and tried to concentrate on what the newsreader was saying, which wasn't easy, because the sound was turned down and the confused voices of the customers in the store were loud, and because a number of confused thoughts were going through his head.

The police are asking for the cooperation of the public, said the newsreader. Anyone who recognises the man in the photograph is requested to call the phone number at the bottom of the screen. Sought as a witness in connection with the murder of the politician Markus Happonen.

Happonen, thought Lassi Anttila.

Sought as a witness.

All around him, the visitors to the electrical goods store were hurrying about on business of their own without giving him a glance, but sooner or later there was going to be someone who had known him an eternity ago. There might not be many, but there would be someone.

He fished his mobile out of his jacket pocket and tapped in the wrong digits twice before he managed to ring directory enquiries. He asked to be put through to an old people's home in the vicinity of Karjasaari.

'In Karjasaari or in the vicinity?' asked the woman at the other end of the line.

'I don't know exactly,' said Anttila.

'I'm afraid I need rather more detailed information,' said the woman.

'Yes, yes,' said Anttila.

'Yes?'

Cunt, thought Anttila. Cunt, cunt, cunt.

He broke the connection and tapped in a number that he knew off by heart. It was ages since he had called it, but he still remembered it. He pressed two fingers to his forehead, and when a strange voice with the right name answered, he said:

'Lassi here. I'd like to have the number of the home where Jarkko Miettinen is living.'

The man at the other end of the line said nothing, and Lassi Anttila thought that he ought to get his ideas in order first. Think about it properly.

'Who is this speaking?' asked the man who had introduced himself as Miettinen. Probably Jarkko's son, who had taken over the nursery garden business. The same firm. The same telephone number.

'It's Lassi. I'm . . . I'm an old friend of Jarkko's.'

'Then . . . do you already know what's happened?'

'Er . . . I'm afraid . . .'

'My father is dead,' said Jarkko's son.

On the TV screens a ski jumper crashed into a barrier bearing advertisements.

'Can you hear me?'

'Yes.'

'The name Lassi means nothing to me.'

'It's . . . a long time ago.'

'Are you a reporter?'

Paramedics were bending over the ski jumper. The red of their jackets stood out in sharp contrast to the snow.

'Hello?'

Anttila ended the call. The ski jumper was being led out of the stadium, his skis still in the run-out position, one lying some way from the other. With a forced smile, the ski jumper waved to the camera.

Dislocated shoulder, thought Anttila.

He called the three digits that every child knew. The answering voice sounded young and pleasingly calm.

'Police emergency number 112, what are you reporting?'

'My name's Anttila. I'm the man you're looking for.'

'Can you put that more clearly?'

'I'm the man you're looking for. On TV.'

'What exactly is this about?'

'On TV. On the news. That photo.'

The man at the police switchboard said nothing for a moment, and Anttila turned his eyes away from the screen and looked into a face that he knew. Or maybe he didn't.

'Mr Anttila?'

'What is it?'

'We have an appointment.'

'Oh . . . do we?'

'What a shame. He's dislocated his shoulder.'

'Excuse me, I must just . . .'

'We spoke on the phone. I'm the security scout.'

'Er . . . you're too early. I . . .'

'No, no, I'm right on time,' replied the man.

The police officer on the phone said something, but all that Lassi Anttila could hear were the words formed by his own lips. He didn't know if he was really speaking them or just thinking them.

All around him it was silent, only the words still hung in the air, like drops that wouldn't fall.

He saw the man making for the exit at a brisk but steady pace, and for a few seconds he felt the soft burning sensation in his stomach as something that he had been expecting for a long time.

62

By the time Sundström and Grönholm arrived, the electrical goods store had been closed off, and inquisitive rubber-neckers had positioned themselves on the other side of the police tape in the entrance foyer of the shopping centre.

A uniformed man led them past the DVDs and CDs and laptops and computers and washing machines and fridges to the dead body, which was lying on the grey carpet at the centre of the extensive shop floor. Sundström put on the overalls and gloves that one of the technicians handed him and bent over the man. He lay on his back, arms spread wide.

'CCTV surveillance?' he asked.

'The recording is being assessed and prepared for you at the moment,' said the man in uniform.

Sundström nodded.

'Lassi Anttila. The store detective.'

'Store detective?'

'Yes, I suppose you could call him the combined security man and cleaner of this shopping centre.'

'I see.'

'Like I said, combined security man and cleaner,' the uniformed man persevered.

Salomon Hietalahti of Forensics was leaning against a desk on the periphery of the scene with a sign saying *Information* in large yellow lettering above it, making notes. Sundström went over to him.

'You're in the right place,' he said.

Hietalahti glanced up and looked at him enquiringly.

'You're in the right place. Information.' Sundström pointed to the sign above Hietalahti's head.

'Ah, I see.'

'So?'

'The man was stabbed. A single stab wound.'

'A single stab wound?'

'Inflicted horizontally. One quick, fast, powerful stab wound.'

'Okay,' said Sundström. Fast and powerful, he thought.

'As far as I can see at present,' said Hietalahti.

'Ah,' said Sundström.

'Come over here, would you, Paavo?' Grönholm called from some way off. He was standing beside a small woman wearing a dark brown trouser suit who came over to him with, in view of the circumstances, a surprising spring in her step. Sundström was already moving in that direction.

'Mr Sundström?'

'That's right,' said Sundström, returning the woman's firm handshake. She introduced herself as Johanna Eklund, deputy business manager.

'We have the CCTV recording ready for you. Would you like to see it?'

'Very much,' said Sundström.

He followed Grönholm and the woman through the concourse to the escalator and down to the basement floor. The little woman, her step still lively, walked briskly ahead and said, as she finally opened a door, 'Sad as it is to say so in the circumstances, this is poor Mr Anttila's domain.'

Sundström looked around the dead security man's office, and nodded to the man standing bent over a keyboard.

'I'll be with you in a minute,' he said.

'This is Tommy Timonen. A colleague of Mr Anttila's.'

'That's right.' Timonen turned away from the monitor. 'Do sit down. I've looked through it once . . . that was okay, I hope?'

'Hmm?' asked Sundström.

'Okay that I've looked at it myself? I had to look for the right place.'

'Yes, yes, that's fine,' said Sundström.

'We have several cameras. I'll just show you what I've spotted so far.' He typed on the keyboard, and a grey image jerked into life on the little monitor.

'That's the camera fitted over the information desk. There, in front of the widescreen TV. See it?'

'Yes.'

'And there's Lassi.'

'Oh, yes?' Sundström leaned forward, and sensed Grönholm beside him doing the same.

'He's standing in front of the TV set looking at the camera.'

'Ah, yes, I can see him.'

'And it's odd, because Lassi stands there for quite some time. He seems to be watching what's on the TV screen.'

'Yes,' said Sundström.

'Then it all gets kind of fast and furious. Just a moment.' He wound forward a little way.

'He's phoning,' said Grönholm.

'Exactly. And now . . . in a minute . . .' The voice faltered slightly, and out of nowhere a man came into view. He seemed to be speaking to Lassi Anttila, and at the same moment he struck him down. Although from the bird's-eye view they had here, they could hardly see that any physical contact had taken place at all.

A single quick stab wound, thought Sundström.

'There . . . now . . . somehow it got Lassi, and the other person disappears from the picture.'

On a grey, coarse-grained screen, Lassi Anttila was in his death throes, and all around him people stood looking at the electrical goods on display and noticed nothing.

'Good heavens,' said Grönholm, sighing.

'Do you have a larger or clearer picture of the man?' asked Sundström.

'Yes, at the exit. Wait a moment.' He typed on the keyboard again, and other grey pictures came up on the monitor.

'That's the camera trained on every customer leaving the sales area,' he said. He pointed to a small line on the screen that quickly came closer and took shape. 'Here he comes.'

Sundström and Grönholm leaned forward again. The figure on the screen was looking down and wore a hooded jacket; he had drawn the hood over his head. It was impossible to guess whether he was young or old. The way the figure walked looked as if he was indeed a man, but who could tell even that for certain?

The man, assuming he was a man, walked on with remarkable composure, considering what had just happened.

'Do you have one of him coming into the electrical goods store?' asked Grönholm.

'Yes,' said Timonen. 'Here you are.'

Seconds later, a new picture flickered into life on the screen. The hooded man was approaching from the opposite direction, moving with equal composure.

'If I didn't know what was going to happen next I'd have said he was just strolling casually along,' said Grönholm.

The man disappeared, and Timonen froze the picture. 'That's all,' he said.

'Outside cameras? In the car park?'

'I haven't checked them yet,' said Timonen.

Sundström nodded. Something else seemed to him considerably more important. 'Thanks,' he said, and went quickly ahead along the dark corridor to the escalator, through the concourse and back to the large, brightly lit store in the middle of which the body of Lassi Anttila was still lying.

He knelt down and bent over the dead man. Anttila's mobile lay half covered by his right leg, level with the back of his knee. Sundström pulled it out without touching the body and studied the display before bringing up the record of calls. He stared at the number.

'What is it?' asked Grönholm behind him.

'Just before his death he called the police emergency number,' said Sundström.

'What?'

'But that's not the really surprising thing.'

'What is, then?' asked Grönholm.

'Before contacting the police he called a number with an area dialling code that I've known for some days, because that's where Kimmo always calls from.'

'Kimmo?'

'Karjasaari,' said Sundström.

63

A dead man whom no one has reported missing. He is sitting leaning back against a tree, in summer, in autumn, in winter. He doesn't feel the rain, the snow or the cold any more.

But I wonder whether the shoebox will keep out the water. For a little longer, that ought to be enough.

Sometimes I search the Internet for any indications that the dead man in the forest has been found. There's nothing of the kind. Maybe he doesn't exist. Maybe my memory is a fantasy. Maybe I didn't sit with him for a night and a day. Maybe I'm just imagining that I did because it seems to me appropriate.

Dear diary. 16 December.

I'm on the way back to Helsinki, sitting in the dining car drinking coffee with plenty of sugar and plenty of cream.

The woman sitting opposite me thinks that's amusing, and has given me the biscuit served with her own espresso.

Lassi Anttila, cleaner, store detective. Surrounded by TV sets showing his face. I didn't have much time. Unfortunately I had no chance to give him the business card, but he paid me the compliment of recognising me.

There was perplexity in his eyes, but also, in that last long second, the dawn of understanding.

64

Kimmo Joentaa looked at the multicoloured muesli flakes in Seppo's bowl, thought of Larissa, and called Tuomas Heinonen in hospital yet again.

Tuomas did not reply, and he decided against leaving another message, since it would only have been a repetition of the one he had left in the small hours. *Hello, Tuomas, thought I'd just call and ask how you're doing.*

The last he had heard from Tuomas had been the alarming message about a big win. Tiger Woods. Record for the course broken. In spite of everything. Tuomas had called in the middle of the night to share his delight with him.

He looked for Heinonen's landline among the stored numbers, and called Paulina. Getting to his feet, he walked a few metres away from the muesli-eating Seppo. One of the twin daughters answered.

'This is Vanessa at the Heinonen home,' she said.

'Hi . . . this is Kimmo. Kimmo Joentaa. I'm a colleague of your father's,' said Joentaa.

'I know,' said the little girl. 'Daddy isn't here.'

'Er . . . well, I wanted to speak to Paulina.'

'I think she's in the bathroom. Wait a minute.'

He heard her calling her mother.

'She's just coming,' said Vanessa. Then she took a deep breath, noisily. 'Hear that? Did you notice I'm sick?'

'Yes, you sound sick,' said Joentaa.

'Tonsillitis. Both of us.'

'Then I hope you get well soon,' said Joentaa.

'That's okay. School can wait.'

'I see.'

'And we're really feeling fine because of the antibiotics.'

'Glad to hear it,' said Joentaa.

'But we have to stay at home all week.'

'Have a nice time,' said Joentaa, and then Paulina was on the line, and Joentaa realised that he didn't know what he wanted to say to her.

'Kimmo?' said Paulina.

'Yes . . . hello, Paulina. I . . . I just wanted to give you a call.'

'Tuomas is still in hospital. But you know that.'

'Mhm. I couldn't reach him this morning and I just wanted to hear how . . . how things are looking.'

Paulina did not reply. Whether because she was searching for words, or because there weren't any. Or because the twins were hovering near her . . .

'This is probably a bad time to call, with the girls at home,' said Joentaa.

'Could be,' said Paulina.

'I've been calling Tuomas now and then, and I just wanted to tell you that he sounded cheerful but . . . but pretty unstable all the same.'

Paulina laughed. 'Unstable,' she repeated.

'I wanted to say you both ought to make sure he really does get a good rest in the hospital.'

She laughed again, this time it was more genuine, heartfelt laughter. 'Kimmo, I think you want to tell me that Tuomas has his laptop in his room and . . . you see what I mean?'

She fell silent, probably because of the twins.

'Yes,' said Joentaa.

'I know all about it,' said Paulina. 'And unfortunately there's nothing I can do. I can only keep asking him to think carefully about everything before he does what he's doing.'

'Ah.'

The little girls were giggling in the background, and Joentaa wondered if tonsillitis had been such fun in his own childhood. But it was good to hear the two of them laughing.

Paulina sounded both harried and calm as she went on. 'Kimmo, it's nice of you to call. And I think it's nice that Tuomas confides in you. I think you're the only person he's talked to about all that.'

'I . . . I'm glad,' said Joentaa. 'I'll go and see him again very soon.'

'Do that,' she said.

'I will. See you soon,' said Joentaa.

'See you soon,' said Paulina, ending the call.

Joentaa lowered his mobile and looked at the flashing poker machines. During the phone call he had kept walking, and had ended up in the lobby.

He went back to the breakfast room. Westerberg and Seppo were deep in conversation, maybe about the muesli flakes, and his mobile played its usual tune. Joentaa stared at the number for a few moments, trying to persuade himself it was the sequence of digits for the number of Larissa's disused mobile. But it was an entirely different number.

'What kind of a village is this place where you're hanging out?' asked Sundström, without wasting any time on a greeting.

'Hmm?'

'That rustic place you're in. Karjasaari.'

'Yes . . .'

'Because I'm standing here in a shopping centre in Raisio and I've found your fourth man. From that photo.'

'What?'

'Unfortunately he's dead.'

Joentaa thought of the giraffe. And the apple tree.

'Stabbed in a department store. Seconds earlier, he'd called the police and told them he was the man they were looking for.'

'Aha,' said Joentaa.

'He'd seen his own face on TV.'

'Mhm,' said Joentaa.

'And just before that he called a number in that village of yours. Karjasaari. The number of the nursery garden outfit, what was the name of that guy with dementia? The gardener.'

'Miettinen,' said Joentaa.

'Exactly,' said Sundström. 'So now we have four dead people. No, five if we count our unknown woman.'

'Saara Koivula.'

'In all probability,' said Sundström.

'That's right,' said Joentaa.

'The man's name is Lassi Anttila. He has two daughters, and as far as we can find out at present one of them lives in Karjasaari. Eva Anttila.'

'Good,' said Joentaa.

'Right now Nurmela is involved in a dispute over jurisdiction: the question is in which city the central investigation will be located. We ought all really to come and set ourselves up in that village of yours, but it looks like being Turku's jurisdiction after all because we have the privilege of the latest body. Three cheers for our suburb of Raisio and its shopping centres.'

The privilege of the latest body, thought Joentaa. He imagined Nurmela, cover name August, arguing with his typical dynamism and eloquence over jurisdiction, presumably with the police in Tamisaari and particularly Helsinki.

'I'll send you the audio data,' said Sundström.

'The what?'

'Kimmo, you're not listening again.'

'Sorry.'

'Never mind. It's at your moments of mental abstraction that you usually get interesting ideas.'

Joentaa did not reply, but he felt a touch of pleasure at this praise, although he doubted whether the idea of Nurmela's cover name was going to get the investigation anywhere much. Although who knew?

'What was that you said about audio data?' he asked.

'We have the emergency call or whatever you like to call it on record. Lassi Anttila's last words.'

Joentaa nodded, and felt a tingling in his stomach. 'Good,' he said softly, more to himself than to Sundström, although he didn't know just what the man's last words might be expected to tell them.

'I'll send it over as soon as it's been prepared. The technical guys are on the job.'

'Good,' said Joentaa.

'I'll call again,' said Sundström, breaking the connection.

Joentaa looked up, and saw that Westerberg was also talking on his phone. Seppo gesticulated as Joentaa came closer.

'Seems to be about the fourth man in our photo,' said Seppo.

'Yes,' said Joentaa.

Westerberg looked profoundly relaxed, and was doing more listening with his eyes closed than talking, while whoever was on the other end of the line was presumably saying the same kind of thing as Sundström.

He sat down, and noticed that Seppo's bowl of cereal was only half eaten, and Westerberg's hadn't been touched. Then he heard the tune of his phone again. Once more he looked for a number that he knew was now unavailable. And once more it was Sundström.

'Paavo here again,' he said. 'We've got something out of that emergency call now.'

'Yes?'

'Although I don't know if it can be right.'

'What is it?' asked Joentaa.

'The model student,' said Sundström.

'The model student?'

'That's what Anttila said just before he was stabbed. The model student.'

65

The model student. Words coming, muted, through walls. Out into a wonderful summer's day.

And you must be the model student.

An unsuitable term. In every respect.

The terrace door is open, there's a mild breeze, a thin film of sweat covers your skin. It's very quiet, only the bed is creaking in a room that I can see into only with difficulty. Suppressed laughter, suppressed moans. Risto is giving a running commentary on proceedings in the flat voice of a man on whom alcohol no longer takes effect.

Seize the day. Revive it, live it again, and then again and again.

Always the same day.

The bike ride, accompanied by a hot bright sun warming your back. The piano playing. Close your eyes and wait for the notes to die gently away and come together again on the floor, in the silence. Saara's voice, very low, so low that I'm not sure if I'm hearing her or if I only think I'm hearing her.

Stop as soon as Risto comes into the room.

End the day and begin it all over again.

Begin it again and again, always beginning with the bike ride through the summery forest.

The model student. Inappropriate as the description is, it also strikes me as appropriate that those were Lassi Anttila's last words.

Presumably I ought to be uneasy in view of the fact that my planning no longer stands up to reality, but ultimately I quite like that. The gardener Jarkko Miettinen died too quickly. Against all probability, with no regard for the statistics. Even his previous illness doesn't adequately explain the considerably accelerated course of his symptoms of poisoning.

I thought, on the other hand, that I could spend considerably more time on Lassi Anttila. I was sitting with Koski this morning in his office on the Stock Exchange, and Koski was saying something about the share prices running past at the bottom of the monitor when a photograph I knew appeared higher up on the screen.

I don't know how that photo came to be on the TV news, but it made me think about the other side for the first time. So there are people out there trying to find me. Trying to understand. I like that. They'll never understand, but I like the idea that they're trying, and the fact that they've put a picture of the shopping centre detective and cleaner on the news suggests that they've made some connections.

In the opinion of the analysts at Kengen & Koski, a close valid-ation of recent long commitments in the shares of Nieminen OY offers an attractive chance-to-risk ratio. Stress test, lows, closing rates.

Send an email off to Koski.

'Thanks!' Koski writes back seconds later.

On the basis of rumours of the certification in the near future of a highly effective gene test relating to inherited illnesses, shares in the biotechnology company Sedigene were the winner on the OMX 25 today, with a surcharge of around 25%.

Before I went home I met a remarkable man who does remark-able things in a remarkable location among the handsome ships in the West Harbour. His manner was brusque, but he seemed to know what he was talking about, and he needs only a small photograph in JPEG format and a name. Excellent. The world is a big village, and identity means nothing. It doesn't come cheap, but it should pay off in the end.

Leea stands in the doorway and says she's just off to do some shopping. Can she get anything for me.

I say no.

Olli is in the doorway where Leea stood just now, asking me if we can play a game.

'Do you have time?' he asks. 'Or are you working on some kind of . . . project again?'

Time describes the sequence of events, and accordingly, by comparison to other physical quantities, it has a clear and irreversible direction. A project is a unique plan consisting of a set of agreed activities with a beginning and an end, and is carried out, taking into account constraints such as cost, time, etc., in order to achieve an aim. Projects are not infrequently undertaken by project teams.

'What about it?' asks Olli.

Police officers who are looking for me while I am looking for Risto. The projects are similar, only the aims are different.

'What about it?' asks Olli again.

'Of course I have time.'

'Hurrah!' says Olli, clenching his fist in triumph, and he runs off, no doubt to find the game.

66

K immo Joentaa drove the way he knew, over the bridge that got narrower and narrower until the car seemed to be gliding over an endless expanse of water.

After about an hour he reached terra firma, and a little later Ristiina. He parked in the same place, and instinctively sought the window behind which the young psychiatrist, Arja Ekström, had been sitting a few days ago laughing heartily at something. The same porter was also on duty, and even the words with which he asked Joentaa to wait a few minutes seemed to be much the same.

He had leafed through the school magazine without any conclusive results, and had had a brief phone conversation with Xaver Blom, who had been unable to remember any pupil in their year making his specific mark as a model student. 'Markus Happonen was a model student, of course,' he had said. 'But it wasn't his nickname. On the contrary, he didn't really come over as a model student.'

Joentaa saw Arja Ekström coming towards him, enveloped in a large green coat. 'Ms Koponen is in the garden. We were expecting you,' she said.

She went ahead, and Joentaa followed her into the garden, which was more like a picturesque park. Anita-Liisa Koponen was sitting in a circular clearing under a roof formed by the snow-laden branches of trees, and she smiled at him as he came closer. He felt a tingling inside him, and a sense of pleasure that was hard to grasp.

'It's good to see you again,' she said.

'Yes.'

'Let's sit down,' said the psychiatrist.

'Thanks, I will,' said Joentaa. He thought of Tuomas, whom he would visit again soon, as soon as he was back in Turku, and he looked at the woman who had lost her own way and had shown him the way to Saara Koivula. He didn't know exactly how to begin, and she got in first.

'How are you?' she said.

'Fine,' he said. 'How about you?'

'Better,' she said.

'I'm glad of that. Very glad,' said Joentaa.

He fell silent again. Suddenly he wasn't sure whether he wanted to confront Anita-Liisa Koponen with the subject again. He waited, and she asked, 'What are you thinking?'

'I'd like to show you a photograph,' he said. 'And ask you whether you recognise anyone in it.'

She nodded. He took the photo out of his coat pocket and handed it to her. She nodded as she looked at it.

'Well?' asked Joentaa.

'I know the two boys,' she said, but she still seemed relaxed. 'They were at our school. Several years above us.'

Several years above us, thought Joentaa. Which meant . . . that she had been even younger at the time than he had thought, much younger.

'How . . . how old are you?' he asked.

'Thirty-seven,' she said.

Joentaa nodded, and concentrated for some time on what was really a simple calculation. It meant that she had been twelve years old in the summer of 1985. When she was raped. In the music teacher Saara Koivula's house.

'And over behind there . . . yes, that's her.'

'Who?'

'Yes,' she said.

'Saara . . . Saara Koivula?' said Joentaa.

'Yes,' she said.

'How do you . . .'

'That's her. That's the way she moved.' She imitated the body language of the woman in the picture. Sat up a little way, propped her head on her hand, and did what the woman in the photograph was doing: she looked at him and past him at the same time.

'Ah,' said Joentaa.

'She always moved like that, you couldn't help noticing,' she said.

Joentaa nodded. He thought of the funeral. The pastor's quiet voice and the empty place left for a name on the cross. An unknown woman, found in a roadside ditch with severe injuries to her skull, and brain damage. Without personal details. With traces of physical violence in the distant past.

Anita-Liisa Koponen offered him the photograph back, and Joentaa quickly put it in his pocket.

'Thank you,' he said.

She smiled.

'I have one more important question to ask you. Does the phrase "the model student" mean anything to you in any connection?'

She did not reply.

'I'm only asking whether, maybe . . . it sets off a memory.'

'Yes, it does,' she said.

'Yes?'

'Yes, Teuvo.'

'Teuvo?'

'A boy in my class. He went to piano lessons too.'

'Lessons with Saara Koivula?'

'Yes. All the others were girls, but he went for lessons as well.'

'Teuvo . . .'

'Of course he wasn't a model student. Far from it, he was rather . . . unruly. That was probably just why everyone laughed when he signed up to piano lessons. Because it wasn't like him. And because everyone thought it could only be because of her . . . do you see what I mean?'

'Yes. And so he was called the model student? Because he went to piano lessons?'

'I think so, yes. For a while some of the others tried annoying him by calling him that.'

'Teuvo . . . and what else?'

She thought. 'Teuvo Manner. I liked him very much. I even asked him about Saara several times. Asked if he knew how she was.'

'You did?'

'Yes, because she'd stopped coming to school. And I . . . I wasn't going to piano lessons with her any more.'

'I see,' said Joentaa.

Teuvo Manner. He had a name.

He struggled with himself. With himself and with the next question he must ask. She spoke of Saara Koivula quite naturally. Even the angel had a name now. 'I have to ask you something,' he said. 'It's a question that frightens me but it's important, perhaps for all of us.'

Beside him, Arja Ekström had straightened up slightly. Anita-Liisa Koponen, on the other hand, was still relaxed. 'I know what you're getting at,' she said.

Joentaa did not reply.

'You want to ask me . . . about Risto.'

R. says I'm not to worry about it.

Risto.

'Yes, I do,' said Joentaa.

'I don't know anything about him. Risto. That's the only name he has. If he has another I don't know it. I only saw him once. On that day.'

'Yes,' said Joentaa.

'He was a friend of hers. I don't understand why, but he was a friend of hers.'

'Yes,' said Joentaa. He felt helpless, and saw, in a few long seconds, a shadow come over her face. Instinctively he put a hand out to her, and laid it on her arm.

'Will it soon be lunchtime?' asked Anita-Liisa Koponen, without taking her eyes off Joentaa.

'Soon,' said Arja Ekström. Her voice seemed to come from far away.

'Then I must go,' said Anita-Liisa Koponen.

'Of course. Thank you very much indeed,' said Joentaa.

'Will you be coming back?' she asked.

'Yes, I will . . . and not to ask any more silly questions.'

She laughed. A brief laugh, but genuine.

'I promise,' said Joentaa.

'See you soon, then,' she said, without standing up.

'See you soon,' said Joentaa, getting to his feet. 'And I wish you very well, with all my heart.'

Arja Ekström was on her feet too, and he followed her to the exit.

'She still hasn't told us what she told you,' said the psychiatrist as they were saying goodbye.

Joentaa nodded.

'It strikes me as remarkable but right that you don't tell us yourself. The initiative must come from her.'

'Yes, probably. And I don't know . . .'

'What?'

'I don't even know whether it's something that she can get over at all.'

Arja Ekström gave him a long look.

'What I mean is, I don't know whether she can come to terms with it, by talking about it. I don't know my way around this field as well as . . .'

'Well, in any case you're the most thoughtful police officer I ever met,' she said.

Joentaa looked for amusement in her eyes.

'Not that I've met so very many,' she said, laughing. 'No, seriously, do come again when you like, because it's just as you say. Talking is only part of coming to terms with a problem, but at the moment she'd rather talk to you than to the doctors. And we long ago left behind the days when psychiatrists and psychotherapists thought they knew everything and were superior to lay people.'

Joentaa nodded.

'See you soon,' she said, shaking hands.

'Yes, see you soon.'

As he made for his car through the biting cold and the snow that was beginning to fall, he tried to imagine a summer. The summer that Anita-Liisa Koponen had forgotten, suppressed, denied so that she could go on living, and yet it had come back to haunt her.

67

Westerberg had worked out what he was going to say. He would inject considerably more authority into his words, and leave the woman in no doubt of the fact that he wasn't going to spend even a single day longer trying to chase her up on the phone. He took a deep breath and was just preparing to utter those words when Kirsti Forsman herself called him.

Her voice was calm and friendly.

'Mr Westerberg, good to hear from you,' she said.

'Er . . . well,' murmured Westerberg.

'You tried to reach me several times over the last few days,' she said.

'Yes,' said Westerberg.

'I didn't have the time to speak to you then,' she said.

'I see,' said Westerberg.

'Or the inclination.'

'Ah.'

'But in the end, it's no use,' she said.

'Well, that makes me feel hopeful,' he said.

'What is it you want so urgently?'

Westerberg closed his eyes and tried to recall the woman at the other end of the line. Lawyer. Dairy products. Advises the company's management on legal questions. A woman who seemed dynamic, and had stood in Forensics for a long time beside her dead brother, saying nothing. Who had bought a suitcase on the way to a place she had wanted to leave again in a hurry.

'Do you remember that photograph?' asked Westerberg.

Kirsti Forsman did not reply.

'The one I showed you the day after your brother's death.'

'Yes,' she said.

'Your brother is in it. And a school friend. And two other men.'

'Yes,' she said.

'It has now become . . . a central factor in our investigations.'

'Yes,' she said.

'What do you know about it?'

'About what?'

'About the photograph,' said Westerberg.

There was a long silence.

'Nothing,' she said.

'That's . . .'

'Nothing and everything.'

'That . . .' said Westerberg, but then Kirsti Forsman began telling her story, and Westerberg sensed the change in her voice and sat very upright as he listened.

68

S he was sitting in her office, at a clean, smooth desk, in front of the files in a legal dispute over a low-fat strawberry-flavoured yoghurt in which a consumer had found an insect. The man had taken the insect for a strawberry and bit into it with relish before turning to the editorial staff of a popular tabloid with his unusual discovery.

Westerberg was waiting at the other end of the line.

'Nothing,' she said.

'That's . . .'

'Nothing and everything.'

She thought of the insect in the yoghurt, and the photograph. A central factor, as Westerberg called it. Kalevi had looked different in that photo, but she had recognised his smile, and it had looked as if Kalevi was pleased about something. Although the date had been on the back.

19 August 1985.

'That . . .' said Westerberg, but she didn't want to listen to what he had to say. She began talking, listening to herself as she did so. Westerberg said nothing at the other end of the line; she only heard him breathing quietly now and then, and the words felt like something she had wanted to get rid of for a long time.

An August evening. She is sitting in the garden at the rather wobbly table among the flowers and shrubs and trees, and her mother is humming as she serves the meal.

Her mother asks where Kalevi is, and she says: In his room, I think.

Then they sit together for several minutes before, hesitantly, they begin to eat. Cucumber soup, potatoes, fish, beetroot sauce made with milk. Then her mother stands up and goes into the house, and she hears her calling to Kalevi.

The chilled soup tastes good. When her mother comes back she is just putting some potatoes on a plate and pouring the milky red beetroot sauce over them.

There's something the matter with him, says her mother.

Something the matter with who? she asks.

With Kalevi.

What is it? she asks.

He's locked his door, says her mother.

They go on eating for several minutes.

Then Kalevi comes out. That image is clear before her eyes. The first thing she thinks is that Kalevi has forgotten to wipe the tears off his face. Only then does she really notice that he has been crying. She has never seen Kalevi crying before. Big brothers don't cry. He says something, but his voice has lost its resonance, and her mother asks a question because she didn't understand him.

She asks what's going on, and Kalevi eats. He eats the soup and then the potatoes with the sauce and the fish.

What's going on? her mother asks several times.

Then Kalevi stands up and goes away. Her mother clears the table, and she helps a bit and then goes to the playground with two girls who are friends of hers. To smoke in secret up there, under the little wooden roof above the slide.

When she comes home it is still very warm. She opens the door and means to go to the kitchen to get herself a drink, but she stops because she hears Kalevi's voice, that new, toneless voice, and her mother's weeping.

He'd only been there, that's all, he is saying. He couldn't have done anything. What's he supposed to have done?

He doesn't scream those words, he says them very quietly, murmuring. Rather pitifully. Plaintively.

Yes, they'd been playing football and volleyball down on the beach a lot over the last few weeks, he'd told her so, hadn't he? There was a net set up there, and the field, and the music teacher had often been there with her boyfriend, and some time ago the boyfriend had asked if they'd like to play too, and of course they hadn't said no.

Well, and last time the teacher's boyfriend had offered them something to drink, and he, Kalevi, had drunk something, but only a few sips. Everyone does that, it's no big deal. But somehow the teacher's boyfriend was in such a funny mood, maybe because the teacher herself wasn't with them on the beach that day, and as for the other two who are always there, the gardener and the guy who cleans the supermarket floors, in his opinion they were falling-about drunk, and then they all ended up at the house. The boyfriend's house. How often does he have to say he had no idea what it was all leading up to? And no, he doesn't know where the music teacher suddenly came from and just as suddenly the others kind of . . . started pulling her around. No, he didn't do that. And nor did Markus Happonen.

Yes, in the bedroom. Yes, on the bed. No, the woman hadn't objected, she had gone along with them. Yes, he was sure of that, because after all she hadn't done anything. What did he mean, do anything? Well, she didn't scream or complain . . . yes, of course, what else? No, he just stood there and didn't understand what was going on. Yes, exactly. Yes, the music teacher, he'd said so three times already. Yes, her boyfriend. No, then he came home. Yes, alone. No, Markus had already . . . had already left earlier. Yes, he had gone directly after that. Yes, he keeps telling her so. What stain? What sort of stain in what underpants?

Suddenly his voice is rather louder.

Kirsti Forsman stands on the steps and wonders what it would be like to be caught smoking by her mother. In the playground, up there in the shelter of the little wooden roof of the slide.

What was she doing, poking around in his underwear, asks Kalevi. No, he doesn't see why it matters. No, it isn't a stain, and he doesn't know why it's so important . . .

A conversation between her brother Kalevi and her mother Ruut.

Kalevi in his toneless voice, her mother in tears.

About something she couldn't grasp.

She stops talking and waits. She doesn't know what she is waiting for until Westerberg speaks.

'Rape,' he says.

It sounds as if he is talking to himself more than her, and what he says seems to her very serious and sober in view of what she'd just been pouring out.

'Three men. Two schoolboys,' says Westerberg.

She thinks of the photograph. That normality. Kalevi smiling at the camera and writing on the back of the photo that he doesn't have to worry about it. Because R. said so. Kalevi smiling into the camera, so distraught that he can't even bring himself to write the name out in full.

Risto.

'Risto?'

'Yes.'

'What do you know about this Risto?'

'Nothing,' she says.

'Nothing . . . and everything?'

'No. Really nothing. I'm sorry.'

'The music teacher's boyfriend?'

'Yes.'

'And that's all you know about him?'

'I think I saw him from a distance a few times.'

'Yes?'

'On the bathing beach. Playing volleyball.'

'With your brother?'

'Yes, but I never went any closer. I certainly wouldn't have wanted to play volleyball with my brother. I liked to go swimming with my school friends.'

'But you saw him?'

'If it was him, yes. A tall man who laughed a lot, loudly. But he never looked happy.'

'Ah,' said Westerberg.

'As I said, I don't even know if he was the one.'

'And you never . . . talked to your brother about all this?'

She laughed. 'Of course not. I went very quietly downstairs to my room that evening. To the day of his death Kalevi wasn't aware that I knew anything about it at all.'

'And your mother?'

'She fell ill and died.'

Westerberg said nothing.

She was trying to remember Westerberg. Another tall man. But one who neither laughed a lot nor seemed unhappy.

Westerberg still said nothing, and for a while she tried to think what she would say next, until she realised that there was nothing more to say.

She broke the connection and turned her mobile off.

69

'A tall man who laughed a lot, loudly. But he never looked happy,' said Westerberg that evening, as they sat at their table in the dimly lit breakfast area near the fruit machines. The same band was playing the same tango music in the restaurant next door.

Westerberg seemed tired. Genuinely tired, not secretly wide awake, and he asked Kimmo Joentaa to make the phone call that still had to be made.

'Offer to go into his study or something,' he murmured as Joentaa tapped in the number that Seppo had spelled out from behind his well-organised laptop.

The father of the politician, Joosef Happonen, answered in a voice that sounded sceptical. Probably because he didn't recognise the number on the display.

'Kimmo Joentaa from the Turku police,' said Joentaa. 'We spoke to each other yesterday.'

'Yes,' said Happonen.

'I have to speak to you again. Only briefly. And perhaps only to you, without your wife.'

Happonen did not reply.

'Did you hear me?' asked Joentaa.

'Yes. My wife is out visiting a friend to play cards,' he said.

'Good,' said Joentaa.

'Yes. Very well,' said Happonen.

'It's about your son. And the music teacher whom I was asking about yesterday.'

'I know,' he said.

'We know now that something happened in the summer of 1985. I believe that you too know something about it.'

'Yes,' said Happonen.

'What do you know?'

Happonen said nothing. Joentaa thought he could hear him walking up and down.

'Mr Happonen?'

As Happonen went on, his voice sounded businesslike again, as it had directly after his collapse the day before. As if he were discussing something entirely different.

'In the summer of 1985 my son took part in the rape of a woman. His music teacher. He told me about it several weeks later because . . . because he couldn't bear the thought of it. We agreed to keep the whole business to ourselves. Do you understand?'

'Yes,' said Joentaa.

'His best friend Kalevi was also involved, as well as several men. Markus really had nothing to do with them. They probably met on the beach. There was evidently a man who took the lead, a . . . friend or acquaintance of the teacher . . . and Markus didn't have the courage to intervene.'

Joentaa made no comment.

'I don't know . . . whether he told me everything,' said Happonen.

'I have an important question to ask you,' said Joentaa. 'Did Markus ever mention another boy? A younger student at the school who was involved in one way or another?'

'Yes,' said Happonen.

'He did?'

'But how do you know about it?'

'What did Markus say about this boy?'

It was a long time before Happonen broke the ensuing silence. 'I watched him,' he said at last. 'For months on end.'

'You watched him? The other boy?'

'Yes. I waited outside the school in my car and tried to work out what was going on in his mind when he left the school building. Then I drove after him. I accompanied him on his way home, if you like.'

'You're talking about Teuvo Manner?'

'Yes, that's right. That was his name.'

'Why did you . . . accompany the boy home?'

'Because I wanted to be sure that he . . . he could live with it. He didn't have to say anything.'

'Didn't have to say anything about what? About the rape?'

Once again Happonen said nothing. The word lingered in the air as if three-dimensional.

'Yes. About the rape.'

'You wanted to reassure yourself that the boy Teuvo Manner was carrying on with his life, and saying nothing to anyone about the rape in which your son took part.'

'Yes.'

'Which means that the boy was there. He saw it all too.'

'Yes. He had a piano lesson that day. A younger boy from the school. And the music teacher's boyfriend . . . probably thought it would be particularly amusing if that boy had to watch as well.'

Particularly amusing, thought Joentaa.

'The man . . . well, he must be out of his mind.'

'Did you talk to the boy?'

'No. Of course not. I followed him for several months. At increasingly wide intervals. In a way they were only spot checks, and then I had a feeling that everything was all right with that boy. And then we all forgot it. Markus forgot it. I forgot it. And I think the boy did too.'

Forgot it, thought Joentaa.

'I could have been wrong,' said Happonen.

'What do you know about the music teacher?'

– 262 –

'What would you expect me to know about her?'

'Didn't the question of what became of her bother you?'

'She stopped coming to the school. Markus told me that.'

'Is that all?'

'Some time that winter Markus came to me and said the woman had gone. And her boyfriend as well. They'd moved away.'

'What do you know about the boyfriend?'

'I know his name was Risto,' he said.

'That's all?'

Happonen seemed to be thinking it over. Then he said, 'That's all.'

Risto, thought Joentaa. If names don't matter, then why was this man reduced to a single name?

'I didn't want to know any more,' said Happonen. 'Surely you can understand that. The man must be out of his mind. Dangerous. I didn't want to know anything about him, I just wanted my son to survive what happened.'

'Yes,' said Joentaa.

'And as for the woman . . . Markus dropped a few hints. Said that up to a certain point she went along with it.'

'Went along with it,' said Joentaa.

'Yes. Went along with them touching her. Well, that boyfriend of hers did it, and the others could watch and that didn't bother her. Do you see what I mean? The whole thing . . . well, the woman wasn't . . . wasn't normal.'

Normal, thought Joentaa.

'Do you understand me?'

'No, Mr Happonen. I don't understand you. I understand that you wanted to be there for your son, but I don't understand any of the rest of what you're telling me.'

Happonen did not respond.

'Thank you. I'll call again if I have any more questions,' said Joentaa.

'Yes,' said Happonen. 'Of course. I'm at your disposal any time.'

'Thanks. Goodbye.'

He put the mobile down on the table in front of him, stared at it, and felt a sudden barely tolerable longing, a painful wish that Larissa would call. Now, at this very moment.

'Kimmo?' asked Westerberg.

Joentaa picked up the mobile and tapped the number in. Larissa's number. Quickly, because he felt there was no time to be lost. Quick, quick, quick. Talk, laugh, laugh together, explain it all, understand it all.

He waited, although he knew what was going to come next. The friendly, impersonal voice of the recorded message. *The number you have called is not available.*

'Kimmo?' asked Westerberg.

'What?'

'Are you crying?'

'Sorry,' said Joentaa.

'Not a problem,' murmured Seppo.

'I . . . I'll make you a tea,' said Westerberg, getting to his feet. 'Camomile?'

Joentaa nodded.

'Coming right away,' said Westerberg.

'I'll be okay in a moment,' said Joentaa.

'What . . . what's the matter?' asked Seppo.

Joentaa shook his head. 'Difficult to explain,' he said, and then Westerberg came back with a cup of steaming hot water and a camomile tea bag.

Joentaa put both hands round the cup and felt his tears die down. Only to come back later some time. He breathed steadily in and out.

'I'll be okay in a moment,' he said.

'Take your time,' said Seppo, and Westerberg smiled.

'Good tip, Seppo.'

Joentaa stared at the mobile lying dark and silent on the table in front of him. He ran his hands over his face, and thought of Teuvo Manner, a boy of twelve. Who had gone to piano lessons because he'd fallen in love with his teacher.

'The boy was there,' he said.

'The model student,' said Westerberg.

'Yes. Teuvo Manner. He had a piano lesson that day. Then Risto and the others came in.'

'And . . . the boy had to watch it all?' asked Seppo, without expecting an answer.

They sat for some time in the silence that had fallen, and then the band in the restaurant next door stopped for a break.

After a while Seppo cleared his throat. 'So . . . if I have the right idea of it . . .' he said.

'Yes?' asked Westerberg.

'We're looking at a kind of . . . campaign of revenge. On the part of the boy. Teuvo Manner.'

'Who isn't a boy any more,' said Westerberg.

Or maybe he is, thought Joentaa. Maybe he stayed a boy for ever, a child. Experiencing the same thing over and over again, until at last, decades later, it's over. He thought of Anita-Liisa Koponen. Westerberg stood up and threw a coin into the machine, which thanked him with a metallic sigh. Seppo sat up and tapped with flying fingers on the keyboard of his laptop. 'Let me bring you up to date with the latest developments,' he said.

'Go ahead,' said Westerberg.

'We still haven't found Saara Koivula's last address, although we're looking for it. But we now know – the information came in about half an hour ago – where she was living in the months she spent here in Karjasaari.'

The summer of 1985, thought Joentaa.

'Where?' he asked.

'Well, judging by the address it's in a place that's part of the municipality but even smaller than Karjasaari itself. Apparently just a few farms and small houses, otherwise only fields and forest. Number twelve Metsänkatu, in the Majala district.'

Joentaa nodded.

'There's a search on for Teuvo Manner. No results so far, but only a few hours have passed since we had the name.'

Revenge, thought Joentaa. The word seemed to him curiously inappropriate.

'There's still Risto,' said Westerberg.

'Manner's next victim,' said Seppo.

'I don't know that victim is the way to put it,' said Westerberg.

Risto. A shadow. A tall shadow, laughing loudly.

Seppo held the photo up to the faint light and seemed to be looking for something. 'What I've been wondering all this time . . .' he murmured.

'What have you been wondering?' asked Westerberg.

'Two boys, two men. Happonen, Forsman, Miettinen, Anttila. We know them all now.'

'Yes,' said Westerberg.

'They're all dead.'

'Yes,' said Westerberg.

'The whole gang, but where the hell is Risto?'

R. says I'm not to worry about it, thought Joentaa. The man pulling all the strings.

If no one says anything, nothing happened.

The woman in the background is turning to the sun and trying to forget it, but an impulse makes her look in the direction of the camera.

Seppo's question was a good one, and the answer suggested itself.

'Risto was taking the photograph,' said Joentaa.

CHRISTMAS

70

Risto Nygren was sitting in front of his screen and keyboard in the dim light, writing.

Today, Christmas Eve, went to see Julia. You know who I mean. THAT Julia. Can't confirm the comments of our fellow-punter. Short personal description. Origin: Russia; age: c. 18 (if that's true, Smiley); height: c. 1.60 m; figure: dress size 10; small tits, skinny, wide hips, flat bum; hair: long and red; other features: a piercing in her navel. As for the action – not all that sexy to look at, but she has the charm of the girl next door; a girlfriend attitude, slightly forced; kind of depraved naivety in her eyes, just my kind. Tried to make a little conversation at first, wasn't easy because I found that Julia speaks very little German and English . . . and as for Finnish, forget it. You all know I'm from the far north. Agreed on blow-job, straight, anal, fisting for 100, and guess what, she provided what she promised, a little too much use of hand in the blow-job, but she's a good girl, doesn't use her teeth, and threw in a little squeal when she came. Not really included in the price, but fine by me. So much for now. Details later.

He read this through twice, correcting a couple of spelling mistakes before sending it to the forum. Minutes later the first thumbs-up messages came through. Greg and whorefucker25 liked his account of the experience.

Risto Nygren ran his hands over the mouse, let them rest there for a moment and wondered what sort of guys they were, Greg and whorefucker25.

He had an image before his eyes. Greg was a student. First semester, philosophy or maybe literature. Greg had already posted 113 accounts of his experiences on the forum, and was always particularly pleased to get an unprotected blow-job at a price that didn't seem too steep for small, fat students.

If he was not much mistaken whorefucker25, on the other hand, was an old man always trying to seem young. Presumably that was one of the reasons why none of his twenty-three accounts was about a prostitute any older than nineteen. He too was a happy man if the ladies offered him an unprotected blow-job, and he liked the riding-astride position. He had once tried S & M and spanking, but something had gone wrong, he had sounded quite upset, and ended his account with the hesitant remark: *Likelihood of going back unfortunately only 40%.*

A third virtual thumb went up. Loverboy-5000 was enthusiastic and announced that he was going to visit the lady in question today.

Good luck, thought Risto Nygren. He doubted whether Julia had recovered from the going-over he'd given her yet. Loverboy-5000 had better wait for the details.

But he didn't feel like writing up the details now. He stood up, put on his jacket, went along the corridor and took the lift down. Christmas music was being played in the big golden lobby. A huge, lavishly decorated Christmas tree stood in the front hall of the hotel, and the mad-sounding laughter of Asiatics relaxing came from the hotel bar.

He sat down at one of the tables, looked at the brightly lit city in the dark from behind the big windows, and for reasons he didn't entirely understand he thought of Saara. Of that strange last day. The last blow, which had been struck too hard. His headlong departure. And the way he had felt so bad about it.

He had sensed the tears come into his eyes during the

flight, and the attendant had asked if he was all right as she brought him a drink. He had only nodded, but for several moments he had felt an impulse to tell her the truth.

The whole truth, whatever that was.

The air ticket had been very expensive, because he had booked it only on the day of the flight. For now, it was a one-way ticket.

He thought of Saara coming back, and yet again he wondered why. What had she really wanted of him after so many years? And what kind of a conversation was it that they'd had? What kind of a woman had it been sitting opposite him? With age marks on her hands, and a voice that was calm and controlled as she told him that she had seen him by chance in that stupid TV programme on a special-interest channel, about the tradition of family firms, and she had suddenly known that nothing was forgotten, and he would be called to reckoning for it all.

She had sat opposite him, smiling when he told her he was going to kill her. Right away. If she said a word about anything to anyone.

She had smiled, and he had almost felt a little panic, because he had seen no fear in her eyes.

Outside the hotel, twilight was falling, and the red-light district was lit up. A city of opposites, he thought, the luxury hotel and bank tower building next to the drugs advisory centre and the brothel. He liked that.

If he leaned very far to the right he could look out and guess at the window of the place where little Julia worked. Maybe Loverboy-5000 was already with her. The Asians were laughing at the bar, a little boy in the hall looked up as far as he could stretch, maybe so that he could see the star at the top of the Christmas tree.

Nothing was forgotten, Saara had said.

The waiter came over and asked if he could bring him

something, but he didn't want anything to drink. He wasn't thirsty. He stood up and went to the lift, and with the little boy and a woman who was holding the little boy's hand he went up to the twenty-fourth floor. He nodded goodbye to them.

There was a post on the forum, flickering on the screen of his laptop. From Loverboy-5000. Either he had used a five-minute number or he was sending his account in real time on his iPhone. Possibly both.

Hi guys. Was just with her, can't go along with Old-Finn's report. Julia looked like she hadn't slept for two days, and if you ask me she was stoned out of her mind. Action as good as a valium tablet, doggy-fashion she almost fell off the bed, and when I came she didn't even seem to notice. Likelihood of going back: 0%. If you ask me, there's something the matter with her.

Oh, well, thought Risto Nygren. A sudden vague sadness came over him; in a way it somehow felt good. He hadn't thought of Saara for a long time. Really, not since the day when he left her in the ditch and drove on to Helsinki and the airport.

His last thought of Saara had been when he felt an impulse to tell the flight attendant, the girl who looked at him with such concern, all about it, 10,000 metres above the ground.

Tell her everything. How he had killed a woman who had meant something to him. How it made him sad. The flight attendant in her smart uniform had looked as if she would understand him.

There's something the matter with her, he thought.

Likelihood of going back: 0%.

He tried to form a picture of Loverboy-5000. A banker. Between twenty and thirty. Who had something important to do at the office on 24 December, and then quickly saw to little Julia. And then, in the subway, gets out his iPhone or iPad, to send like-minded guys a report on his recent experience. Before Mama served the Christmas goose at seven and made him try on his new tie.

He logged out and closed the system down. Sat in the silence smiling slightly to himself.

Outside, idiots were throwing fireworks. At Christmas.

He closed his eyes.

After a while, as the image of Saara withdrew into mist, and made way for little Julia's faint smile, he fell asleep.

71

Kimmo Joentaa spent Christmas in the small house in the forest, now standing empty, where the piano teacher Saara Koivula had lived twenty-five years ago.

The present owners of the property, a young married couple with a three-year-old daughter, had moved out a few months ago taking everything with them, except for a table and a chair, both made of pale wood the same colour as the floorboards.

Joentaa had had a short phone conversation with the young husband, and ended by asking him if, by any chance, he knew where the piano had stood. The man didn't understand, and when Joentaa had finally managed to convey what he meant said that there had been no piano in the house, at least not when he and his family moved in. Joentaa had thanked him and apologised for his silly question.

He had been here several times in the last few days, trying to imagine what it had looked like in the summer of 1985. He assumed that the piano stood against the wall with the window next to the door to the terrace, which led straight out into the garden. He had a feeling that that would have been a good place for it.

He opened the terrace door, sat down on the wooden chair, and looked around the living room, which was small and square. A narrow corridor led to the kitchen, a small bathroom with an even smaller sauna, and another room that had presumably been the bedroom. Another door led from the bedroom out into the open air and the garden, which seemed to merge with the forest after about 20 metres. Snow blew in through the open door; the air was cool and clear.

A little way off a church bell rang, and a few minutes later the muted sound of Christmas carols being sung could be heard. Joentaa had seen the church when he turned off the narrow road along the even narrower track through the forest leading to Majala and Saara Koivula's house.

He closed his eyes and thought of the telephone conversation he had had with Sundström that afternoon. The country-wide search for Teuvo Manner was turning out, so far anyway, to be a complete failure. Teuvo Manner didn't seem to exist. All trace of him was lost in 1991, after he left school here in Karjasaari. Manner's mother had died in 2003, also here in Karjasaari, and her son had obviously not been to the funeral. He had gone away, he was always going away, a friend of his mother had said.

It was a real problem, Westerberg had commented, and Joentaa had thought: Another shadow.

He thought of Seppo, spending Christmas in his hotel room and thereby probably annoying his fiancée and several family members who had expected him back in Helsinki for the holiday season. But Seppo was a man possessed by the idea that he could make a name emerge from a sea of photographs. He had been back to the local journalist to borrow her extensive photographic archive, had returned to the hotel with three large boxes, had dragged them up to his room, and announced that he was going to find what he wanted at any price.

However, he hadn't found it yet, nor had Joentaa found anything out, although he had had many conversations over the last few days: with Happonen's father again, with Miettinen's son, with Anttila's daughter and other people who had been in Karjasaari long enough to remember the summer of 1985.

Teuvo Manner had disappeared.

And Risto was still just Risto. A single name.

At least their colleagues in Helsinki, to which Westerberg had now returned, had found out Saara Koivula's last address. She had lived a quiet life on her own in a one-room apartment in the city centre, with a view of the sea and the ferries going out and coming in.

She had last worked several years ago, teaching music and several languages at evening classes for adults, and after that she lived on state benefits, which had been paid up to and including December, because the state bureaucracy had not yet realised that Saara Koivula was dead.

Former students at her evening classes had been questioned. They had reacted with dismay to the news of her death, and were very positive in what they said about her. She had been a good, kind and patient teacher. None of them had connected her with the photograph shown in the media, the woman lying dead in the Turku hospital. The photograph hadn't looked at all like her.

Westerberg had sent Joentaa a picture by email, a digital photograph taken by a woman who had attended her classes. Saara Koivula laughing among her students. If you looked very closely, you could just about see the laughing woman in the picture as the dead one in Turku hospital, but in a certain way they really were two different faces.

One laughing woman, one dead woman, Joentaa had thought, and then thought the idea was both true and stupid.

No one had noticed Saara Koivula's disappearance. She hadn't taught evening classes for years now. There seemed to be no relations or close friends who would have noticed that she was missing.

His mobile lay on the wooden table in front of him. He picked it up and called a number, the one he kept on calling recently. His own. No one answered. The house was empty, the giraffe was lying in the snow.

He thought of Tuomas Heinonen; he had phoned him the day before. Heinonen had said he was spending Christmas Eve at home with Paulina and the twins, and Joentaa had said he was very glad about that. He wrote a message: *Dear Tuomas, a very happy Christmas to you and Paulina and the twins. See you soon, Kimmo.*

Then he leaned back on the chair and closed his eyes. The cold came in through the open door to the terrace. A text message from Tuomas came in: *Dear Kimmo, I wish you a happy Christmas too. We're at home, it's all lovely. I have a silly question to ask, and I really do ask you only because I know you won't take it the wrong way – can you lend me a little money in the next few days? 500 euros?*

Joentaa stared at the text message. For a few minutes he wondered whether it was possible that Tuomas Heinonen really did just mean to crack a joke.

Then he leaned forward, laid his head on the top of the table and closed his eyes. He tried to think about the boy Teuvo Manner, but the thought eluded him. He thought of Larissa, and that thought eluded him as well, and he dreamed of a woman who looked like Larissa.

When the familiar melody of his telephone roused him from sleep, he was sure that the call came from Sanna. Sanna had risen from the dead and had a mobile on which she was calling him now, at this moment, in the dark beside the red wooden church, standing beside her grave.

He raised his head from the table and reached for the phone. Put it down, picked it up again.

'Hello,' he shouted.

No one answered.

'Yes!' he shouted.

'Er . . . Kimmo?' asked the caller. He sounded uncertain.

'Yes . . . sorry!' shouted Joentaa.

'Er . . . Kimmo, you're shouting.'

'Sorry,' said Joentaa.

'Never mind. Did I wake you up?'

'Yes, but it doesn't matter.'

'I thought I'd give you a call at once,' said Seppo.

'Yes?'

'Kimmo . . .'

'Yes, what?'

'I've got him.'

Now Joentaa heard the new tone in his voice. Triumph and excitement.

'Risto Nygren.'

Joentaa said nothing.

'Winner of the beach volleyball tournament on Karjasaari bathing beach on 24 July 1985. Captain of the team that won not only the honour but also a voucher for brunch at the fish restaurant there. In the photo Risto is holding the cup up to the camera, with the others in the background grinning for all they're worth.'

R. says I'm not to worry about it, thought Joentaa.

'Do you understand? All four of them. Happonen, Forsman, Miettinen, Anttila.'

The entire volleyball team, thought Joentaa.

'We've got him, Kimmo,' said Seppo again.

'Yes,' said Joentaa. A puddle had formed on the square metre of floor in front of the terrace door, and Joentaa wondered vaguely if it would damage the floorboards.

'I'll call when we get more concrete facts,' said Seppo.

'Right,' said Joentaa.

Then he sat in the silence again, in the empty house where Saara Koivula had lived with her boyfriend Risto Nygren. A brilliant volleyball player. He got up to close the terrace door, but when he reached the door he decided to go outside. Into the garden that merged with the forest after about 20 metres. There was a swing to one side of the garden; it looked home-made. Probably by the young father of the family, the man who wanted to sell this house.

Joentaa brushed off some of the snow and sat on the swing. He swung back and forth a little, looking through the windows into the living room of the house. After a while he heard the sound of his ringtone again. He walked in, slowly, and when he got to the mobile the display told him a call had been missed. Seppo's number. He called back.

'Kimmo?'

'Yes. You called.'

'I did. Well, we're scoring hits thick and fast here.'

'Okay.'

'Risto Nygren. A Finland Swede with German roots.'

'Aha.'

'Originally comes from Laappeenranta. Fifty-seven years old. Paper manufacturer, one of the four largest in Finland. Sold the firm a few years ago, seems to be living on the interest from the proceeds. A millionaire, I assume. Unmarried, no children. Has a handsome house near Turku, but he isn't there now.'

Another house standing empty, thought Joentaa.

'Our colleagues disturbed several Christmas parties in the area, and found out that Nygren hasn't been seen since the summer of this year. That wouldn't be considered anything unusual, though, because Nygren's former company has branches in various countries, and he always spent a lot of time travelling.'

'Hasn't been seen since the summer of this year,' said Joentaa.

'Exactly. And it all began in summer when Saara Koivula was found in the roadside ditch.'

Joentaa remembered the conversation with Rintanen, the doctor in the Turku hospital. Apallic syndrome as the result of severe trauma of the skull and brain. Lack of oxygen, circulatory arrest.

'And here it comes,' said Seppo. 'We've scored another hit, with luck the crucial one. Risto Nygren flew to Germany on 24 June. The first findings are that he's been living there ever since, in Frankfurt. He's taken a suite in a five-star hotel for an indefinite period.'

'That's . . .'

'Marko Westerberg and I are flying out tomorrow. I'll go back to Helsinki first thing after breakfast, and our flight for Frankfurt takes off at eleven thirty-five. Shall we see each other first? At seven, maybe?'

'I'd like that,' said Joentaa.

'See you tomorrow,' said Seppo, and then, once again, Joentaa was sitting in the silence that was filled with something he couldn't yet pin down. Risto Nygren, Germany, five-star hotel. Paper manufacturer. Millionaire, Seppo assumed.

He closed his eyes, and when he opened them again he had a feeling for some moments that he could see it all. The shimmering heat, the garden in flower, the film of sweat on the forehead of the boy who has struck a wrong note, but is happy all the same. For those moments he could see it, even the absent piano. Then everything was back to how it had been before.

An empty house in winter, snow blowing in through the terrace door. Risto. Manufactures paper.

A white sheet of paper. Nothing written on it.

A woman with no expression in her face any more.

A giraffe that won't be able to breathe if the snow doesn't stop falling.

He heard a sigh, and not until seconds later did he realise that it had come from his own mouth. He stood up and went to close the door carefully before he went down the slope to his car.

72

On the morning of 25 December Kimmo Joentaa was slowly eating a bowl of multicoloured muesli flakes, looking at the empty chair where Seppo had been sitting just a moment ago.

Seppo had said goodbye and taken a taxi to Laappeenranta station, and Kimmo Joentaa felt as if he were now not just the only guest but the only human being in this hotel.

The old man who often breakfasted here, doggedly reading a newspaper, was not in evidence, and the young woman who had served them coffee had also said goodbye, taking care to wish him all the best in the New Year. Joentaa had returned her good wishes.

He went to his room and sat on the bed for a while before he began packing his few things in his travelling bag. When he had packed the bag he sat down on the bed. After a few more moments he pulled his laptop close to him and opened the email program. He had one new message. Not a lottery win, not a phone bill. A message from veryhotlarissa instead. Sent at 04.27 hours last night.

Happy Christmas, dear Kimmo.

He sat looking at those words for a little while. Looked at them and looked through them. Now and then a colourful ad popped up in the picture, exploding into a thousand sparks like a firework, only to come back a few seconds later. Joentaa tried to bring himself to obliterate the ad from his screen, but he didn't have the strength. At some point a message came up saying that battery power was running low, and then the screen went black and the computer stopped humming.

Joentaa put the computer in his travelling bag and lingered in the doorway for a while before he left. He took the lift down. There was no one at the reception desk, but the old man who spent hours every day reading his newspaper was sitting in a niche in the breakfast room. So he had come after all, but a little later today, the first day of Christmas.

Joentaa left his key on the counter at reception; the police expenses department in Turku would deal with everything else. Then, on impulse, he went over to the old man and wished him a merry Christmas and a happy New Year.

'Thank you, thank you,' said the old man, without looking up from his paper. 'And the same to you.'

As Joentaa stepped out of the hotel his mobile rang.

'Yes?' said Joentaa.

'Moisander, remember me? From Karjasaari police station.'

'Yes, I do,' said Joentaa. He had met Moisander once, and had talked to him on the phone several times when he wanted information on addresses and contact data in Karjasaari.

'We spoke on the phone several times,' said Moisander.

'Yes, I know. What . . . what is it?' asked Joentaa.

'We have something here. Something that might interest you,' said Moisander.

'You do?'

'I'll pick you up,' said Moisander, 'if that's okay with you.'

'Yes, fine, no problem. I'm outside the hotel here, I was really about to . . .'

'I'll be with you in five minutes,' said Moisander.

'Right,' said Joentaa.

He went to his car, put his travelling bag in the boot, and waited for Moisander, who did indeed turn into the hotel car park with verve a few minutes later. The light on top of his patrol car was blinking, but the siren wasn't sounding.

'Hello,' said Joentaa. 'What's happened?'

'We none of us know for sure at this point,' said Moisander. 'I haven't been to the scene yet. We'd better drive there and take a look for ourselves.'

Joentaa nodded and leaned back. He was feeling leaden weariness, and thought of the euphoric Seppo, who had sounded so triumphant first thing this morning. He closed his eyes, thinking that in a certain way everything, while still in progress, had come to a halt.

Those involved had been named, and now had only to be found.

Moisander took the car along increasingly narrow tracks through the forest, and Joentaa thought of Nurmela's birthday party on the summery autumn day that now seemed so long ago. Maybe because Larissa had still been there that day, and next day she had gone. He thought of the last dance – of August Nurmela's offbeat music in the night – a dance that came to an early end when Grönholm threw up on Nurmela's fitted carpet.

'Nearly there,' said Moisander, beside him.

'Isn't this . . .' Joentaa began.

'Hmm?'

They went along another forest track, this one covered with snow, and some way off Joentaa saw two more police cars and another used by Forensics.

'It's over there,' said Moisander. He expertly drove the car through the deep snow and parked beside one of the police cars. Joentaa narrowed his eyes and peered through the windscreen.

'No, that way,' said Moisander, pointing in the opposite direction, but Joentaa was climbing out and went a few steps up the slope. The trees grew very close together here, but he made his way through them.

'Okay?' called Moisander.

'Just coming,' said Joentaa, climbing on. He had not been mistaken. He had thought he saw the swing through the branches of the trees, and now the house itself was ahead of him. He went on, although Moisander was calling something or other, and then at last he was in the little garden and sat down on the swing where he had been sitting last night. Only a few hours ago. The windows were like mirrors, he could see nothing. But he knew what was on the other side of them. A chair, a table, no piano.

'I'm here,' called Joentaa. 'Coming down again now.'

Moisander waved to him and nodded, and Joentaa walked towards the scene. After a few metres a strange feeling came over him, one that he didn't understand. It was a feeling that with every step he was coming closer to a truth that he ought to have recognised long ago. Moisander was waiting for him, holding a pair of gloves provided by Forensics and a shoebox.

'What's that?' asked Joentaa, putting on the gloves.

'We . . . we don't know yet. It was beside the body.'

Joentaa followed Moisander's eyes, but he saw no body, only trees and wet leaves and snow, and people crouching on the ground going about their work, and then the body obviously covered up.

'The dog's owner thinks it must have been the stress of Christmas,' said Moisander.

'What?' asked Joentaa.

'The . . . er, the stress of Christmas. The dog ran away from him, which it never usually does. And the owner puts it down to all the stress at their Christmas family gathering, because it seems there was an almighty quarrel.'

'I see,' said Joentaa.

'Anyway, the dog found the corpse. Otherwise I suppose it could have lain there for ever; there's no real path that way. The dog's owner is in shock because the body . . . well, it's not a pretty sight by now.'

'And what's that?' asked Joentaa, pointing to the shoebox.

'It was lying beside the body.' Moisander took the lid off and handed him an exercise book. A school exercise book, with lined paper.

Joentaa read the words on it, and thought of the giraffe. And the snow. And the night in the hospital where Sanna had died, and her smile that he hadn't seen for too long.

He took the exercise book and walked away. Moisander said something, but he wasn't listening. He walked on until he felt he was somewhere peaceful at last. Somewhere very peaceful.

Then he sat down on the ground, leaned back against a tree trunk, and read the words again, just to make sure they were really there. A simple, memorable heading that someone had written in careful handwriting on the lined paper of a school exercise book, many years ago.

Summer 1985.

73

Westerberg and Seppo were met at Frankfurt airport by a German colleague, who drove them along a smooth, wide, almost empty motorway to the city centre without asking questions. His replies to their own questions in English, the language in which the three of them conversed, were brief but to the point.

Risto Nygren. Six months ago. Checked into the hotel in June, moved into a suite on the twenty-fourth floor, at an all-inclusive price, so it seemed, but he didn't really know much about these things.

Westerberg looked at the slushy snow piled high to the right and left of them, and listened to the noise of the windscreen wipers squeaking on the glass. Presumably it was the squeaking that caused his German colleague to utter a quiet, half-hearted curse now and then.

He parked the car right outside the hotel entrance, to the displeasure of a doorman standing there stiffly in the cold, showed his ID and said something that Westerberg didn't understand in German. It seemed to make the right impression on the doorman, for he stepped aside and nodded to Westerberg and Seppo as well.

The hotel was red, gold and large. Westerberg looked up, trying to make out the windows of the suite on the twenty-fourth floor, before joining the others in the lobby, in the middle of which a gigantic, brightly lit Christmas tree stood.

The German officer spoke to a young woman at reception, and Seppo breathed audibly in and out and seemed to be shivering, although it was very warm inside the hotel. During the flight and on the drive to the centre of Frankfurt, Seppo had hardly said a word, and Westerberg too had been silent.

Presumably Seppo's mind was on the same thing that had been occupying his own, and that ultimately consisted only of a name. Risto. And the fact that at last they would be able to put a face to that name, and associate it with the unimaginable.

'He's right here now and doesn't know anything,' said their German colleague in English. 'Room number 248.'

Westerberg nodded.

The German offered to wait for them in the lobby, and Westerberg and Seppo took the lift up. Meditative music came over loudspeakers, and Seppo breathed in and out again audibly before he walked fast and purposefully along the corridor. Westerberg followed him. The droning of a vacuum cleaner came from one of the rooms. But all was quiet behind the white door on which there was a gold plate bearing the number 248.

Seppo hesitated, looked at his colleague, and Westerberg knocked. He thought he heard footsteps, but that could have been his imagination. Seppo breathed audibly in. Westerberg waited for Seppo to breathe out, but he held his breath and compressed his lips.

'Seppo?' said Westerberg.

Seppo abruptly turned away from the closed door. 'Hmm?'

'We'll take this very calmly. You look kind of . . . tensed up.'

'Yes, I am. But as you say . . . of course.'

'Fine,' said Westerberg. The man who opened the door to them was wearing a white bathrobe and did not seem at all pleased to be disturbed. He snapped something in German, but then his expression changed, presumably because neither Westerberg nor Seppo looked like members of the hotel staff.

'Mr Nygren? Risto . . . Nygren? Resident of Turku?' Westerberg asked.

The man did not reply, but stared at Westerberg in silence.

'Risto Nygren?' Westerberg asked again.

'Yes . . . that's me,' said Nygren. His Finnish sounded a little strange, with touches of various different accents.

'My name is Westerberg, this is my colleague Seppo, and we are police officers from Helsinki, Criminal Investigation Department.'

Nygren nodded. Nodded and nodded, and seemed to be thinking intently of something or other.

'May we come in?' asked Westerberg, and Nygren smiled suddenly, just as suddenly adopting a different tone of voice.

'Of course. Visitors from Finland are always welcome.' He stepped aside, and made an inviting gesture.

'Thank you,' said Westerberg. Seppo just nodded.

'Excuse the untidiness,' said Nygren, a remark that Westerberg waved away, wondering what untidiness he meant. To Westerberg's way of thinking, the hotel suite which Risto Nygren had been inhabiting for months was meticulously neat and tidy.

Nygren opened a connecting door to a large and comfortable living room, and asked them to sit down as he took juice and a bottle of water out of the mini-bar and put them on the table. Then he fetched glasses. And then he sat down in an armchair, let himself sink back into it, and gestured to the drinks.

'Help yourselves,' he said.

Westerberg declined with thanks, while Seppo beside him suddenly straightened up and reached for a bottle of orange juice. He poured the bright yellow juice into one of the glasses, and Nygren said, 'Well . . . of course you make me curious.'

'Do we?' asked Westerberg.

'Yes. Very curious. What . . . brings you here to Germany?'

'Happonen,' said Westerberg, watching Nygren's face for any reaction. At first there was none. Then surprise.

'Happonen,' he said in a toneless voice.

'Happonen, Forsman, Miettinen.'

Nygren said nothing.

'And Anttila.'

'Ah,' said Nygren. He seemed to be genuinely surprised. As if he had been expecting another name. Westerberg guessed what name, and Seppo spoke it aloud.

'And of course Saara. Saara Koivula.'

Leaning back in his armchair, wearing a white bathrobe and white slippers, Nygren nodded.

'Does that mean anything to you?' asked Westerberg.

'I'm not quite sure,' said Nygren.

'Not quite sure?' asked Seppo, and Nygren seemed to be thinking. Then he stood up.

'Excuse me,' he said as he left the room. 'I'd just like to get some clothes on.'

'Of course,' said Westerberg, and sensed Seppo beside him straightening up as if to get to his own feet.

'I'll be right back,' said Nygren, and then Westerberg and Seppo were alone sitting on the sofa, which for reasons that Westerberg could not plausibly explain smelled of lemon.

'Is that wise?' asked Seppo.

'Our friend will hardly be stupid enough to think he can simply walk away now,' said Westerberg.

Seppo nodded, drinking his orange juice, and Westerberg looked at the armchair, now empty, where Risto had just been sitting. A tall man with short hair, wet and smoothly combed back, and a curiously composed expression in his eyes and on his lips. His smile non-committal, and doled out in small portions. Not a trace of aggression. His face was slightly bloated and marked by the passing of time, but only if you looked very closely.

'At least I understand that now,' murmured Seppo.

'Hmm?' asked Westerberg.

'All through the flight, I was wondering what Nygren would say when he heard that name. Saara Koivula. And I couldn't think of any words.'

'Ah.'

'I understand that now, because when Nygren heard her name, he didn't say anything, he only . . . nodded . . .'

'In agreement,' said Westerberg.

74

Risto Nygren sat on his bed in the next room, his fingers busy with the keyboard, his eyes running over the letters. What a good thing his laptop had been here on the bedside table. And that the Internet connection was as fast as the hotel brochure said.

He read and read, and felt he had only seconds to catch up with what he had failed to do for six months. He urgently needed some information.

He had flown to Germany, getting out of Finland physically and also putting Finland out of his mind. He had consumed exclusively German television and German news and German papers and magazines, and even that only now and then, because he had had more important things to do. That was how he had acted again and again over the past years and decades, but this time it really mattered.

He had laid Saara in the ditch, leaving her dead body behind along with all the damn rest of it. Although her body, as he now read, had not been dead at all.

He hadn't killed Saara, only injured her severely. Left her in a comatose state, according to the newspaper report flickering on the screen. He had found it, after specifying more and more details, by entering the words *accident, woman, Turku* and *roadside ditch* in the search line.

And then, long after he had come to Germany, Saara had died after all in hospital in Turku, in circumstances that had not yet been conclusively established. The newspaper report contained a picture of Saara, and he clicked on it and looked at it for a while, although he had no time to spare.

Happonen, Markus. Rising politician. Also dead. Murdered. With bottles of whisky.

He searched for *Kalevi Forsman*, and found the home page of a computer company, although the name of Forsman as a partner was only to be found in archival hits. The name had been removed from the up-to-date page. Under *Kalevi F.* in the search line he found the reason; Kalevi F. was also dead, victim of an unusual murder in a Helsinki hotel.

Miettinen, Jarkko, Jarkko M., former gardener, dead. A small announcement in the Laappeenranta local paper.

Anttila, Lassi, Lassi A., cleaner and store detective in a shopping centre, dead. The home page of a tabloid newspaper illustrated the news with a wobbly photograph, probably taken by the camera of a mobile. A grey, then yellow store full of TV sets. The man lying on the floor some way off was barely recognisable, presumably the reason for the red circle drawn round him.

He leaned back, passed his hands over the keys carefully, and tried to think, but it was no good. As soon as a thought had formed in his mind, other and unwanted ideas made their way in. He thought of Greg, of whorefucker25, of Loverboy-5000, and for a moment felt an absurd impulse to log into the forum and read the experiences of its contributors. Had anyone else tried out little Julia?

A drink, he thought, a drink to bring him back to his senses. But the mini-bar was in the living room where those two police officers were sitting, the tall one and the short one, who had come to . . . yes, why had they really come? What were those freaks doing in his hotel room?

Think, he thought, think, but it was no good. He went into the bathroom, ran cold water over his hands, and passed his wet hands over his face. Looking at himself in the mirror, he realised that he hadn't yet done what he had said he wanted to do: put some clothes on.

He put on his trousers and jacket. He stood in front of the laptop for a while, in front of the picture of the unrecognisable dead man encircled in red, then he took hold of the handle of the connecting door and after a few seconds went through it.

The police officers were still there. Of course. The younger one had emptied his glass of orange juice, the older man was sitting exactly as he had sat before. As if he hadn't moved during his own absence of several minutes.

He went to the mini-bar, opened it and took out the drink that he needed. 'One for you too?' he asked the policemen, but he neither expected nor got any answer. 'I understand,' he said. 'You're on duty.'

'That's right,' agreed Westerberg, and Risto Nygren sat down in the armchair again, and looked at the clear liquid in his glass, trying to concentrate on Westerberg's voice as the man began talking about a volleyball team.

A volleyball team.

'What?'

'You captained the winning volleyball team, didn't you? Back in Karjasaari. In the summer of 1985.'

What a summer, he thought. What a summer that had been. Little Forsman, little Happonen. Although Happonen had grown into a giant. He'd known, even then, that little Happonen would amount to something, and on one of those evenings, just as the sun was sinking into the water and when the others had gone, little Happonen had said he'd like to be like him, Risto, some day, and have a woman like Saara.

'And so you will,' Risto Nygren had replied. 'So you will.'

The volleyball tournament. They'd won a brunch in the fish restaurant. A very hot summer. Risto Nygren remembered how he had sweated that summer, he had been sweating all the time, and he was sweating now, probably because the memory of it was coming back.

'Mr Nygren?' said Westerberg.

'Yes?'

'I am asking you questions, but I'm not getting any answers.'

He did not reply.

'I'd like to know when you last saw your friends. Kalevi Forsman, Markus Happonen, Lassi Anttila . . .'

'Oh, not for a long time,' he said.

'Is that so?' said Westerberg.

'I can hardly remember them,' said Nygren.

'But in the summer of 1985 in Karjasaari, you were all very close.'

He nodded. He had no idea why now. The focus had been Saara. He had driven out to that dump from Laappeenranta every day, just to fuck Saara, that damn . . . woman, she'd made him crazy. The woman had turned him into a cripple, an emotional cripple, but no one understood that, only Risto himself, and he didn't recognise the name that the younger police officer now mentioned at all.

'Who did you say?'

'Teuvo,' said Westerberg. 'Teuvo Manner.'

'Who's he supposed to be?'

Westerberg just looked at him in silence, waiting, and Risto Nygren felt a memory begin to stir, and thought yes, he must know the name after all. He only had to answer that question to their satisfaction, and then Westerberg and his colleague would thank him warmly and go away. Back to Finland.

'Teuvo Manner was twelve years old in 1985. He took piano lessons from your girlfriend Saara Koivula.'

Too hot, that summer, thought Nygren. Crickets chirping, mosquito bites all over his body. The smell of the insecticide that the gardener Miettinen kept spraying around, sticky insecticide spray.

'She was your girlfriend, wasn't she? Saara Koivula.'

'Yes,' said Nygren. 'Yes.'

'And she taught the piano,' said Westerberg.

'Just a moment,' said the younger police officer.

Nygren looked up. He thought he heard a door opening. The terrace door in Majala, a mild breeze blowing in. The little house, the sofa beside the piano, Saara with her legs drawn up and her eyes closed, smiling as he penetrates her.

'Excuse us, please, we are in the middle of . . .' said Westerberg.

'Room service,' said a voice behind Nygren's back. He turned round and saw a man he didn't know. He watched him bringing a knife towards his neck, all very slowly. He turned back to Westerberg, who had risen to his feet and seemed to have frozen in mid-movement, while his young colleague walked past him in slow motion. Then Westerberg's face was above him, curiously close and intimate.

Westerberg was phoning. Said something he couldn't hear. Nygren's head fell to one side, and he saw the connecting door swinging back and forth, a chair that had fallen soundlessly to the floor lying in front of it. He heard a humming, and now, very quietly, like a distant, muted murmur, he did hear Westerberg's voice after all.

Room service. But the man hadn't been wearing the green-and-white uniform of the hotel staff, and he hadn't ordered anything from room service.

Above him, Westerberg seemed to be shouting. He looked at the man's distorted face and his wide-open mouth.

He thought of little Julia, sitting on the bed counting the banknotes. The goodbye kiss, once on the left cheek, once on the right cheek. One day Saara had tried showing him how to play the piano. His hands had lain on the keys, but he hadn't been able to move them, and Saara had laughed and said he was afraid of music.

Saara's passport and Saara's driving licence, both in his wallet. Now and then, before going to sleep, he had looked at the photos, running his fingers over the paper.

The voucher for the team's brunch at the fish restaurant on the bathing beach at Karjasaari had never been cashed in.

Westerberg lowered his mobile, stood up and moved out of his field of vision.

Afraid of music, thought Risto Nygren, and then, after a while, the humming that had drowned out the silence also died away.

75

K immo Joentaa sat on the ground, leaning back against the tree and reading.

From time to time Moisander came over and said something, and then the forensic pathologist from Laappeenranta came over and said something, but Joentaa listened only cursorily and never took his eyes off the lines.

A blue school exercise book. The words were very carefully written, by someone who wasn't used to producing fine handwriting. *Summer 1985. Dear diary.*

Twilight seemed to be falling at midday, and Moisander came back again, bent down to him and gave him some transparent film folders containing various items, documents that the forensic technicians had found. Most of them were wet or softened by rain and snow.

'Thanks,' said Joentaa.

'Is that . . . important?' asked Moisander.

Joentaa followed his glance to the blue exercise book, and nodded.

'In that box, I mean the shoebox, there was also a receipt from a stationery store.'

Joentaa looked enquiringly at him.

'A bill for copying forty pages. Eight euros.'

'Copies?'

'Maybe someone wanted this exercise book copied.'

Joentaa looked down again at the fine letters written so carefully, forming the words.

Moisander went back to the forensic technicians and medics

going about their work, calm and concentrating hard. Joentaa could see the swing and one of the windows of the little house through the branches of the trees. He read the diary again, and felt that now he would remember every word of it, that the text irrevocably made its own mark on the reader's mind.

Summer 1985. Winter now. And nothing in between, only the long gap torn open on one of those dates.

His mobile rang. Sundström. He sounded excited.

'Kimmo, we've got him,' he said. 'Teuvo Manner. He's obviously been at sea over the last few years. Mechanical engineer on one of the Baltic ferries.'

Joentaa did not reply.

'Are you listening to me?' asked Sundström.

'Yes,' said Joentaa.

'Then pay attention. Manner was probably out of Finland for several years, but he came back this summer. On 27 June.'

27 June, thought Joentaa. Saara Koivula was found in a roadside ditch in the summer. A little later her photo was published by all the major Finnish newspapers.

'We haven't laid hands on him yet, but we're working on it, and we have it in black and white that he's come back to Finland,' said Sundström.

'Paavo, not only is Teuvo Manner in Finland, to all appearances he's here. In Karjasaari.'

Sundström did not reply.

'And he's dead,' said Joentaa.

Sundström still said nothing.

'He's been dead for months,' said Joentaa. 'The forensic pathologist thinks for about six months.'

Still no reply from Sundström.

For about six months. Teuvo Manner had come back in June; he had died shortly afterwards. Joentaa's eyes rested on the words that he didn't have to read any more, because he knew them all.

'But . . . who . . .' said Sundström.

Dear diary. That's what people say, don't they? Dear diary. Hi, dear diary. I'll have to ask Lauri tomorrow if you really do put it that way.

76

Yes, Teuvo, that's what people say. I told you so at the time, and I tell you so today. 25 December. Christmas Day.

Dear diary.

Not that it seems appropriate. A book is not a human being, not a person, not a living creature.

The writer talks to himself, and because that doesn't work, and he can't think of a name for the imaginary person he's talking to, he turns to a diary.

Or so I assume. That's one of my theories, nothing more.

However, I think I'm right.

77

Risto Nygren died before the emergency doctor arrived. Westerberg had sat down again on the sofa where he had been sitting during the interview, and the arrival of the doctors, various members of hotel staff, his bewildered German colleague who had been waiting down in the lobby, and finally Seppo, who told him breathlessly that he had lost their man, passed him by like a scene in a film.

A satire. A carefully staged farce, so absurd that you felt like yawning because things like that didn't happen, so you didn't want to be offered them as a spectator.

No one went into a hotel room and cut a man's throat in the presence of two police officers sitting directly opposite the murder victim. No one did it, and no one got away with it.

'I missed him by a second. He blocked the lift with a laundry cart,' said Seppo, bending double as he tried to get his breath back. 'Couldn't get at it, the bloody cart was in the way. He simply rode down in the lift himself and then he'll have taken the first taxi to come along.'

Westerberg said nothing.

'Sorry, but it all happened so fast, and there was no emergency button I could press to stop the lift. I ran twenty-four floors downstairs, but of course I was too slow to catch up.'

'That's no problem, Seppo,' said Westerberg. 'Not your fault.'

He was afraid he hadn't noticed anything, said their German colleague. Westerberg nodded. Colleagues of their German colleague arrived at the crime scene to look at the body.

Risto Nygren.

R. says I'm not to worry about it.

A search operation was set up, taxi drivers over a wide area as well as German police officers at railway stations and the airport were informed.

For some minutes the name Teuvo Manner was bandied around the room, and if Westerberg interpreted it correctly their German colleague was having some difficulty in giving another officer the correct spelling of the first name over his mobile.

A laboriously staged farce, thought Westerberg again, far too studied, and then Kimmo Joentaa called to tell them that he was in the forest, and Teuvo Manner was very probably dead.

'Aha,' said Westerberg.

'The man we want is a school friend of Manner's. Lauri Lemberg.'

'Lauri Lemberg,' said Westerberg.

'I have the boy's diary here. Teuvo Manner's diary, I mean. It seems to me that Lemberg made a great impression on Teuvo, who related strongly to him. Almost as if Teuvo was writing his diary first and foremost for Lauri. Presumably someone read the diary later, and I think it was Lauri. Because it is really addressed to Lauri, do you understand?'

'No,' said Westerberg.

'We should be looking for Lauri Lemberg.'

'Oh,' said Westerberg. Seeing Seppo's enquiring glance, he wondered what Kimmo was really telling him. He had the feeling that he didn't understand any of it. The German investigators were kneeling on the floor, bending over the body, and Westerberg said, 'Risto Nygren is dead. Murdered in front of our eyes.'

At the other end of the line, Joentaa did not respond, and the words that Westerberg had just spoken echoed on in his ears.

'Whoever the man was, he's gone. It was so crazy and it happened so fast that we couldn't . . . couldn't react at all.'

Kimmo's silence dragged on, and a small woman in a headscarf appeared and talked excitably to one of the German officers. After a while he came over to them.

'I'll call you back, Kimmo,' said Westerberg, breaking the connection, and the German told him that the key-card of one of the cleaning staff had gone missing. He probably got in like that, with her key, he suggested in broken English, and Seppo nodded. So did Westerberg, and then he tried to tell the German officer that another name should be introduced into the search action, Lauri Lemberg.

'Lauri who?' asked Seppo, looking so baffled that it almost made Westerberg laugh.

The German police officer seemed at a loss too, and Westerberg spelled out the name. He thought there could be only one possible spelling. Lauri Lemberg, Lauri whoever. A name dug up by Kimmo Joentaa, who was sitting in some forest or other reading a diary. If he had all that straight.

Seppo was still standing opposite him, his mouth slightly open and a frown on his forehead, apparently waiting for explanations.

'Seppo,' he said.

'Yes?' asked Seppo.

'I miss that woman. The one in our car.'

'What?'

'The woman. In the patrol car. Who always tells us the right way to go.'

'Ah . . . the satnav system?'

'Exactly. That's what she's called. I miss her more than anything else in the world.'

78

Milestones. It's a word I heard recently in connection with projects and carrying them out. You get to your destination by reaching milestone after milestone. I suspect that all the milestones of my project have been reached. Project teams are often set up to carry out a project. People who are looking for me while I am looking for Risto. The projects are similar, only the aims are different.

So I probably ought to be grateful to the two Finnish police officers, because without them I wouldn't have found Risto. In his nice suite, 2,000 kilometres from Finland.

In the two press conferences that the news channel transmitted in full, Westerberg appeared very reserved and very tired. I noticed how seriously and thoughtfully he answered questions. Suddenly I was convinced that he if anyone was going to find Risto, and so he did.

It's very easy to shadow police officers, I suppose because they don't expect the person they're looking for to be following them. They were standing at the check-in counter talking about Risto, quietly but sounding a little harassed. Risto. In Germany. Frankfurt. A hotel. The lady at the airline counter smiled and told me I was in luck, there weren't many seats still vacant.

In the plane I sat right behind the two of them, and I sensed their uneasiness, their tension, their hunting instinct now that it was aroused, although they said hardly anything, but I understood them very well.

However, back to the diary – a diary serves to reflect what its writer has experienced, so it is meant exclusively for the diarist himself. I told you that clearly, Teuvo. But I can understand now why you sent me your diary, and sad as your story is, I am even glad to have it.

It was strange, because on the day in summer when your diary reached me, my sister's husband died. In a car accident. He drove into a crash barrier and the car somersaulted several times because he was trying to avoid a drunk driver. The drunk was uninjured.

Since then I've been staying with my sister Leea and her son Olli. You'd have liked Olli. He reminds me of us at that time. Well, perhaps of myself more than you. He's just as stubborn, and hates to lose, and he also seems to have my preference for subjecting everything to stringent logic.

I am sorry that I was never honest with you, but unlike you I lacked the strength. Or the courage. I don't know exactly what I lacked; it must have been something fundamental.

I was there, Teuvo, I was there every time. I always got there fifteen minutes after you, and stood in the flower bed in the garden, and watched the two of you playing the piano. And listened. I was there on the day when it happened.

For a long time I tried to find a way of talking to you about it, but I never did, and then you lived your own life and I lived mine, and in the end you were a memory, a memory of someone I had liked and whom I was endlessly sorry for, but also someone who wasn't part of my life any longer.

I stood out there in the sun that day, and looking through the window I saw the men and the two boys go into the bedroom. I heard Anttila, the man from the supermarket – we always laughed at him – when he called you a 'model student'.

What a misjudgement! Don't take this the wrong way, but you were really not a model student, Teuvo. However, you know that yourself.

Do you know what Anttila said, instinctively and entirely automatically, when I last met him only a few days ago? 'The friend of the model student.' Yes, he recognised me. He could remember me and, above all, you, although so many years have passed.

The friend of the model student, those were his last words, and if you were still alive that might possibly comfort you, although I suspect not. That's not the way it works.

For instance, there isn't anything in the least logical about my writing to you now, because one can't talk to someone who is dead. But I can find no other way to write this down. If it was not meant for you I couldn't write it. And I have to write it.

When your letter arrived this summer, with the letter accompanying it that told me you were planning to take your own life, of course I began looking for you.

It didn't take me long. My first thought was the same as yours – to go to Karjasaari. To Saara. The house was empty. A young family seems to have lived there last, but they had just moved out. It's a very remote place; I had the feeling that most of the houses and farms there are uninhabited now.

I went into the garden and looked through the window. I didn't find the piano, but I found you – again, that didn't take long – I went into the forest and saw you sitting down there, leaning against a tree. I went down myself and sat with you, and stayed for quite a long time. A day and a night.

You said in your letter that you had seen Saara in the paper, that you had found her. Without looking for her. And that it was too late. You were right. I saw her myself once more, in the hospital, and it was too late for anything. I ended it.

Can you remember that dictation? You wrote something about it in the diary. You couldn't write any more, you were sweating and breathing heavily, and in my opinion you were having a breakdown of some kind, I don't know just what but a breakdown in the clinical sense, so I wrote it out for you, and we laughed about it a bit in break, because old Itkonen didn't notice, and I even seriously thought I had helped you. But I never did the one thing I really ought to have done, definitely ought to have done long ago: I ought to have talked to you in peace, with all the time in the world, about everything.

Perhaps it's as simple as I sometimes think, perhaps I was afraid of your questions.

I think you would like to ask, even now, why I stood in the flower bed while you and Saara were playing the piano. I don't know. All that occurs to me is the word longing, and I can't explain what the longing was for.

You will laugh, but some years ago I went to see several doctors, and one of them confirmed that I had a defect, one that to the best of his knowledge was not to be found in any medical textbook. He seemed fascinated, and was probably disappointed when I stopped going to him, but that was only because I thought his diagnosis was quite conclusive enough. I like the word defect, and I think he was right.

At that time my sister Leea, who sometimes says wise things, contributed to our discussion of it over her kitchen table one night – her impression, she said, was that it was difficult for me to take hold of life. To have it in my hands and be aware of that. I know so much, she said, and I would always find categories and concepts, but everything would slide off them. I would find concepts but not the lines holding them together and relating them to each other.

That's my sister Leea.

Her son Olli will amount to something one of these days.

I don't mind that you mention in your diary my failed attempt to kiss fat Satu Koivinen. You're right, it really was a failure, but that was partly Satu's fault, honestly.

I've always wondered what you were doing, and when I read that you have been at sea all those years it seemed to me convincing. Logical in the best sense of the word. Travelling over the water back and forth, there and back, without ever coming to your journey's end.

In all these last eighteen years I have practised any number of professions, all of them ultimately stupid stuff. Recently I've been working for a news agency, writing things about the Stock

Exchange. An absurd but lucrative job, although only if you go about it circumspectly.

This is where boarding ends. Passengers are standing in line waiting. A funny thing happened just now, while I was writing this. A name was called, telling its bearer that the gates would soon be closing, and I wondered how often they would have to call that name before the right person finally reacted. And then, finally, I realised that it was my name. My new name, mine from now on, so I still have to get used to it, although it's very memorable, and I've already used it on various business cards.

So I'm going now. I can see the ground staff at the boarding desk getting impatient. I'm looking forward to the flight and my arrival, perhaps because I have never been in that city, and I left the choice of place to chance. A few weeks ago I asked Olli to tell me the name of a city beginning with S, not in Finland. It's compulsive. The initial S. And the silly name I've given myself, and that in fact is already on a passport that I can use for travelling. I can't travel everywhere on it, there are places I shall avoid, partly on the advice of the odd but friendly man who prepared the document for me. And I wouldn't have thought that, ultimately, it would be easy to travel with an invented name. It somehow makes me hope that the world is really in order.

Araas Aluviok.

Leea thought it sounded Norwegian or Latvian. Olli thought it sounded Greek. They both asked whose name it was, and I almost laughed.

I know it's silly, really, but I've always liked pseudonyms, names behind which people can hide. Not just any old invented names, but names that make sense, and this one makes sense, even if it's simple and slightly pathetic.

An ananym is always simple and pathetic, perhaps even childish, but I like this one, perhaps that's what it's about, Teuvo – about our childhood. I just wanted them to have to read Saara's name once more, although they didn't understand what they were really looking at.

I spent a day and a night with you, Teuvo. You sat leaning against a tree, not alive any more, and no one had taken any notice because no one ever seems to walk in the part of the forest just beyond Saara's house.

I left you sitting there – telling someone might have endangered my plan to bring this all to an end, and I also felt that you were in the right place.

I gave you back the diary, because it's yours. I made a copy for myself, because it seemed to be important to you for me to have it.

Well, now they are about to close the gate.

Dear diary, 25 December.

I don't know what will happen next.

Contrary to all logic, that's not a bad feeling.

79

That afternoon Westerberg stood beside Seppo in an office with large glazed windows providing a good view of Hall A of Frankfurt airport, looking alternately at the passengers hurrying by and the names coming up on the small monitor.

Lauri Lemberg.

Next to the names, they could see a cross-section of the aircraft and seats in various different colours, occupied and vacant, and the seat that had been occupied by Lauri Lemberg a few hours ago was highlighted in a different colour again, orange, close to the front of the screen.

'Actually he was sitting right behind you,' said the friendly man from the German airline in English, a comment very much to the point, and Seppo tilted his head to one side as if he hoped he would understand it all better if he read Lauri Lemberg's name at a different angle.

'Yes,' said Westerberg, and he thought of Kimmo Joentaa sitting in a forest, leafing through an exercise book and coming up with names that were hard to grasp.

Lauri Lemberg, Helsinki to Frankfurt. A one-way ticket, so no return journey, just like Risto Nygren several months earlier. Lauri Lemberg had arrived in Frankfurt, but he had booked no flight back or onward. At least not for anyone bearing that name.

'Thanks,' said Westerberg, and Seppo still had his head on one side, but tilted the other way. Their German colleague's handshake was firm as they finally parted between Arrivals and Departures, wishing each other luck, assuring each other of close cooperation, and then Westerberg and Seppo flew back to Helsinki early in the evening.

At least the investigations in Finland had swiftly come up with results. The last privately registered residence of the wanted man, Lauri Lemberg, had been in Naantali near Turku, but he had been staying recently with his sister in Helsinki, in Länsisatama to be precise, a prosperous residential district in the west of the city.

They arrived on time, the snow was whiter, the street lighting brighter and the evening darker than in Germany as, led by the woman's omniscient and gentle voice, they drove along the street to Länsisatama.

There was a light on in the house where Lauri Lemberg was staying, and as Westerberg followed Seppo up the drive he thought for a split second that Lauri Lemberg would open the door, smile and ask them in.

Seppo rang the bell and a boy opened the door, flinging it wide. He had been expecting someone else.

'Oh. Who are you?' he asked.

I'm beginning to ask myself that question, thought Westerberg, and then a young woman appeared behind the boy. Seppo asked her name, got an answer, showed her his ID and hummed and hawed for a while, because he wanted to let her know their business without upsetting the boy.

'Lauri . . . isn't here,' said Leea Hankala-Lemberg.

Westerberg nodded.

'But do come in,' she said.

An aroma came from the kitchen that, curiously, reminded Westerberg of his childhood, although he couldn't have said what his memory consisted of. Leea Hankala-Lemberg took them into the living room, suggested that they should sit down, and then asked if everything was all right . . . with Lauri. There was a Christmas tree with real candles against the wall with the windows in it. Westerberg liked that.

'We'd like to talk to him. Do you know where he might be?'

She seemed to be thinking about it. 'No,' she said. 'He's made an office for himself in the loft here, and he has another at the Stock Exchange in Helsinki. He works for an online investors' magazine.'

'Aha,' said Westerberg.

'He's been away a good deal recently. Olli, go to bed, please.'

The boy was standing in the doorway.

'I'll come and see you in bed in a little while,' said Leea Hankala-Lemberg.

Olli rolled his eyes and put his head on one side, just like Seppo that afternoon at Frankfurt airport.

'Say goodnight to these gentlemen,' said Leea Hankala-Lemberg, and Olli lingered in the doorway for a few moments, then said, 'Goodnight,' and went away.

'Can't you tell me what's . . . what's happened about Lauri?' asked Leea Hankala-Lemberg.

'Do you know whether he was planning to fly to Germany? To Frankfurt?'

'What?'

'Then the answer is no.'

'Of course not. Why would he do that?'

'In fact he did fly to Frankfurt today.'

She gave Westerberg a long look. 'It could have been on business,' she said at last.

Westerberg nodded. 'Do you have a photograph?'

'Of Lauri?'

'Yes,' said Westerberg.

She went away and came back with an iPhone. 'There are a good many here, I think,' she said. Concentrating, she searched what was obviously an extensive picture library and handed him the device. 'Here, this is Lauri,' she said, and Westerberg looked at the smiling face of the man who had cut Risto Nygren's throat that afternoon. Seppo leaned down to him, and gave a start of surprise on seeing the picture. Lauri Lemberg in front of a wintry scene, pulling a sledge behind him.

'Can you show us his office here, please?' asked Westerberg.

'Yes, of course.'

They followed her up to the top floor of the house. The room looked like a hotel room that had just been cleared; the narrow bed was made up, the desk uncluttered by anything.

'Does he have a PC?' asked Westerberg.

'A laptop. But he always takes it with him when he . . . goes away.'

'Did you speak to him this morning?' asked Westerberg.

'Yes.'

'Yes? And what did he say?'

'Nothing,' she said.

'Nothing at all?'

'He didn't say he was flying to Frankfurt. I thought he was simply going away and would be back. He said he had to go to the office, and I did think that was funny. On Christmas Day. But as I said, he's been away a lot. Particularly over the last few days, when he seemed to have . . . something important and time-consuming to do.'

'Yes,' said Westerberg. And someone to shadow, he thought.

The boy Olli appeared in the doorway.

'I'll be with you in just a minute,' said his mother.

'Is something the matter with Lauri?' he asked.

'No. We're going to talk a little longer up here, and then I'll be with you,' she said.

Olli left them, and they stood in the empty room, rather at a loss. Another empty room, thought Westerberg.

Lauri Lemberg's sister opened the wardrobe. A single jacket hung in it. 'Most of his things have gone,' she said. 'And his travelling bag, but he usually keeps that in his car. As if he were somehow . . . always on the move.'

Westerberg looked at the freshly made bed. Neat and clean.

'Can't you please tell me what's going on?' asked Lauri Lemberg's sister.

An investigation full of empty rooms.

'Your brother . . .' Westerberg began.

'Yes?'

'Tell us something about him. Anything that occurs to you.'

'Anything?'

'Yes, please.'

'He's the dearest, craziest person I know,' she said.

Westerberg tried to meet Seppo's eye, but Seppo was looking at the woman and seemed to be waiting for her to go on. He looked strangely sad.

'Lauri is . . . special. Very clever. Top grades in his school-leaving exam, top results in his university studies.'

'Please go on.'

'What am I to tell you? He's a dear. He seldom does anything you'd expect. In fact never. But he's always there when I need him. He has four university degrees, all with distinction. Since my husband died he's been living with us, helping out. He does relatively odd things that no one else understands. For instance, he once spent a year working as a waiter at an igloo hotel in the north of Finland – with his four brilliant degrees.'

Westerberg nodded.

'I don't suppose you can understand that, can you? I can't either. But that's how he's always been.' She looked at him enquiringly, in search of help.

'Do you remember a friend of his, a school friend? Teuvo Manner?'

'Teuvo . . . yes, certainly.'

'You do?'

'Yes, they were close friends, but that was ages ago. As you said, when they were at school. I was Lauri's little sister, but I do remember that Teuvo sometimes visited us.'

'Yes?' asked Westerberg.

'In retrospect, they were an odd couple. I remember they once let me play Monopoly with them, and Teuvo made sure that I could go safely down Lauri's streets on the board. In the end, thanks to Teuvo, I even won the game, and Lauri's feelings were slightly hurt, but not for long.' She smiled, and Westerberg could see the scene before his eyes. Teuvo Manner, Lauri Lemberg, Lauri's little sister Leea and a board with small green houses and red hotels, and a Lauri who didn't want to lose.

'If your brother comes back or gets in touch with you, please let us know at once,' said Westerberg.

'I really would like to know what's going on,' she said.

'I can understand that. Your brother is suspected of killing a man today in Frankfurt. And that's linked to further investigations on which we're working at the moment.'

She said nothing. He thought he could see how hard she was trying to understand that, but she didn't. Of course not. Westerberg walked a little further into the room, looked round him, and sensed that they were not going to find anything here. Although of course they would try.

'Is your son on holiday?' he asked.

'Of course,' she said.

Of course. Christmas. 'I'd like you to take him out on some kind of excursion tomorrow. A team of forensic officers will have to spend a few hours in your house, and there's no need for him to see that.'

She nodded.

'I'll call you at about eight, and we'll discuss the details then. Is that all right? And I'll need this iPhone, with the photos on it. You'll get it back tomorrow,' said Westerberg.

She nodded.

They went downstairs, and when they were finally trying to find words to say goodbye, Westerberg had a feeling that Olli was with them. Standing in a doorway somewhere, making no noise, trying to hear words that were left unspoken.

80

Leea Hankala-Lemberg read Olli a bedtime story about a little boy fearlessly putting monsters to flight.

At the end Olli asked if Lauri would be coming back soon, and she said yes. A few minutes later Olli was asleep. She waited there for a while, looking at her sleeping son. Then she carefully rose to her feet, tiptoed to the door and then went straight to the kitchen, because that morning she had left something there, next to the fruit and vegetables, and now it was urgent for her to take a closer look at it.

There was only one word on the slim package – *Infopost*. She held it in her hands for a while, looking at the brown envelope, reading the single word again and again, and remembering the conversation she had had with Lauri some time ago. Lauri had been amused by her credulity, and suggested that junk mail should go straight into the recycling bin rather than being opened.

She opened the envelope, and then stared at its contents for several minutes before spreading them out on the kitchen table and reading the handwritten note.

Dear Leea,

We won't be able to see each other for some time. I've left you the money I made on the Stock Exchange. Please use it mainly for what Olli will need in the next few years. I'll visit you both as soon as the whole thing has stopped mattering, but that could take some time. I'm fine. I'll call you and Olli, but I have yet to work out a clever way to do it. Oh, and another thing – if Koski phones or even turns up on your doorstep, he could be a little angry. The Securities and Exchange people will probably want to investigate me for helping a biotechnology company to show a sudden leap in profits, but in the circumstances that's the least of my worries, and the money in this envelope was worth it to me.

See you some time, love to Olli and to you, from Lauri.

She read the letter twice, then put it down on the table and began counting the money. Mauve notes, yellow notes that looked like play money, and to Lauri that was all it would have been. She counted until at last a round sum began to emerge: 100,000 euros. For Olli. Whatever he wanted them for.

She thought of what the police officer had said and that had been going round in circles in her mind ever since, a few centimetres away from her ability to take in its meaning. *He's suspected of killing a man today in Frankfurt.*

She went on sitting at the table for some time, thinking of toy money and the game of Monopoly that she had won, thanks to Teuvo and to Lauri's annoyance. In the end Lauri had swept the hotels off the board, torn a 10,000 note in half, and told Teuvo not to laugh in that silly way.

She tried to hold the picture in her mind: Lauri, Teuvo and herself, as children.

She closed her eyes.

For some seconds she thought that the voice speaking to her from a little way off was part of the memory.

'Is that money real?' asked Olli.

81

Kimmo Joentaa drove through the night over the water and over the apparently endless bridge, and then followed the blue-and-green signs purporting to direct him to Turku.

There was very little traffic on the roads. Now and then he met snowploughs clearing the carriageways of the large amounts of snow that were falling thickly, snow in large flakes.

He phoned Sundström in Turku and Westerberg and Seppo in Helsinki. In turn, they brought him up to date with the latest developments, and they had various questions to ask about Teuvo Manner, the diary and the summer of 1985.

The diary, the blue exercise book, lay on the passenger seat beside him, and as he drove and talked and most of all listened, a picture began to emerge.

Lauri Lemberg, thirty-seven, born 17 February 1973, resident in Naantali and recently in Helsinki with his sister Leea and her son Olli; graduated with distinction in biochemistry, Finnish literature, economics and jurisprudence, subsidiary subjects physics, mathematics, cultural history and psychology; several years as a lecturer at Turku university; broke off studying for a doctorate in biochemistry after a few weeks and went to north Finland to work as a waiter for a year; then occasional jobs, after that journalistic work for a cultural journal in Turku, then a post he held for rather longer as representative for the pharmaceutical products of the firm of Kloks OY. Fired from that post, according to the CEO, for telling the firm's indignant customers that the medicinal drug it was offering was useless and not worth their money.

'Oh,' said Joentaa.

'Yes,' said Seppo. 'But he was right. The drug in question was taken off the market a little later.'

Seppo said goodbye and promised to phone again, and Joentaa thought of Larissa riding a moped through a snowstorm, and then his mobile rang, and this time it was Westerberg, who immediately began talking about Lauri, going on from where Seppo had left off.

Lauri Lemberg, representative for pharmaceutical products; then economic journalist on the investors' magazine succinctly entitled *Shareholders*.

'And here comes the crunch,' said Westerberg. 'He made money out of insider knowledge. I don't quite understand how, but he ended up giving false information and writing reports that were pure imagination.'

Must ask Lauri tomorrow, thought Joentaa.

'Kimmo?' asked Westerberg.

'Yes?'

'I can't think of anything to say, can you?'

'No,' said Joentaa, and then he went on driving by himself, missing Westerberg's voice. Then Sundström called to say that Saara Koivula had gone to see Risto Nygren a day before she was found unconscious and severely injured in the roadside ditch.

Joentaa did not reply, but tried to concentrate on the road ahead of him.

'The surveillance cameras caught her. Nygren convicted himself, so to speak, because his house has a lot of expensive security fitted to deter burglars. The cameras show Nygren putting the unconscious Saara in the boot of his car that evening, a few hours after she arrived, and then driving away.'

Joentaa still said nothing, and concentrated on the road.

'Next morning he flew from Helsinki to Frankfurt.'

'Yes,' said Joentaa.

Sundström ended the call, and Joentaa drove on by himself thinking of the dead man in the forest, Teuvo Manner, who had been a boy and perhaps had stayed a boy, always hearing the last chord that Saara Koivula had played.

After some more time had passed, it was Seppo who told him that a letter had been found in Lauri Lemberg's office on the Stock Exchange in Helsinki.

'The desk was empty, just this letter in it. For us,' said Seppo. 'A letter from Manner to Lemberg.'

From Teuvo to Lauri, thought Joentaa.

'Dated 27 June. It must have been with the diary. Manner writes that he saw the photograph of Saara Koivula in the paper, and indicates that he meant to take his own life.'

Like a whispered scream, thought Joentaa.

'He got off his ship, came to Karjasaari, went into the forest and killed himself,' said Seppo.

Joentaa was silent.

'And Lemberg read the diary and . . . cracked up.'

Lauri. Must ask Lauri tomorrow.

'He must have been there,' said Joentaa.

'What?'

'Lauri Lemberg. He must have been there, with Teuvo,' said Joentaa. 'The receipt for the pages copied was made out on 29 June. Judging by the letter, Lauri must have had the diary before that.'

'How do you mean?'

'Lauri copied the diary, so Teuvo had sent him the original. Lauri looked for Teuvo, found him dead and gave him the diary back. Getting a copy made for himself.'

'Gave it back . . . to the dead man?'

'Yes.'

'And then he just left him . . . the dead body . . . there in the forest?'

'Yes.'

'Oh.'

Joentaa reached Turku just as night was giving way to morning. He did not drive straight home, but went to the city centre and withdrew money from a cash machine. Then he drove on, going a way that he had not taken for some time.

The last phone call that night came from Sundström, telling him that Saara Koivula had made a will a few weeks before her death.

'A will,' said Joentaa.

'Yes. Handwritten, but properly witnessed by a notary. I think she knew or guessed that she would be in danger if she sought out Risto Nygren.'

Joentaa said nothing, but parked the car by the side of the road and wondered what he could put the money in. There was a CD sleeve in the glove compartment. The CD was in the player, a compilation that Larissa had made that summer when she was still around. Melancholy disco music, strong basses, atmospheric sound.

'It's about a small plot of ground, a kind of . . . meadow,' said Sundström. 'She left it to that woman . . . Anita-Liisa Koponen. The nutcase.'

Joentaa said goodbye to Sundström and wished him a good night. He felt the soft, fluffy snow underfoot as he went up to the house. He put the CD sleeve with 500 euros inside it into Tuomas Heinonen's letterbox: *Dear Tuomas, here's the money you asked for. Let's have a drink and talk in peace some time soon. I hope you and Paulina and the twins are well, and having a good holiday.*

He drove home along increasingly narrow roads and thought of what he could ask Lauri tomorrow.

Maybe whether it was right or wrong to give Tuomas the money.

Or why Larissa always switched off the light when she came home.

82

6 December 1985

Lauri and I went to the Christmas fair. Lauri was talking all the time, and was kind of excited, and says I'm sad but I can't show it.

Then something funny happened, and that's why I'm writing now, although I wasn't really going to write any more.

There she suddenly was. Saara. In a thick coat and a big cap, and she'd been drinking mulled wine and looking at the guys riding motorbikes on the ice rink.

She saw us and smiled for a second, and then she took several steps back as if she was afraid of something. Then I went up to her, because I couldn't help going towards her, and she said I should run away. At once. Now. She screamed it.

Then she was gone, and I went after her. I couldn't help it. She turned and shouted to me to stop following her.

Then Risto was there. He was pushing a motorbike and had probably been one of the bikers on the ice. He smiled, turned off the engine of the bike, came towards me quickly and bored into my ear with his finger until it hurt, and I thought I might pass out.

And then the funny thing happened. Lauri grabbed Risto's hand and pushed it away from my head. It all seemed so easy. Risto stood there staring. Little Lauri, big Risto. Saara was standing beside Risto, and her eyes were gleaming so sadly, as if she was going to cry but she couldn't.

Lauri let go of Risto's hand and they stood facing each other. Lauri was trembling, I could see that, but he stayed put.

'And who are you?' asked Risto, and it sounded quite friendly. Lauri didn't answer. Then Risto swung his arm back and punched Lauri in the face with his fist, with all his weight behind it, really hard, making Lauri's head wobble, and flinging him backwards. But he still stayed put.

Risto asked Lauri if he wanted to die, and Lauri turned round and told me we'd be going now. He said it perfectly calmly, but then he began running and I ran too.

When we cycled home I suddenly had to cry because of everything, and because Saara had looked so sad, and Lauri's face was red as a tomato, and his nose was bleeding because of the punch in the face.

Lauri asked why I was crying, and I couldn't explain. Why was I sad, he asked, and I said I wasn't sad. Then if I wasn't sad there was nothing for me to cry about, he said.

Logical, Lauri, only logical.

Tomorrow I'll tell him that he's my best friend, but I'm sure he knows that anyway.

83

When Kimmo got home, the giraffe had woken up and got to its feet and gone away. He looked for it in the snow under the apple tree for several minutes, but he didn't find it.

He went back to the car, sat in it looking through the windscreen for some time, wondering how long electric light bulbs last. Wondering how long they would burn before giving up the ghost.

How many days and weeks?

How many days and weeks was it since he had switched on the light and locked the door and driven to Karjasaari? He didn't know. He tried to think about it, but it was no good.

He thought of the Christmas tree, the fir tree a metre high that Larissa had carried out of the forest into his living room exactly a year ago. They had stood side by side looking at the tree, and he had felt a certain kind of smile come into his face.

A smile that now, at last, came back.

He got out and went up to the house that lay there in the dark.

THANKS

My thanks to Niina and Venla, Georg and Wolfgang, Christian and Klaus, Esther and my parents.

A special thank-you to Stefan Scheid, who had the idea of taking up music together. Dear Stefan, it was fun and gave me new strength for writing – and now at last I know what songs Kimmo listens to in the evening in his house by the lake. When he thinks of the people he misses.

Jan Costin Wagner was born in 1972 in Langen/Hesse near Frankfurt. After studying German language, literature and history at Frankfurt University, he went on to work as a journalist and freelance writer. He divides his time between Germany and Finland (the home country of his wife). His previous crime novels featuring detective Kimmo Joentaa are *Ice Moon*, *Silence*, which won the 2008 German Crime Prize, and *The Winter of the Lions*.

Anthea Bell is a freelance translator from German and French, specialising in modern and crime fiction.